WITHDRAWN

Also by Stuart Kaminsky:

Inspector Porfiry Rostnikov Mysteries

DEATH OF A DISSIDENT

RED CHAMELEON

A FINE RED RAIN*

Published by Ivy Books

BLACK KNIGHT IN RED SQUARE

Stuart M. Kaminsky

IVY BOOKS • NEW YORK

Ivy Books
Published by Ballantine Books
Copyright © 1984 by Stuart M. Kaminsky

ISBN 0-8041-0405-0

Manufactured in the United States of America

First Ballantine Books Edition: June 1989

FOR DOMINICK ABEL

It is a matter of indifference who actually committed the crime; psychology is only concerned to know who desired it emotionally and who welcomed it when it was done. And for that reason all of the brothers (of the family Karamazov; or of the human family) are equally guilty.

—Sigmund Freud, "Dostoevsky and Parricide."

ONE

WARREN HARDING AUBREY THOUGHT HE WAS FEELING the effects of a trio of double vodkas on the rocks. Actually, he was dying.

His once hard belly ached slightly as he got on the elevator of the Metropole Hotel and told the young woman he wanted *vosem*. When she pressed the button marked eight, he knew his minimal Russian had not failed him this time.

The girl on the stool was named Maria Nevanskaya. She had been riding up and down for almost fourteen hours a day five days a week for three of her twenty-five years. Normally it would take the appearance of a babbling ax murderer or of the general secretary himself to draw her attention. But this was not a normal week. It was the first week of the Moscow Film Festival, and the hotel was filled with foreigners. The lobby elevator dispatcher, Verochek, had abused Maria about her lack of courtesy to the guests. She guessed, quite correctly, that Verochek had himself been abused by Karlenko, the Metropole's Communist Party supervisor. So as the elevator slowly rose to the sound of the weary restaurant orchestra playing "I Want to Hold Your Hand," Maria turned to her drunken passenger and asked, in what she thought was French, if he was ill.

Aubrey was lost in thoughts of 1954, when he had

1

begun the metamorphosis from Pulitzer Prize–winning war correspondent in Korea to hired typist who would cover anything anywhere in the world for a standard fee and all he could drink, which was an impressive amount. The French word *mal* got through to him, though, and he grinned at the woman and shook his head. He wanted to say something to her, but the taste of blood in his mouth and her apparent indifference stopped him. His hand went to his mouth and came away dry.

As the elevator door slid open on the eighth floor, Aubrey took a step forward feeling as if he were wading in knee-deep water. He almost collided with the desk of the *dezhurnaya*, the floor woman who sat watching him. Her hand automatically went up to protect her key box from his potential drunken onslaught. Each floor in each hotel in Moscow, with the exception of the gargantuan Rossyia, had an old *dezhurnaya* to guard the keys, the morals, and the sanctity of the establishment and to serve, when necessary, as the eyes and ears of the KGB. As Aubrey knew, these old women could shift from motherly sympathy to matronly scorn without apparent reason. None could speak any language but Russian. This *dezhurnaya*, Vera Olganova, eyed Aubrey suspiciously, and with little of the Party's careful courtesy to the foreign visitor, found his key and reluctantly handed it over. Aubrey clutched the key, took a step, began to fall, and tried to steady himself by grabbing the nearest object on the woman's desk, which happened to be a small framed portrait of Lenin.

Vera Olganova snatched the portrait from him with a grunt, and Aubrey had to hold the edge of the desk to keep from falling. She decided that the foreigner had intentionally and politically reached for the picture, which she now clutched to her cascading bosom, saving it from desecration at his capitalistic hands. He merited a report to the proper authorities even if he was drunk.

"Sorry," Aubrey said, hoping he wouldn't throw up.

She placed Lenin safely on the far end of the desk, facing away from the disrespectful Westerner.

Aubrey, praying that he would make it to his bathroom,

took a dozen steps, inserted the key into the lock of room 808, turned it, and pushed open the door. With a great effort, he managed to raise his hand and flick on the lights. He was unaware that he'd left the door open behind him and that he had dropped the key.

The nausea subsided slightly as he found himself eye to eye with a painting of a thin man with his bushy head held high and a stern expression on his face. Aubrey put out both hands and leaned against the wall, trying to outstare this figure from the past.

"Just a few too many tonight, Comrade," he confided to the severe revolutionary. He wanted to say more, but the taste of blood rose again in his dry mouth. This time it was mixed with bitterness. Another wave of nausea came, accompanied by a dull pain in his head and chest. He shuffled toward the bathroom.

"After I get the booze out of my stomach," he called back to the portrait, "I'll take you on."

He rested his sweating hand on the bathroom door, light-headed. The feeling of falling that surged over him was so vivid that he felt a warm breeze against his cheeks. Then it struck him that he was actually falling, but so slowly that he must be defying the law of gravity. He marveled at how long it took him to hit the cold tile of the bathroom floor. I should put out my hands, he thought, break the fall. But his hands didn't move, though he was pleased that he'd been capable of the thought.

His head hit the porcelain toilet, opening a deep gash over his right eye, but he felt no pain as he rolled heavily under the sink. The nausea and headache were gone. The hell with it, he thought. I'll just sleep here and check the damage in the morning. The floor tiles felt cool against his hot cheek, and Aubrey closed his eyes.

At nine the following morning, Irina Marmontov, one of the maids, pushed her cart past the dozing Vera Olganova and down the hall to begin making up the rooms in her section. She noticed that the door to room 808 was open. The light was on, and she could see that no one had slept in the bed. But she had been working at the Metropole for almost thirty years and had seen far stranger things, particularly from the Cubans, Americans, and Italians. The worst times were during the Moscow Film Festival. In 1971, during the festival, a rainy July morning, she had opened the closet door and found a fat, naked man grinning at her. The man said something in a strange language, stepped past her, and sat down cross-legged on the floor as if he had been waiting for hours for someone to come and release him so he could engage in his meditation. But the door to the closet had not been locked, and the closet was covered with blood, though the naked man was apparently unwounded. Irina had hurried to the *dezhurnaya*, who had called the security office. The police eventually arrived and discovered that the man had not been found in his own room but in that of a Latvian clock factory representative whom they found in the dining room calmly awaiting his breakfast. The Latvian claimed that he didn't know the naked man and had no idea what he was doing in the room or how the blood had come to be in the closet. The fat man had been of no further help. He had no identification, and he said nothing, but simply grinned. The police kicked him a few times in irritation and then covered him with a robe and took him away. That was the last Irina had heard of the mystery, but the memory had stayed with her, and an unpleasant feeling went through her whenever she opened a closet door.

Although Irina could not remember who was in room 808, she was not particularly intrigued by the open door. She went about her business, cleaning the other rooms, working slowly as always. She didn't have too many rooms to clean, for the hotel, like most Moscow hotels, was ridiculously overstaffed. Irina, however, did not work slowly out of boredom or lethargy, but rather in the hope that the occupant of a room was a foreigner who might come back while she was working and give her a tip. During one film festival, an Italian actor had given her a tip of a thousand lire. A bartender she knew had given her four rubles for the colorful piece of paper. Irina knew there were movie actors, directors, producers, and writers in the Metropole right now, maybe on her floor, in this section, but she would not recognize a foreign movie star.

She walked through the open door of 808 at about nine-thirty and asked, "Anybody here?" No one answered.

Clothes hung on hangers; a suitcase sat on the chair. There was nothing to empty from the wastebasket. Irina bent to pick up the room keys from the floor near the door. She put them on the nearby table and got a cloth from her cart. The routine was automatic. Clean the room, replace the towels, check the toilet paper. The light was out in the bathroom, and she flipped it on.

There was blood on the toilet seat, bright red against the white plastic. Under the sink a drunken foreigner was sleeping. She wanted to simply walk out after changing the towels, but he might be someone important, and he might be hurt.

"Gospodin," she said, "you all right?" He didn't move. She reached down to touch his shoulder, but what she felt made her pull her arm back with a jerk. He is not a man, she thought. He is a body. She touched him again, and he rolled away from the wall to stare at her with unseeing eyes.

Irina jumped back quickly, banging her shoulder against the open door. Although the face of death was a shock, it was not death but the look of pain on the man's face and the blood on his lips that terrified her. He was pale and cold, and the light from the sputtering bulb danced on his bald head.

Irina backed out of the bathroom, fighting her panic and the desire to run. She left the room as calmly as she could and hurried to Vera Olganova, whose eyes opened wide at this breach of routine. She reached for the phone, dialed a number, couldn't get through, and dialed again.

"Comrade Verskov," she said, proud of the control in her voice.

"What room?" he answered. Vera's eyes rose and met those of Irina, who was looking back down the corridor.

"I—we just found a dead man in eight-oh-eight."

"I know," said Comrade Verskov, his voice cracking.

"There's blood on his mouth."

"How did—?" she began, but Verskov's quavering voice cut her off.

"We now have four of them in the hotel." There was a silence, and she could hear Verskov trying to pull himself together. "Don't touch anything. Close the door. The police will be there in a few minutes."

On the sidewalk in front of number 16 Kalinin Street, three boys about fifteen years old were jostling a younger boy between them. The younger boy wanted to get away without looking too frightened, but the tears were forming. From the window of the first-floor apartment, a pair of dark eyes watched the struggle with detached interest. The viewer saw the event as an experiment carried out many times before from São Paulo to Helsinki. The outcome was statistically inevitable. The tormented boy saw a slight opening and tried to step through the small circle of his tormentors' legs, but one of the older boys tripped him, and he fell on the sidewalk, taking part of the impact with his face. He stood up bewildered, examining the blood on his shirt. Instead of arousing sympathy in his tormentors, the sight of blood seemed to anger them, and the shortest of the three attackers stepped forward and slapped the bleeding boy hard with the back of his hand.

The dark eyes turned back to the near-darkness of the room.

"The time must be exact," said a male voice in too precise German.

The dark eyes turned slowly to the speaker, a thin, dark Arab in his late twenties.

"Four days from today on Sunday at six, seven, and eight P.M. Moscow time," said the one with dark eyes. "That is exact." The eyes coolly examined the four others in the room. Besides the young Arab, Ali, there was a short, muscular Arab in his late forties named Fouad, a nervous type who had to have something in his hands to keep them quiet. There was a blond man in his thirties with a French accent. The others called him Robert. He appeared to be the leader, but he seldom spoke. The final member of the quartet had made most of the arrangements. She was a woman in her late twenties with thick blond hair who identified herself as Seven. She had once been beautiful, but now she was consumed by a neurotic hatred that the man with the dark eyes had seen often before. She had a slight British accent, but the dark-eyed one knew it was a fake. The conversation was conducted in German.

"You are sure," said Seven, "that nothing has changed because of the Metropole business?"

"I am sure," said the one with dark eyes. "Business is going on as usual. Now I'll have the rest of my payment."

"We think," said Seven, rising, "it would be better to pay you when we are finished."

Fouad leaned against the door, and Ali backed into a corner, his hand in his pocket. The dark eyes moved to Robert, who sat impassively, arms folded, a slight smile on his lips.

"I get it all, and now," said the one with dark eyes, "or you can forget about the agreement."

"If the KGB knew about our meeting," said Seven, "you would not be seeing anyone for a long time. You might not live very long."

"You are not very good at this," said the dark-eyed one, "not good at all. If you get away with the plan, it will be because of what I do, what I plan. You're wasting time with these games. I've got to get back or someone might grow suspicious about where I've been. The cash now, and all of it."

Robert nodded to Seven, who went to a briefcase on the table and extracted a package.

"If you—" Seven began, but a gesture from Robert stopped her words. She handed the package to the visitor.

The dark-eyed visitor took it and left, thinking that the money was good and the challenge interesting, but that as a group, the terrorists were far below even the clumsy Japanese airport group and the inept Italian quartet, both of which had bungled their tasks miserably. Robert was more interested in self-image than ideology. Seven was all fire and no brains. Ali was an idealist with no experience. Only Fouad had the makings of a good terrorist; he was unconcerned about self-image and able to control his fire and strength. If the four of them had plans to dispose of their visitor eventually, Fouad would be the one to keep an eye on.

Outside the sunlight was bright. Across the street, the three youths had given up their game with the younger boy and were looking for something else to fill their empty day. They spotted the one with the dark eyes and started to move forward. When their quarry did not run or even walk away, they paused in the middle of the street.

The smile on the face of the one with dark eyes told the three boys they were like insects to this lone, well-dressed foreigner. The stranger walked directly toward and then past them without hurrying or looking back. One of the boys muttered the only words he knew in English: "Fuck you."

The dark-eyed one felt the packet of $150,000 in American dollars and didn't bother to reply.

TWO

PORFIRY PETROVICH ROSTNIKOV REALIZED THE IMPORtance of what he was about to do this Thursday morning. There had been several such crucial moments in his fifty-two years. The first had occurred in 1941 when he was a boy soldier who had stepped out from behind a doorway in Rostov to face a German tank. He had destroyed the tank with a lucky grenade and a hail of bullets from the machine pistol he had taken from a dead German. The cost had been a nearly destroyed left leg, which he had to drag slowly and often painfully behind him throughout the rest of his life. The second such moment happened when, as a young policeman in Moscow, he had caught a drunken thief named Gremko assaulting a young woman outside the Kursk railway terminal. The drunk had nearly killed Rostnikov with his bare hands, but fortune and a well-placed knee to the groin had turned the tables.

At that point Rostnikov began to lift weights. At first he did so to gain strength and then as a means of relaxation, a way to escape from the pressures of living in Moscow. Eventually, lifting weights had become an end in itself. It demanded his total attention and he gave it willingly. His body had begun to expand with musculature as he lifted, and before he was named a chief inspector he had already earned the nickname "Washtub" among his fellow police and also among full-time criminals.

Rostnikov gripped the metal tightly in his hand and moved slowly up the stairwell of the apartment on Krasikov Street, again going over what he would say. His wife, Sarah, had tried to talk him out of this, but he had worked too hard, prepared too well. He moved resolutely upward, dragging his bad leg behind him, and opened the door on the seventh floor. There were no elevators in the apartment building; few apartment buildings in Moscow had elevators.

Going down the corridor, he took a deep breath. No turning back, he thought, and then he paused before the door and knocked. Beyond the door he could hear two voices, one a man's, the other a woman's. He could not make out what they were saying. He knocked again, and a voice answered, "Coming."

It was early in the morning, more than two hours before Irina would discover Aubrey's body, half an hour before Inspector Rostnikov was due in his office at Petrovka—barely enough time to do what must be done. The door opened.

"Yes?" A thin man in an undershirt stood at the door. His wife, standing behind him, was extremely plump, with her orange hair pinned in an untidy bun.

"I live in the apartment below you," said Rostnikov, adopting the official voice he used in dealing with those who appeared frightened.

"We are Bulgarian," the man said.

"I know," Rostnikov replied.

"I am here for six months for a machine trade exchange," the man said.

"That's not important," replied Rostnikov, shifting the tools in his hand. Both the man and the woman looked down as the tools clanked together.

"You are a policeman," said the woman.

"Yes." Rostnikov spoke softly, almost with resignation, trying to give the impression that what he was about to do was regrettable but inevitable.

"What have we done?" said the man, touching his chest and looking at his wife.

"Your toilet," said Rostnikov.

"I'm what?" said the startled man, stepping back.

"Your toilet is broken," explained Rostnikov. "It is causing a massive leak in our apartment below. We cannot use our toilet."

"You cannot use your toilet," echoed the man dumbly.

"We can," Rostnikov went on, "but we are not willing to clean up the floor each time we flush."

"No one told us," said the woman apologetically, putting a hand to her breast and discovering that her dress was not fully buttoned.

They had not been told, Rostnikov knew, because a decision had been made, in spite of Rostnikov's threats and pleas to the building manager, a thin Party member named Samsanov, to avoid telling the Bulgarians that their toilet was faulty. Apparently the local political decision was that it would not do to let the Bulgarians see how defective the plumbing was. They might go home and ridicule their Moscow hosts. Rostnikov, in spite of his position with the police, had been told to forget it till the Bulgarians left, but they showed no signs of leaving. So Rostnikov had begun reading plumbing books. For four weeks he read plumbing books. The library was filled with them. There were more books on plumbing than on plastering, cooking, radio and television repairing, automobiles, and crime. He now felt himself capable of repairing whatever the problem might be, if his tools were sufficient and his resolve to defy the local Party decision held firm.

"No one told us," the man repeated his wife's word.

"There are reasons," Rostnikov said mysteriously. "I will repair the problem, and you must promise to tell no one I have done so. It is forbidden for one in my station to do this, but I did not want the problem to get worse and affect you, visitors to our city."

With this he stepped past them into the replica of his own apartment. The central room, a combination living room–dining room–kitchen, was well furnished, including a small television set. There was a foreign odor, which was not unpleasant but which Rostnikov could not place. To the left of the entrance was the even smaller bedroom. He marched toward it with the Bulgarians behind, mumbling to each other frantically.

"I'll take no more than a few minutes," he said, pushing open the door. The window was open, and sunlight was pouring in on the unmade bed. Rostnikov stood before it trying to imagine the unmatched Bulgarians making love. They made little noise during the night. He knew this because his and Sarah's bedroom was right below theirs. He moved to the bathroom, turned on the light, and removed an oversize pink slip from the toilet seat. The woman, closing in behind him, reaching over to take it from him like a nurse retrieving a scalpel during surgery.

"I'll not be long. Just leave me alone."

They backed out, mumbling again in their native language, and Rostnikov went to work. From his pocket he withdrew a long, coiled plumbing snake, unwound it, and began to force it down the toilet. He eased and worked it but struck nothing.

Next, he turned off the water and, with the wrench that he had taken from the confiscated burglar tools in the basement of police headquarters in Petrovka, he removed the pipe behind the toilet seat. When it was removed, he found a cup on the nearby sink, filled it with water, stomped his foot on the floor and poured the water down the pipe. Almost instantly, Sarah in the apartment below pounded on the ceiling with the signal.

"Fitting," muttered Rostnikov on his hands and knees, peering down into the dark pipe.

"What is?" said the Bulgarian behind him. The man was standing back in the bedroom, unwilling to intrude but equally unwilling to leave this barrel of a man alone.

"There is a loose fitting in the pipe," Rostnikov explained. "I'll have to go down to my apartment, unscrew the coupling and pull it up here to fix it. If it's just a fitting it won't be difficult. If there is a leak in the pipe, we have a more serious problem."

Using the sink to steady himself, Rostnikov rose. There was a smile on his lips. He might be a bit late for work, but he would lick this. Triumphs were few in his work and even fewer in the tasks of getting through the day, but this would be a triumph.

The knock at the door jerked him from his near triumph. He turned to face the Bulgarians, who looked at him.

"Answer the door," he said, stepping into the bedroom. Had someone actually called Samsanov? Did the little man have a spy on the floor? Rostnikov began to think of a lie and decided that his best chance to get through would be to bluff Samsanov, to tell him this was a police matter, that the toilet had to be fixed, that national security was at risk. That, of course, superceded even local Party decisions. The Bulgarian opened the door, and Rostnikov wondered how national security could be involved in fixing a toilet.

"Chief Inspector Rostnikov," came a familiar voice from the doorway.

"In here," said the Bulgarian, and Emil Karpo strode into the room to further confound the man and the woman.

The man who strode into the room was about six feet three, lean, and quite hard. Because of his slanted eyes, high cheekbones, tight skin, and expressionless dark face, he had been known in his early police career as the Tatar. But twenty years of fanatical pursuit of enemies of the state had given him the pale look of the obsessed and earned him the more frequent nickname of the Vampire among his colleagues. The name seemed particularly appropriate when a peculiar look crept into Karpo's eyes and at those moments even those who had worked with him for years avoided him. Only Rostnikov knew that the look was caused by severe migraine headaches, which Karpo refused to admit to. Rostnikov knew quite a lot about his junior colleague. Survival in the Soviet Union often depended on how many secrets you knew and could call upon. Rostnikov watched Karpo with interest, glancing at his left arm, which was stiff and still. Karpo had been shot several months earlier and then had injured the arm again while chasing a petty criminal. He had almost lost the arm that time, but a surgeon who had just had a good meal and a few hours' sleep had worked harder than usual to save the limb. So the two men shared something—one with a bad leg, the other a bad arm—though they never spoke of their common bond.

"Yes," said Rostnikov.

"You're to come to Comrade Timofeyeva's office. It is urgent. There's a car downstairs waiting."

Rostnikov looked at the Bulgarians and back over his shoulder at the toilet.

"Karpo, what do you know of plumbing?"

"I'm a police investigator," Karpo replied.

"That does not preclude your knowing something," Rostnikov said.

"You are joking again, Comrade Inspector," Karpo said expressionlessly.

"Why is it you can recognize a joke, Emil Karpo, but you cannot engage in one?" Rostnikov said, walking past him toward the door.

"It is not functional to engage in jokes," Karpo said. "There is too much to do. Lenin had no sense of humor either."

"I know." Rostnikov sighed, and then said to the Bulgarians. "Do not touch the toilet. Use the one at the end of the corridor. Above all do not tell anyone of this." He put his fingers to his lips. "I'll be back tonight to fix it."

"But—" the woman began. The thin man tugged at her sleeve to quiet her.

"Security," said Rostnikov, allowing Karpo to precede him through the door.

"We understand," said the Bulgarian, rushing to close the door behind the two policemen.

As they walked down the corridor, Rostnikov said, "Are you curious about that?"

"No," said Karpo, and the conversation ended.

Twenty minutes later, after getting his jacket and saying good-bye to Sarah, Rostnikov arrived with Karpo at the entrance to Petrovka in a yellow police Volga with a blue horizontal stripe.

Petrovka consists of two ten-story L-shaped buildings on Petrovka Street. It is modern, utilitarian, and very busy. It is prominent—everyone knows where it is—and so are the thousands of gray-clad policemen who patrol the city. The ratio of police to civilians is higher in Moscow than in any other major city of the world.

In spite of this, crime, while it does not flourish, exists. Files of *doznaniye* or inquiries, cover the desks of the procurators working under the procurator general of the Soviet Union. The police work with the procurators in the twenty districts of Moscow and are responsible for all but political crimes, which fall within the sphere of the KGB (Komityet Gosudarstuennoy Besapanost) or State Security Agency. It is a constant puzzle to both procurators and police what qualifies as a political crime. Economic crimes are generally political because they threaten the economy of the state and thus are subversive. In fact, any crime can be considered political, even the bludgeoning of a husband by a jealous wife. Officially, the procurator general's office is empowered by the constitution of the U.S.S.R., Article 164, to exercise "supreme power of supervision over the strict and uniform observance of laws by all ministries, state committees and departments, enterprises, institutions and organizations, executive-administrative bodies of local Soviets of People's Deputies, collective farms, cooperatives and other public organizations, officials and citizens."

Which was why Procurator Anna Timofeyeva, a thick box of a woman, about fifty, spent at least fourteen hours a day, seven days a week in her office in Petrovka, trying to shorten the pile of cases on her desk. She looked quite formidable in her striped shirt and dark blue procurator's uniform. She drank gallons of cold tea, did her best to ignore her weak and frequently complaining heart, and went on with her massive task.

Procurator Timofeyeva was in her second ten-year term of office. Before that she had been an assistant to one of the commissars of Leningrad in charge of shipping and manufacturing quotas. She had no background in law, no training for her position, but she was dedicated, reasonably intelligent, and, above all, a zealot. She was an excellent procurator.

She was behind her desk as always when Rostnikov entered her office after knocking and being told gruffly to enter. Then the ritual began. Rostnikov sat in the chair opposite her, glanced up at the picture of Lenin above her head, and waited. As always she offered him a glass of her room-temperature tea.

"Murder," she said.

Rostnikov sipped his tea and waited.

"Poison," added Procurator Timofeyeva.

Rostnikov looked down at his glass, hesitated and again sipped at the tea. He liked sugar in his tea, or at least lemon. This had neither and very little taste, but it kept his hands busy. Procurator Timofeyeva's one vice was her taste for the dramatic in assigning cases.

"An American," she went on. "During the night, at the Metropole."

"An American," Rostnikov repeated, shifting his left leg. Keeping it in one position for more than a few minutes always resulted in stiffening and at least minor pain.

"And two Soviet citizens. And a Japanese."

"Four," said Rostnikov.

"Let us hope our powers of addition are not taxed beyond this number," she said, sipping her own tea.

"And the inquiry, I take it, is now mine?" said Rostnikov.

"It is yours, and it is, once again, delicate. The American was a journalist here for the Moscow Film Festival. The Soviets were businessmen. The Japanese was also here for the festival, but it is the American who causes concern. It seems he was well known in his country."

"An accident?" tried Rostnikov.

"According to the preliminary medical report from the hotel, this poison could hardly have been an accident. So, you must work quickly. There are several thousand visitors in Moscow for the festival from more than a hundred countries. There must be no rumors of a poisoner, no panic to spoil the festival. It is an important cultural event, a world event. The Olympics as you know were successfully sabotaged by the Americans and their puppets. Moscow cannot be the scene of another such embarrassment."

Comrade Timofeyeva's knuckles were white as she clutched her glass.

"Forgive me, Comrade Procurator, but are not such fears a bit premature? This is but—"

"Sources have informed me that there may be those who wish to embarrass the Soviet Union during the festival and that this may be part of their scheme," she said, looking over her shoulder at the portrait of Lenin as if to seek approval.

"In which case, would this not be properly handled by—" Rostnikov began, but she interrupted him again.

"The KGB wishes us to investigate this as a common crime and not a political one. I'm afraid, Comrade Rostnikov, you have gained a reputation for discretion in such matters."

The meaning of this, Rostnikov well knew, was that if he failed, his enemies could throw him to the dogs. He was expendable, and this precarious state was becoming part of his life with each delicate case he handled.

"I understand," Rostnikov said, rising. "I assume I am to go to the Metropole immediately. I am to keep you informed, and I am to work, as always, as swiftly as possible."

She stood and took the empty glass from his hand.

"An American is dead, poisoned," she said. "It is already an embarrassment."

"And Karpo is to work with me?"

"If you wish," she agreed, sitting again and already reaching for the next file on her desk. "But he must keep up with the rest of his case load."

Rostnikov moved toward the door.

"If you need Tkach, yes," she said.

He opened the door but paused before he stepped out. The next thing he was going to say would surely be dangerous, but it was worth saying, for he both liked and admired the homely, far too serious, and officious woman who sat behind the desk in this hot office.

"How are you feeling, Comrade Anna?" He spoke softly so that she could ignore him if she wished.

Her reaction was to yank off her glasses and glare at him angrily for an instant. But something in his look, the way he stood, the sincerity of his tone, got through to her, and she couldn't sustain the anger.

"I am well, Porfiry," she lied evenly.

He recognized the lie and smiled ever so slightly.

"Good," he said and stepped into the corridor, closing the door behind him.

He knew that she would not take his inquiry as the false solicitude of the underling who coveted his superior's job, for the facts were clear. Rostnikov would never be more than a chief inspector in the MVD, a position higher than might be expected of him considering his inability to control his tongue, his frequent impetuousness, and his politically hazardous Jewish wife—a wife who had no interest at all in either religion or politics. Fortunately, Rostnikov had no ambition; he was politically uninterested. His job was to catch criminals and occasionally punish them at the moment of capture. Usually, however, the game—and he saw it as a game—ended when he caught the criminals and turned them over to the procurator's office for justice. It didn't matter to Rostnikov whether the law was reasonable or not. The criminals knew the law and knew when they were violating it.

Beyond catching criminals, Rostnikov's life was in his wife, his son Iosef who had recently been posted to Kiev with his army unit, weight lifting, reading American mystery novels, and, most recently, plumbing.

Lost in thought, Rostnikov turned the corner and found himself facing Emil Karpo, a startling specter.

"You'll be needing me?" Karpo said.

"For now," answered Rostnikov, continuing to limp down the corridor. "We are going to the Metropole Hotel."

On Sverdlov Square facing the monument to Karl Marx stands the Metropole Hotel, which belongs to Intourist, the official Soviet tourist travel agency. The Metropole was built in 1903. In October 1917 the revolutionary workers and soldiers fought fiercely to capture it from the White army troops who had barricaded themselves inside. On the side of the hotel facing Marx Prospekt is a plaque commemorating this battle. Near the entrance to the hotel, on the square, are other memorial plaques, reminding people that the hotel for a time housed the offices of the All-Russia Central Executive Committee of Soviets of Working People's Deputies under the chairmanship of Yakov Sverdlov after whom the square had been named. Lenin often spoke in the ballroom of the Metropole.

The Metropole has been renovated several times. The upper part of the facade is decorated with mosaic panels designed by Mikhai Vrubel on the theme of the play *La Princesse Lointaine* by the French playwright Edmond Rostand, who also wrote *Cyrano de Bergerac*. Feodor Chaliapin once sang in the hotel's restaurant and Maxim Gorky once described the hotel in glowing terms in his novel *The Life of Klim Samgin*.

That is the tourist-book description of the Metropole. In fact, the hotel is dark, dusty, and decaying. The food in the restaurant is poor, the service ridiculous even by Moscow's standards, and the orchestra laughable. In spite of this, many foreigners prefer the Metropole because it behaves like old Moscow and there is so little of old Moscow left. In addition, the Bolshoi is across the square, and the hotel is well located for city-wide events such as the Moscow Film Festival. Another attraction for festival participants is the Stero Cinema on Sverdlov Square, which specializes in 3-D movies.

By 11:40 that morning every room in the Metropole had been searched. Police were guarding the exits of the hotel, and a trio of pathologists from the Kremlin Hospital were examining the four bodies, which were assembled on tables in the ornate but now unused Victorian bar. The bar was decadently ornate with massive mirrors, beautiful chandeliers, and even a gilded foot rail. The door to the dining room was guarded by two uniformed policemen.

Rostnikov looked around the room, ignoring the white-haired man who stood next to the four tables where the corpses lay. Rostnikov was absorbing the place through his pores, beyond his senses. It might be thought that this was part of his method, his secret means of detection that went beyond words, but it had nothing at all to do with the case. Being a policeman, Rostnikov occasionally entered one of the big hotels in pursuit of a criminal. Being a policeman, however, he could not afford to eat in the restaurants of any of these hotels. And being a Muscovite, he could not stay in any hotel in Moscow. It was the law. So he stood and imagined the past.

Karpo, while he did not approve of his superior's lapses into romanticism, did not interfere. In spite of his less than zealous interest in building the Soviet state, Rostnikov was a good policeman who, in his way, probably did far more for the state than so many of the self-interested Party members.

"You are the police?" asked the white-haired man impatiently. His voice echoed through the large room. Rostnikov enjoyed the sensation.

"We are," replied Rostnikov, moving toward the tables and giving up that instant of relaxation he always enjoyed before plunging into a case.

"I am Dr. Gregori Konstantinov of the Kremlin Hospital," said the man.

The import of that statement was not lost on Rostnikov. The Kremlin Hospital was known as the treatment center for the Soviet Union's political and military leaders. Dr. Gregori Konstantinov might well be an important man.

As he came closer to the doctor, Rostnikov could see that he was about seventy, stoop-shouldered, and very irritable.

"They all died of the same thing?" Rostnikov asked, glancing at the four naked bodies on the tables. Karpo had begun examining each one.

"It looks that way," said Dr. Konstantinov, pursing his lips. "If not, we have a coincidence worthy of publication in medical journals. Four men, all dead in the same night. All apparently poisoned. All with blood on their mouths, all pale. All in the same hotel."

"Hmm," grunted Rostnikov standing reflectively as Karpo went from one body to another.

"What's he doing?" asked the doctor irritably. "We'll do a proper medical examination at the hospital. I've already looked at the bodies."

"Magic," whispered Rostnikov.

"Policemen," grunted the doctor.

It was obvious which of the four bodies was the Japanese, and had the other three been dressed Rostnikov could probably have told instantly which were the Russians and which the American. Even so, that determination took little thought; the American was the bald man. His face had none of the squinting hardness of the Soviet male.

"Well, can I take the bodies?" sighed the doctor.

"A moment," said Rostnikov.

"There are sick people back at the hospital who are still alive," the doctor said.

"And they will have to wait for you," Rostnikov replied evenly. "I have never waited less than an hour for a doctor at the hospital. The patients will not notice."

Karpo came away from the bodies to speak to Rostnikov. As he paused in the dusty light of one of the high windows, he looked to Rostnikov like a figure in a religious painting by Rublev.

"They have all been drinking vodka," he said. "All have swelling at the lymph nodes. All have blood in the mouth. All have the smell, the same smell which I cannot place."

"Now can I—" began the doctor, but Rostnikov ignored him.

"So we have four guests in the hotel who have died from the same thing, probably something ingested."

"Quite probably," agreed Karpo, taking notes.

"So now we find out if they had dinner or a drink together last night. Who was with them. What they ate. Get the waiters who were on duty last night. Find out if any of these men were with a group, traveling with anyone. Discover—"

"Chief Inspector," came a voice from the doorway, interrupting Rostnikov.

Rostnikov looked toward the doorway and saw the form of a woman against the light. He could not tell her age, but her voice sounded young.

"Yes?"

"My name is Olga Kuznetsov. I am from the Intourist office in the hotel," she said, coming forward. "Mrs. Aubrey is here. She is demanding to know what happened. What shall I tell her?"

"Chief Inspector," growled the old doctor, "I would like to—"

"Who is Mrs. Aubrey?" Rostnikov asked.

"Her husband is the American who died," said the young woman, her voice wavering. She had seen the four corpses as she came forward, and had taken a step backward and looked away.

"Shall I talk to her?" said Karpo.

"No," sighed Rostnikov. "You find the waiters, check with the elevator operators, cleaning ladies, floor women. We'll meet in the lobby in half an hour."

"Shall we let them open the restaurant?" Karpo asked, putting his notebook away.

"After the good doctor has seen to the removal of the bodies. I think their removal during lunch might affect the customers and cut into the sales receipts." Rostnikov looked at the doctor to indicate that the corpses could now be removed.

"Games," grumbled the old man. "Bureaucratic games. They never change."

"Never," agreed Rostnikov. And then to the young woman from Intourist he added, "I'll see Mrs. Aubrey in your office."

"No need for that," came a voice behind him. It was a woman's voice, older than the Intourist woman and quite startling, for she spoke in English.

Rostnikov turned as gracefully as his leg would allow.

"Mrs. Aubrey?" he said, also speaking in English. "This I think is not a good place for us to talk."

"If you're thinking of my feelings, I can take care of them myself. That is not my husband lying on that table."

"It isn't?" said Rostnikov, giving the woman his full attention now. She was about thirty-five, very trimly built in a blue skirt and jacket. Her hair was black and long, her eyes dark, and her glasses large and quite Western. Her lips were full and pouting. Quite an attractive woman.

"My husband's soul, if he had one, departed when he died." She nodded toward the corpse. "That is the shell only, a symbol. I would like to know what happened. Who killed him and why?"

Karpo nodded and walked out, passing Mrs. Aubrey, who took a step back when she saw the giant figure approach her from the darkness. Then the doctor stalked out in search of attendants to take the bodies away. The Intourist woman stood uncertainly, her hands clasped in front of her. Rostnikov nodded at her, and she left. Then he turned to Mrs. Aubrey.

"If we go slowly," he said, "we can speak in English without a translator. Would you prefer?"

"That will be fine," she said, her eyes fixed on Rostnikov.

Rostnikov did not want to take another look at the body, not because he was squeamish, but because he didn't want Mrs. Aubrey to catch him and possibly figure out his thoughts. It wasn't necessary to look at the body again to know this woman was at least ten years younger than her dead husband, probably much more.

"May I ask you questions?" Rostnikov asked.

"You may ask," she said. "I'll decide if I wish to answer."

Rostnikov did not like the way she was looking at him, the challenging superiority of her attitude. Though he recognized that there were many ways to cope with sudden family tragedy, this American woman provoked him, and he wanted her respect.

"You show no grief," he said.

"I feel it," she replied. "I don't wish to share it with you."

"Why have you not demanded to see the American consul? It is the first thing to do in such a situation."

"I plan to do so in my own time," she said. "What has this to do with my husband's death?"

Rostnikov wasn't sure whether he had caught the meaning of all her words. His English was almost totally confined to reading American detective novels. The spoken words sounded strange to him, and he was always surprised to find that he had been mispronouncing so many of them in his mind when he read them. The word "husband" was not pronounced "whose-bend" but "huzz-bind."

"Your husband," he said, careful to pronounce the word as she had, "was here for the film festival."

"He is—was a writer, a famous writer," she said. "He was covering the festival for several American and English magazines."

"Can you think of reasons why a murder might be done upon your husband?"

"None," she said, turning her head as two young men in white linen uniforms came in carrying a stretcher.

"Would you like to talk in another place?"

"That is not my husband," she repeated, proving her conviction by looking directly at the naked body of Warren Harding Aubrey.

"Would you like to sit?" Rostnikov tried, doing his best to ignore the two attendants at their work.

"No," she said.

"Would you like to cry?" he went on.

She didn't reply. He waited. She still didn't reply.

"Did you have great affection for your husband?"

"Yes, he was a fine journalist," she said softly with something like feeling.

"You had love for him because he was a fine journalist?"

"I don't think I like you, Inspector," she said, and Rostnikov thought he detected the first sign of breaking emotions.

"I am sorry," he said with contrition. "I have my tasks."

The burden of speaking English was making it difficult for Rostnikov to think. The extra step of translation in his mind was giving the woman too much time between questions, too much time to recover. But it was too late.

"You did not share the room with journalist Aubrey?" Rostnikov went on as the two attendants hoisted the Japanese onto the stretcher. They were going to take the lightest weight first, which meant that Aubrey would be last. Unless they were doing this by nationality, in which case Rostnikov had no idea which the second corpse would be.

"I just arrived in Moscow this morning," she explained. "I'm a writer, too, and I finished an assignment. How did Warren die?"

"Painfully, I think," Rostnikov said, purposely choosing to misunderstand.

"That's not . . ." she began, and the trembling started in her lips. She had probably come here directly from the airport, and the disaster was still new and alien. She had taken on a competent exterior as defense, and while it stood, she was of little help. Rostnikov had been trying to chip away at it, and now the pieces were beginning to fall away. It was, he knew, a cruel and unfair battle, but her defeat and subsequent cooperation were necessary and inevitable.

"I think you must sit," he said, stepping forward and taking her arm firmly. She wore some Western perfume and smelled quite nice, he thought. Her arm was firm and she started to resist, but Rostnikov was a strong man. With his free hand he pulled over a nearby chair and guided her into it. She looked up at him, surprised by his action and strength.

"It could have been in the food," he said, looking down at her. "It could have been simply an accident. It could have been he was murdered but one of the other men was the intended victim. You understand?"

She nodded, her eyes now wet, but not so wet that she needed a handkerchief.

"From you I need to know what your husband was doing here. Who he talked to. Who might want to harm him dead. If you will think and answer and not hate me in place of the person who may be responsible, we can be finished quick. You understand?"

"I understand," she said.

"Good," sighed Rostnikov, pulling up a chair for himself so he could get some relief for his leg. "Then we start again."

All four bodies had been gone for half an hour when Rostnikov finished questioning Myra Aubrey. The attendants had taken one of the Russians second, Aubrey third, and then the other Russian. Rostnikov had discovered that Warren Harding Aubrey had been named for a U.S. President who was in ill repute in American history. The idea and the name fascinated Rostnikov, but he could find nothing in Mrs. Aubrey's tale that might indicate a reason for her husband's death.

"I'd like to have my husband's things," she said when Rostnikov finished questioning her. "He didn't have much with him."

"When we have looked through them, I will suggest that they be returned to you," he said. "You will be staying here?"

"Intourist has me at the Rossyia," she said, not looking at the table where her husband's body had been. "I don't . . ."

Rostnikov touched her shoulder. She didn't shrug his hand away.

"You are strong," he said. "Call upon that strength while we discover what has here taken place."

The line had come from some American novel he had read years before. He had always wanted to use it, but now that the time had come it felt awkward. Above all, he did not want this woman to laugh at him.

"The Rossyia is a marvelous hotel," he said.

"It is a massive joke," she replied. "My God, I can't believe I'll never talk to him again. It's like seeing a movie and having the film tear."

The anology made no sense at all to Rostnikov but he nodded knowingly nonetheless.

Miraculously, perfectly, the Intourist woman Olga Kuznetsov reappeared and guided Mrs. Aubrey out the door. She had recovered her composure and turned to remind Rostnikov that she wanted her husband's things. He repeated that he would do his best to get them for her. Then she was gone.

A search of the rooms of the four dead men revealed little. The Japanese had more than a dozen rolls of exposed film in one of his suitcases. He also had a number of pamphlets in Japanese with what appeared to be stills from movies that bordered on the pornographic. Rostnikov wondered if there was a market in Russia for such films. Where would they be shown? Among private collectors?

Investigation of the rooms of the two Russians revealed that one of the men had a small supply of English pounds hidden in his jacket and the other had several boxes of chocolate candy.

The two Russians and the Japanese had been in Moscow alone, no family, no traveling companions.

Aubrey's room revealed little more. There was, however, a notebook in the pocket of Aubrey's jacket with names and comments. It took Rostnikov a few minutes sitting on the bed to decipher Aubrey's scrawl and to discover that in the past two days he had interviewed various people connected with the film festival. The list included James Willery, whose name sounded English or American, possibly Canadian; Wolfgang Bintz, clearly a German; and Monique Freneau, almost certainly French. Rostnikov recognized none of the names, but the notebook gave him an idea. He made a thorough but fruitless search for Aubrey's notes or tape recordings of the interviews. Then he made a note to ask Mrs. Aubrey how her husband took his notes.

The chief inspector placed himself so that he could watch the hotel desk and the people crossing the vast carpeted lobby while he listened to Karpo's report. He did not expect to witness anything directly related to the case, but he was beginning to feel that if he was going to solve this case, he would have to cultivate a more specific understanding of foreigners. As he sat listening and watching, Rostnikov decided that East Germans looked the most like Americans. Several registered and let their accents give them away even across the expanse of the lobby.

He learned in the course of the next twenty minutes that the four dead men had indeed shared a bottle of vodka in the Metropole restaurant the previous night. In fact, they had shared two bottles of pepper vodka, a number of dark beers, a very large order of smoked salmon, and some caviar. The empty bottles and remains of the food were nowhere to be found.

Apparently Warren Aubrey had absented himself from the party for about an hour. A waiter had heard him say something about finding a woman. Under pressure from Karpo, the waiter had explained that it was his impression that the American was going to seek a prostitute.

"And next?" asked Karpo, closing his notebook which, after he copied his comments for official use, would go into the extensive library of black notebooks in his small apartment, notebooks containing every detail of every investigation he had been involved in for the past twenty years. He would index and cross-categorize the notes, and he would later return to the notebooks if more information turned up.

"Next," sighed Rostnikov, "we get something to eat. Then you make yourself ominous at the police laboratory until they give you a report on what killed those men."

Rostnikov also gave him the task of tracking down the prostitute Aubrey might have been with, then added, "Oh, yes. I have some names from a notebook, people who must be interviewed. Foreigners who are here for the film festival. Do you speak German?"

"No." Karpo shook his head.

"Then I'll talk to the German one," Rostnikov said, leading the way to the Metropole dining room. He would personally interrogate the kitchen staff.

"Do we have anyone who speaks French?" he asked.

"Tkach," answered Karpo, staring down a hotel guest who gave them an angry look when the two detectives pushed past him into the dining room.

"Good. Tkach gets the Frenchwoman. I'll find him after we investigate the kitchen."

THREE

THE BEATINGS HAD BEEN PARTICULARLY BRUTAL BUT none of the seven victims had died. Sasha Tkach, though only twenty-eight years old, had seen a great deal in his three years as a police detective. He had seen decayed corpses, old men so frightened that they had messed their pants while being robbed, and even the body of a very young boy whom Tkach had been forced to shoot. But these rape victims were the worst he'd ever seen—their faces swollen, bones broken, teeth punched out, hearing destroyed, ribs cracked. The victims were all women of about fifty.

All—at least those who could speak—told the same story. As they were walking home from a store or from work at dusk, four or five young men had appeared from nowhere and dragged them behind a nearby building or into a hallway. First they beat the women. Then they raped them, robbed them, and left them to be discovered, their clothes ripped, their bodies torn.

Tkach felt sick with rage, especially after talking to the third victim, who reminded him of his wife Maya. Tkach and Maya had been married less than a year, and he worried about her. Moscow was not plagued by gangs and random violence, but such things happened. As a policeman he knew this far better than the citizens, who were given the impression that crime was almost nonexistent in the Soviet Union.

This victim even had Maya's Ukrainian accent. Tkach nervously ran his hand through his blond hair throughout the interview, and by the end of it, he had abandoned all professional detachment. It had happened to him before. Maya had warned him not to become personally involved in a case. So had Chief Inspector Rostnikov. But it was not something Tkach could control.

He had prepared maps of the area where the muggings occurred, charted the times of day, pieced together descriptions of the assailants. He kept all this in a file in the desk he shared with a hulking police officer named Zelach. Though he had other cases, the muggings occupied Sasha's mind. His great fear was that he would be placed on a new case and told to forget this one for a while. He would not forget.

It was only this morning that he began to see a possible pattern. Yes, the time of day was about the same, but the locations were strange—not in a cluster but back and forth along a line, an almost straight line but on different streets. It had struck him in the morning as he rode the metro. Yes, the metro was a series of straight intersecting lines except for the Koltsevaya Line, which circled the inner city.

Now he sat at his desk, a metro map in front of him with the list of locations of the muggings. It was true. Each mugging and rape had taken place within walking distance of a stop on the green line. No two had taken place near the same station.

He marked them off with a pencil by date. The first attack had been a month ago near the Voikovskaya station. The next was a short walk from the Sokol station. The pattern was clear. The muggers were using this line and moving closer to central Moscow. If the pattern held, the next attack would take place near Pushkin Square.

But there was something wrong. There was no mugging near the Byelorusskaya station. Why would they skip that station, if indeed they were working along the line and

using it to escape? The most obvious answer was that Byelorusskaya was their home station, where they worked
from and where they might be recognized. It made sense.
So, what was next? Why did these muggings take place
early in the evening? Wouldn't it be better for the criminals
to wait till total darkness? The answer was almost laughable. They committed these crimes after work; they left
their jobs, went out and beat and raped women, and then
promptly went home.

Tkach could wait at the Pushkin Square metro station
shortly before dark in the hope of seeing a gang of young
men who fit the description of the criminals, but miss them
in the crowds. Or they might change their pattern.

No, it would be better to watch the Byelorusskaya station and painstakingly follow any suspicious group. But
that, too, might take days, weeks, months. The great open
square near the station was especially crowded in the evening.

At that moment he put it together. One of the victims
had told him that she thought she'd recognized one of the
muggers. He was a dark young man who had sold her a
drink near the statue in Gorky Square.

Twenty minutes after the idea came to him, Sasha
Tkach was standing in Gorky Square, eating his lunch and
pretending to admire the statue of Maxim Gorky erected in
1951. Chewing thoughtfully, Tkach pushed his blond hair
from his forehead, skipped out of the way of two little boys
who were playing a game, and pretended to admire the old
Byelorussian railway station, one of the few structures that
remain from Moscow's past. The station is over a hundred
years old with trains leaving daily for Paris, Vienna, London, Oslo, and Stockholm.

Tkach had seen it all before, had been in the garden,
heard his mother's tale of welcoming home the war heroes,
in the square in 1945, but today his thoughts were elsewhere. Several young men wandered by selling drinks, but
all were blond. Then, after about an hour, Tkach saw what
he was looking for. A young man with straight dark hair,
looking very much like a French or American rocker of the

1950s, strode down from Leningrad Prospekt carrying a basketful of bottled drinks. Tkach began following him at a discreet distance. It might be the wrong youth, but Tkach had a hunch. The man was easy to follow. He moved slowly through the crowd and did not seem particularly concerned with selling his wares. Then a second young man joined him. A few minutes later, a third joined them and then a fourth. They laughed, pushed one another, looked at the passing women. Then they checked their watches and headed for the metro station. They took the underground walkway across the street, and Tkach almost lost them in the crowd, but they were in no hurry, and he found them well before they entered the station.

Tkach got on the same car with them and his heart started pounding when, two stops later at Pushkin Square, they began pushing their way off the train. The pattern fit.

Out on the street they hesitated, discussing whether they should move across the square toward the Rossyia Cinema or down Gorky Street. They opted for Gorky Street, and Tkach followed. They turned off at the Stanislavsky Theater, made another turn a block farther on, and stopped. The street was narrow and almost deserted. Tkach kept walking and went right past them as if he were in a hurry to get home. They watched him, he was sure, as he turned a corner. Darkness was coming now, and Tkach started looking for a public building, an open door. It was time to get help. He was confident that he had found the attackers, even though he had no evidence. The victims could identify them. That would be proof enough. He found a small gift shop and ducked inside, watching the window for the approaching muggers.

"Yes?" said the woman behind the counter without enthusiasm, recognizing Tkach for what he was, a Russian and not a foreign tourist.

"Your phone," he said, looking back. The young men had turned the corner and were walking toward the entrance to a building Tkach did not recognize. It was a large new office building.

"We have no phone," the dark-haired shop owner said.

"Then find one." He pulled out his wallet and held his identification in front of the woman's face. "Find one and call Petrovka nine-one-one. Ask for Chief Inspector Rostnikov." The young men had now disappeared into the building across the street. "If he's not there, ask for Inspector Karpo. Or ask for anyone and tell them Inspector Tkach needs help in that building."

He pointed to the building, stuffed his wallet in his pocket and turned to leave. But the woman looked unimpressed, and Tkach said angrily, "I vow to you, woman, if you do not find a phone and make the call, and do it quickly, you will be answering questions tonight instead of going home."

He dashed out of the store and ran across the street.

He was panting lightly when he entered the building. He loosened his tie and looked around the lobby. It was the headquarters of some branch of the railway and transportation system. A guard should have been in the lobby to take names. Even though it was a bit late, some people were still leaving the building. Now, he thought, where are they? Did they spot me? Do they know of some other way out? Or have they already found a victim and pulled her into a stairwell, or . . . One of them was standing around a corner near an elevator door. Where were the others?

The young man pressed the button impatiently, glanced over his shoulder at Tkach, who was walking toward him, and showed no sign of recognition. Tkach waited with him at the elevator. Without looking at the man, Tkach could see that he was about twenty. He outweighed Tkach by twenty pounds, and was a few inches taller. As Tkach recalled, this was one of the smaller members of the group.

Tkach didn't have his gun with him. He had not expected to need it. In truth, he had carried it as seldom as possible since he shot the young robber this past winter. But Tkach knew that he could subdue this one young man.

Looking at Tkach's loosened tie, the young man smiled and said, "I think it will be a warm summer."

"Perhaps," said Tkach indifferently.

"You work here?" the young man asked casually.

"Sometimes," Tkach replied, giving the man an imperious look to indicate that such a question was far too familiar for his taste.

The elevator arrived, and the two men stepped inside. The operator was a woman about fifty. Tkach didn't want to seem reluctant to give his floor number, so he said, "Twelve." The young man said, "Seven."

The elevator rose slowly. The woman adjusted her glasses, and Tkach pretended to ignore the young man. When the doors opened at seven, the young man turned to Tkach and smiled slightly before getting off.

As soon as the doors closed Tkach said, "Comrade, let me off at the next floor. Then take the elevator down to the lobby and wait there for the police, who will arrive soon. Take them up to the seventh floor and tell them to be careful."

The elevator operator looked over her shoulder at him as if he were mad and went past the eighth floor. Tkach, sweating now, whipped out his wallet and showed his identification. "MVD," he said. "There is a gang of rapists in this building. You just let one of them out on the seventh floor. The others are probably there now looking for a victim." They were passing the ninth floor, and she was looking at him stupidly with her mouth open. He went on. "You might be that victim. Let me out. Then go right back down without stopping and do what I said. Do you understand?"

She nodded as they passed the tenth floor. He reached over and pushed the button for eleven. She pressed herself against the wall. The door opened, and Tkach said, "Now go down. Quick."

As soon as he was out of the car, she pushed the doors closed and was gone.

The dark hallway was quiet and deserted. Then Tkach saw a woman of about sixty with a bucket in her hand.

The cleaning women, he thought. They're after a cleaning woman. He dashed past the woman. He ran down the narrow concrete stairs two at a time, almost stumbling.

On the seventh floor the corridor was also dark and deserted. Staying in the shadows, he moved along slowly, listening, and then he heard something, a ticking perhaps, metal hitting metal. He followed the sound, carefully listening for voices, hearing none, trying to keep his footsteps as soundless as possible. It took him a few minutes to determine that the tapping was coming from a room at the far end of the corridor. Perhaps it was a cleaning woman.

He stopped at the door, listening for a moment to the soft clanking, then pushed it open. The office was dark, but the sound was quite clear. And then the lights went on.

One of the men was tapping a knife against a metal desk. There was a man on each side of the door. The one who had been on the elevator stood in the corner, his arms folded, a smile on his face.

The one with the knife stopped tapping.

"You followed like a fish," he said, showing a very poor set of teeth. He was the biggest of the group, quite big and clearly the leader.

"I am a police inspector," Tkach said, trying not to show fear. "There are police downstairs by now. You don't want trouble with the police. Just come with me and answer a few questions."

"About what?" asked the leader, closing his knife and putting it in his pocket.

"Routine," said Tkach, cursing himself for sweating.

"Ah," said the leader, suddenly understanding. "You mean about my selling drinks in the square without a license."

"Yes," said Tkach. "That is it."

"And you followed me all the way here for that great crime?"

"And to see if you were involved in any other criminal activity," Tkach said. "I don't like your looks, but I can see you're not up to anything more than mild hooliganism."

"Do any of you believe this baby face?" the leader asked.

There was no answer. The leader came around the desk and moved in front of Tkach.

"Those women," he said. "That's why you followed us.

We want to know how you got on to us. You tell us. Then we push you around a little, tie you up, and run. We've got places in the North we can go."

It was a lie, a poor lie, a game to give Tkach hope and then take it away. The image of the battered women came back to Tkach and he said, "There is no place you can hide in the Soviet Union. You know that. You might as well give up and hope that you get labor in a detention camp."

"I don't like this," came a voice from behind Tkach. It was one of the men at the door, the one who looked like the youngest. "If the police are coming, we have to get out of here. Let's just kill him and go."

The leader shook his head sadly at the ignorance of his underling.

"There are no police coming. He's the only one. He hasn't had time to call for help. He's alone. We saw he was alone."

Tkach now understood the situation. The leader enjoyed making the victim suffer; they had probably never worked on a man before, and he was trying to decide how to handle it.

He looked at Tkach and suddenly threw a punch into the policeman's stomach. Tkach doubled over, and the man grabbed his hair and pulled him up straight.

"To the elevator," the leader said. "We'll make it a double. Our brave policeman can watch while we show him first hand how we do our work on the elevator operator. Misha, when we get on, you close the elevator doors. Boris, you grab the woman and throw her on the floor. Alexi and I will watch our inspector."

When they turned Tkach around, he was still trying to catch his breath. Breathe slowly, he told himself as they walked to the elevator. As soon as the door opened, he would make his move, try to fight them off and get the door closed. It wasn't much of a plan, but it was the best he could do. At the very least, he would smash the face of the leader before they got their knives into him. May the first punch be wonderful. May it break him, kill him.

He dragged his feet and doubled over, trying to slow

them down, but it didn't do much good. He had told the
elevator operator not to come up here, to wait for the police, but he had little hope that she would obey. And he
couldn't be sure the woman in the gift shop had called.
Even if she had, he didn't know how long it would take for
help to come. It would almost certainly be too late.

The men surrounded him at the elevator door and
pushed the button. Tkach hoped fervently that the elevator
would not come but slowly, steadily, it was coming. He
looked up at the inscription embossed on the panel above
the elevator door: The Revolution Continues. Transportation Forward.

With that, the door of the elevator groaned open, and
two of the muggers stepped forward to grab the operator,
but the woman was not there. Instead, a stubby washtub of
a man with a dark scowl and muscular, hairy arms seized
the two men. Both came skittering out almost instantly, one
thrown across the corridor against the wall, the other sliding back on his rear.

Tkach straightened up and slammed the heel of his hand
into the nose of the leader. The man screamed, and stumbled back, holding his face in his hands.

The other mugger, the one who had ridden up in the
elevator with Tkach, had his knife out and was advancing
on Rostnikov, who stepped out slowly, staring at him.
There was no time for Tkach to move, but neither was
there need. Rostnikov ducked low as the man with the
knife lunged, then grabbed the man's arm with one hand
and his belt with the other. He lifted him and hurled him
against the wall, where he sagged to the floor next to the
man with the broken nose.

Tkach heard a sound behind him and turned to see the
second man, whom Rostnikov had thrown out of the elevator, reach into his pocket. He kicked the man in the stomach and was satisfied to hear an escape of air not unlike the
one he had let out when the leader punched him.

Without a word, Rostnikov herded the four muggers
into the elevator with kicks and pushes and motioned
Tkach in, giving a sour look at the whimpering leader.

Then he pushed the elevator button for the first floor.

"I—" Tkach began, trying to put his clothes back in order.

"Not now," said Rostnikov abruptly, "I have important work for you to do. You do speak French, don't you?"

"I speak French," said Tkach.

"*Bon*," said Rostnikov, turning so that neither Tkach nor the muggers could see the satisfied grin on his face.

FOUR

PROSTITUTION, OF COURSE, DOES NOT EXIST IN THE Soviet Union. It has not existed since 1930. This disease of
exploitative societies, according to the official *Soviet En-
cyclopedia*, "has been liquidated in the Soviet Union, since
the conditions engendering and nourishing it have disappeared." Lenin said that "lack of self-control in sexual
matters is a bourgeois characteristic, a sign of demoraliza-
tion." Therefore, following a brief flurry of free love
movements after the revolution, the Soviet Union effectively ended the sexual exploitation of women.

Which is why it took Emil Karpo almost half an hour to
find the prostitute he was looking for in Moscow. Normally, time and duty permitting, Karpo met Mathilde in the
Café Moscow off Gorky Street at seven in the evening on
the first Wednesday of each month. They would then go to
the apartment Mathilde shared with her aunt and cousin,
who would be conveniently absent for an hour. Mathilde
worked as a telephone operator during the day and as a
prostitute at night. She was a *sekretarsha*, or "secretary,"
not a full-time *prostitutka*.

Mathilde was not at the Café Moscow, but the waiter
who set her up with clients stood leaning against the wall,
his black bow tie clipped on at an odd angle. His name was

Anatoli, and he was somewhere between forty and sixty. His hair was thin, his body sluggish, and his expression sullen. He saw Karpo coming and feigned indifference as he turned to start a conversation with another waiter.

"So," he told his friend, "if I can get an extra ticket, and you want to pay the twelve rubles, you can have it."

"Twelve rubles?" asked the man incredulously, removing the black papirosi cigarette from his mouth. "I wouldn't pay more than seven." The papirosi had a long cardboard filter and smelled like burning rope. Karpo, who never drank, smoked, or even considered abusing his body, was revolted by all smoking and drinking, which meant he had much to be revolted by in Moscow.

"Anatoli," Karpo said, stepping behind the waiter.

The other waiter glanced up at Karpo, smelled cop, and headed for the ktichen. Anatoli turned slowly and gave Karpo a bored look.

"Yes?" he said.

"I must see Mathilde immediately."

"Impossible," said Anatoli with a near chuckle at the absurdity of the request.

"You misunderstand," Karpo said softly, putting his good right hand on the waiter's shoulder. "This is not a request. It is an official police order."

The waiter winced in pain and began to sink, but Karpo pulled him up. A pair of late lunching customers saw the disturbance and, pretending they hadn't noticed, hurried to pay their bill and leave.

"Mathilde," he repeated. "I am not going to arrest her or you."

"You'd better not," said Anatoli, reaching up to massage his aching shoulder. "It would do you no good for your superiors to know about you and her."

He got no further. Karpo's hand was around his neck, and Anatoli found himself looking into the emotionless face.

"That would embarrass me," Karpo whispered, "but it would not cost me my job. It would, however, lead to your detention and sentencing as a panderer, and you are well aware of the penalty for that." He released him roughly. "Where do I find Mathilde?"

Anatoli's clip-on tie had come loose on one side and dangled as he touched his throat and let out a rasping sob.

"Home," Anatoli whispered, and cleared his throat. "She called in sick to the telephone office."

Karpo turned and headed for the door.

"She's not alone," Anatoli said.

Karpo continued on through the door and out into the street. In ten minutes, he was on Herzen Street, heading for a long row of almost identical ten-story apartment buildings. He entered the fourth building at a little before two in the afternoon and began the climb to the seventh floor. His left arm still throbbed occasionally, but the doctor had assured him that the throbbing would eventually go away. Karpo wasn't so sure. He also wasn't entirely sure he wanted it to go away. What he wanted was full use of the hand and arm. A little pain, like the great pain of his headaches, was a challenge to him. It was a test of his endurance, his dedication. The world was full of obstacles, pain, human frailty. The challenge for the state and the individual was to overcome the frailty. Karpo had done admirably with a few minor exceptions. He considered Mathilde, whom he had known for almost seven years, a major frailty.

Karpo did not hesitate at the door. His four knocks were sharp and loud, and the familiar voice called, "Who is it?"

"Karpo," he replied. Behind the door he could hear frantic scrambling and a man's voice, but it took no more than ten seconds for the door to open. Mathilde stood before him, the front of her green dress closed except for one button at the waist. Her dark brown hair fell loose to her shoulders. She was not pretty in the conventional way, but she was handsome and strong. Certainly, she was confident and sturdy. Even now one hand was on her hip as she faced Karpo in the doorway.

"You're a week and five hours early," she said.

"I have some questions to ask you," Karpo replied.

"Send him home." His eyes had not left her face. For a

moment she looked angry, but then she must have remembered that anger had no effect on the man who stood before her. Secretly she felt sorry for Karpo, but she would never tell him so, because she knew that the slightest display of her feelings would send the gaunt, serious man away, never to return. She stepped back, allowing him to enter, and closed the door to the one-room apartment behind him.

"Mikol," she said, without turning around. "Come out."

The door to the bathroom opened slowly, cautiously, and a thin young man came out. He was barely more than a boy, in fact, dressed in work pants and a white shirt. He was trying to put his tie on as he emerged, and his long, straight brown hair fell over his eyes. At first he looked at Karpo with a touch of defiance but on seeing the specter before him, the defiance vanished.

"I'm afraid you must leave now, Mikol," Mathilde said gently. "This man is an old friend. He is in the government, like your father. You understand?"

Mikol finished with his tie, unsure whether he should shake hands, say something to Mathilde, or just make for the door. He did the last, hesitating at the door as if to say something to Mathilde.

"I will talk to you on Monday," she said.

Mikol nodded, glanced at the unsmiling Karpo, and left, closing the door behind him.

"His father is an assistant to the transportation commissar," she said. "I've known the father almost as long as I've known you. Would you like some tea?"

"Yes," he said, ignoring the unmade bed in the corner near the window. "I've come for your help."

She walked into the kitchen alcove and began to fill the teapot. Over the sound of water splashing into the aluminum pot, she said. "Personal or business?"

"I have no personal interests," he said seriously.

Mathilde turned, pot in hand, eyebrow raised, and cocked her head.

"I have personal needs, perhaps," he amended.

"You are a flatterer," she said with a grin. She put the

pot on the burner and turned to Karpo, her arms folded in front of her.

"Do you miss many days at your job?" he asked.

"Mikol's father arranged for me to have the day off," she explained.

Karpo nodded knowingly. He was not at all naive. Corruption was rampant in the Soviet Union. One man, even a small dedicated group of men and women, could not hope to stamp it out completely. But one had to keep trying, keep behaving as if it were possible. That was what gave meaning to one's life.

"I must find a prostitute," Karpo said as Mathilde sat down at the table.

"Well, you have come to the right place," she said, waving him to the seat beside her.

"I did not mean you," he explained. "I must find a prostitute who works near the Metropole Hotel, one whom a man might pick up late at night without attracting notice, one a taxi driver or clerk might have quick access to."

Mathilde looked puzzled. "What—"

"It is part of an investigation," he explained, and she knew she would get no more from him. She shrugged, discovered the open button on her blouse, buttoned it.

"Could be quite a few taxis." She sighed. "There are maybe a dozen who work out of cabs in that area, but if it was late, it would probably be a railroad prostitute, one of the cheap ones who work the stations. More likely, the one you're looking for went to the Metropole restaurant with her pimp or her husband. Probably works the place."

"A name," Karpo said, staring at her with unblinking eyes.

Mathilde smiled. "You don't even close your eyes when you're . . ." She hesitated. She had been about to say "making love," but the act for Karpo had nothing to do with love.

"The name," Karpo repeated.

Behind them, the kettle began to boil, and Mathilde rose to make the tea.

"What night?" she said, her back turned.

"Wednesday," he replied. "Yesterday."

"Her name is Natasha," Mathilde said. "She goes one night a week, Wednesdays, to the Metropole. She doesn't dare go there any oftener than that for fear someone might get suspicious and turn her in. Normally in the afternoons she works one of the railway stations in Komsomolskaya Square. Try the Leningradsky station. She's about thirty-five, on the thin side, short blond hair, fairly good teeth, no beauty, but when she gets dressed for a night at the Metropole, she can pass, especially with a foreigner who is drunk. Is that what you wanted?"

She returned with the tea and placed a cup before him.

"Yes," he said, his eyes meeting hers.

They drank quietly, saying nothing for almost two minutes.

"You've never been here in the daytime," she said finally.

"Until today," he agreed, finishing his tea.

"Since you are here . . ." she began.

Somewhere deep within him, Karpo had the same thought. It was as if she read his mind, exposed his need and turned it into a vulnerability.

"I think not," he said rising. "I prefer our regular arrangement."

"As you wish," Mathilde said with a slight nod.

As it must be, Karpo thought to himself, and he departed without another word.

The Leningradsky station was alive with people when Karpo arrived. He showed his identification to the policeman at the entrance who was posted there to keep out all those without tickets.

The hard wooden benches were crowded with peasants in ragged clothes. Some of them may well have been there for days, unable to find someplace in the city to sleep. All hotels were essentially beyond their means. Even if they were not, the chances of a peasant being given a room were nonexistent. If the peasant knew no one in the city or could find no one who would allow him and his wife and possibly a child or two to sleep on the floor for a few rubles, his only choice was to live in the railway station till his train came. The better dressed travelers sat a little straighter, sought others like themselves, or buried their faces in books to keep from being identified with the lowest levels of Soviet society.

Karpo moved to the dark little snack bar in the corner and watched the woman behind the bar. She had a clear case of asthma, made no better by the smokey station. She was ladling out chicken soup for a man in a rumpled business suit. When she finished, she shouted over her shoulder at one old woman who was washing the dishes.

Karpo caught the attention of the asthmatic woman.

"Natasha," he said softly. Just then another customer, reasonably well dressed but in need of a shave, ambled forward but when he saw Karpo's vampirelike face he decided to wait.

The woman had not been looking at Karpo. As she turned and saw him, her sour expression turned docile.

"My name is not Natasha, Comrade," she wheezed.

"There is a woman who works the station—blond, thin," he explained. "Her name is Natasha."

"I know of no such person," the woman said, looking around in the hope that a customer would save her from this man.

Karpo leaned forward, his eyes fixing on the woman's. He could smell her sweat. There was no room behind the bar for her to back away. Behind her the dishwasher asked if something was wrong. The woman said nothing and gasped at the face before her. Then her voice came out in a small whisper.

"She's here. The far corner, over by the second gate, behind the . . ."

But Karpo had turned and was gone. He pushed through the crowds, moving slowly, his eyes scanning the room. He spotted a prostitute almost immediately, but she was hefty and had dark hair. He went on, and in a few more minutes spotted the thin blonde. She was asking a gentleman for a light for her cigarette. At this distance, she looked rather elegant, but as Karpo pushed toward her, the look of elegance faded. Her face was hard, her hair brittle and artificially colored, her teeth uneven and a little yellow. Looking at her, Karpo thought that her nights at the Metropole were probably numbered. Soon she would be spending more time at the railroad stations, and soon after that she would only be working nights.

Karpo pretended to ignore the talking couple as he strode past them to a newspaper stand in the corner. In spite of the bustle of sounds around him, he caught a bit of the conversation.

"In about an hour," said the man. He had a boyish face and graying temples, and he looked like a professor.

"Plenty of time," said Natasha. "There's a place . . ."

And Karpo was out of earshot. He turned and saw the professor hesitate, heard Natasha coax, though he couldn't make out her words. The professor shook his head slowly, and Natasha grabbed his arm, smiling. Karpo felt confident of his quarry now. He stepped forward behind the couple, dodging a young man with a huge suitcase held closed by rope, and touched Natasha's shoulder. She turned suddenly, surprised.

"I'd like to talk to you," he said.

The professor didn't bother to excuse himself. He simply disappeared in the crowd.

One lost, one gained, she seemed to be thinking as her smile returned. Karpo didn't like the false smile, but he understood it.

"We can't talk very well here," she said, looking around.

With that she lifted her left arm so he could see the number 20 clearly written on her flesh. Karpo knew that street prostitutes put their prices on the soles of their shoes, on their arms, or on the palms of their hands. Her price was high for a railway station prostitute, but that was only the initial asking price.

"I'm a policeman," Karpo said softly.

Natasha's pale face went ghostly white.

"I've done nothing," she gasped. "I've broken no laws."

It was true, for there were no laws against prostitution. Since it doesn't exist, the argument goes, there need be no laws against it. However, as both Natasha and Karpo well knew, there were many sexual crimes in the nation's criminal code, including infecting with venereal disease, illegal abortion, sexual relations with a minor, and depraved actions. Natasha could be charged with several of the crimes, and the penalties could include a number of years in a penal colony.

"If you answer quickly and honestly," he said now, holding her arm, "I will turn in a minute or two and walk away. If you do not, I arrest you."

Natasha didn't respond.

"Last night at the Metropole. You were there?"

Natasha was about to tell a lie, but Karpo's face was inches from her own, and what she wanted most was to escape from this man.

"Yes," she said.

"There was an American. His name was Aubrey. He was looking for a woman. He found you."

Karpo was not at all sure that Aubrey had been with Natasha. If it turned out that he had not, Karpo would pressure her for another name, follow another lead.

"Yes," she said.

"Where did you go with him?"

"In a taxi," she said. "My husband is a taxi driver."

"What did the American say to you?" Karpo went on. A couple passing by looked at Karpo and the transfixed and frightened Natasha, considered intervening, and changed their minds.

"Nothing," she said. "He just got in. We . . . he couldn't do it so I helped him. He said nothing."

"Nothing?" asked Karpo. "A drunk who had minutes before been babbling?"

Natasha's eyes darted back and forth. Then, suddenly remembering, she cried, "Oh! He did say something. It was nonsense. Something about having them now, having the biggest story, having the liars. My English is not good, but something like that. He kept saying he had them now, and he would show them. But he didn't seem happy about it. More, you know, angry. Spiteful."

"Names?" Karpo went on.

"He mentioned no names," she said. "I swear. No names. He did say something strange, though. Something about a frog bitch. It is drunk talk. Dogs are bitches in English, I think. Frogs are not spoken of that way. He was drunk."

Karpo let her go, and she almost fell. Natasha's automatic reaction was to offer herself to the policeman for nothing, but Karpo was gone before she had a chance to speak the words.

The normal waiting time at the stone pyramid of the Lenin Mausoleum is half an hour, unless it is a holiday, in which case the wait is four times that. The line stretches several hundred yards across Red Square outside the Kremlin, but the people waiting are patient and respectful. Guides from Intourist usher foreigners and soldiers to the head of the line.

The one with dark eyes was a foreigner but chose not to seek help from Intourist, instead preferring to stand at the end of the line, facing resolutely forward. There was plenty of time, the day was pleasant, and the line was moving. There were a number of foreign visitors in line speaking languages the dark-eyed one understood but pretended not to. A young man directly ahead in the line was playing chess with a companion, a young girl, on a small board he held in his palm. An old man in front of the couple kept frowning at them as if they were committing an act of blasphemy in the sacred line. He looked over at the dark-eyed one for support but got none.

A guard stepped forward to tell a Japanese man to put his camera away. He told another man to remove his hands from his pockets. The crowd moved slowly, single file, down the steps and into the crypt. The temperature dropped with each step. No pausing, no talking. Hats off as the line passed the rigid soldiers standing a yard apart.

And then the dark-eyed one stood before the crystal sarcophagus containing the body of Vladimir Ilich Lenin. In the pinkish light, the seemingly perfectly preserved face was peaceful and calm. The dark-eyed one leaned toward the sarcophagus as the line shuffled forward and then stumbled.

The young man who had been playing chess with his girlfriend picked the stumbling visitor up. A guard moved forward to help, but the dark-eyed visitor waved him away with a nod of thanks and moved on into the daylight. There was no pausing on the tree-lined walk at the base of the Kremlin Wall. The crowd moved past the Mausoleum of Joseph Stalin; past those of Sverdlov; Dzerzhinsky; Irene Armand, the Frenchwoman who was Lenin's close friend; Soviet cosmonaut Vladimir Komarov; John Reed; Lenin's wife, Nadezhda Krupskaya; and Maxim Gorky. It was 2:00 P.M. The dark-eyed one held back a smile. It had been quite easy. The compact bomb, encased in soft plastic, now clung to the underlip of the tomb no more than two feet from Lenin's head. Provided the public transportation ran smoothly, the other two bombs would be in place by 5:00 P.M.

FIVE

WHEN PORFIRY PETROVICH ROSTNIKOV ENTERED HIS apartment shortly after eight that night, his thoughts were a random bombardment of fragments. He knew he would have to put them in order, and he could think of only one thing that would help him. He greeted Sarah who, he could tell, had something on her mind. He could tell from the hand she placed on his right cheek when she kissed his left cheek. He could tell by the bustle and light talk as she prepared dinner. She told him about the letter from their son Iosef, which described a weekend in Kiev with two friends. Iosef would say nothing in a letter about his three months in Afghanistan. That would have to wait till he came to Moscow on leave.

Rostnikov grunted appreciatively as he changed into his sweatshirt and pants, leaving the bedroom door open so he could hear Sarah continue her chatter. Sarah was not a chatterer. The bomb, Rostnikov knew, would eventually fall. He glanced into the kitchen to see what she was cooking. It was his favorite dish, chicken tabaka, a Georgian specialty, which Sarah prepared to perfection when she could buy chicken.

She carefully removed the backbone, flattened the bird and fried it under a heavy metal plate weighted down still further by a hand iron. She would then serve it with a prune sauce and pickled cabbage. At that point he would be most vulnerable, and that's when she would speak.

Rostnikov moved to the weights, and Sarah stopped talking, knowing that she would not get through his concentration. Rostnikov turned on the radio, opened the cupboard, rolled out the thin mat, carefully removed the heavy weights, and, enjoying the music of Rimsky-Korsakov and the smell of chicken tabaka, began his routine. He had one more day to prepare. No one but Sarah knew that he had entered the annual weightlifting competition in Sokolniki Recreation Park. The competition was for men and women over fifty, and the participants, he well knew, were often remarkable. He had seen the competition every year for the past seven years, with the exception of 1977 when he was being held at gunpoint by a pyromaniac in the basement of the Moscow Art Theater.

This year, Alexiev was to give out the trophies. Rostnikov imagined standing next to his idol, accepting a trophy from him, clasping his huge hairy hand. The fantasy was overpowering. Rostnikov had never entered the competition before, because his leg would make it nearly impossible for him to participate in many of the events. To clean and jerk 200 pounds, he had to move in a strange swoop, and this put him at an immediate disadvantage. To win the event, he would have to do far better than the other competitors. Even the dead lift would be a problem, since he could bend only one knee. He would have to do on one leg what others did on two.

In moments, Rostnikov was happily sweating and straining. The music danced around him. He counted without having to think about counting. His body, arms, legs, and chest told him how close he was to exhaustion, and when that exhaustion came he would strain through it, his face turning red, his veins mapped along his furry arms, his breath coming in short puffs. Sarah always turned away from him at this point. In spite of his assurance that this was natural, she was convinced that he was doing terrible things to his body. She never tried to talk him out of it, for she realized how much he needed those weights. But still, she would not look.

Rostnikov had spoken on the phone to the partner of the dead Japanese filmmaker. The partner had spoken no Russian but could get along in English, so Rostnikov had conducted the interview in a language that was awkward for both of them.

The dead Japanese, Yushiro Nakayama, knew no one in Moscow. He had been in town only two days when he died. His film production company was small and produced soft-core pornography as well as one general release film each year. This year's film, *Green Days in Kyoto*, was an entry in the film festival. Nakayama and his partner, however, were less interested in the chances of winning a prize than in finding markets for their other films.

The partner might have been lying, but Rostnikov didn't think so. Like most Russians over forty, Rostnikov harbored a deep suspicion of the Japanese. The Japanese had been one of the few nations to clearly defeat Russia in a war. Of course that had been under the czarist regime, but it was a crushing defeat nonetheless. The Russians had done their best to avoid conflict with the Japanese during the Second World War, Rostnikov's war, leaving them to the Americans and the British. Rostnikov didn't trust the Japanese, though he grudgingly admired them. In fact, from his reading he had decided that the Japanese were clearly the most intelligent people in the world, which made him even more suspicious. Thus, though he felt confident that the dead Japanese film producer was the victim of an accident, still he decided to assign a junior officer to continue investigating his death.

He was waiting for reports on the two dead Russians. Neither one seemed likely to have been the intended victim. But, just in case, Rostnikov had called the home towns of both men and asked for a local inquiry and investigation.

No, he thought, transferring a weight to his right hand, the American journalist was the most likely target. Karpo's report had led him to that conclusion. Karpo's prostitute had said that Aubrey, the American, spoke of a frog bitch. Rostnikov remembered that Americans and Englishmen used the word "frog" in a pejorative sense to mean French. He had read that in one of his American detective novels. So the drunk and dying American in the back seat of a Moscow taxi had referred to a Frenchwoman. According to Aubrey's notebook, he had interviewed a Frenchwoman the day before his death. After the encounter outside the elevator, Rostnikov had dispatched Tkach to interview this Frenchwoman, Monique Freneau.

Yes, Rostnikov thought, he had done the right thing. Now the investigation could wait till morning when he would talk to Tkach, interview the German, and have Tkach interview the Englishman.

Rimsky-Korsakov and Rostnikov finished at almost the same time. Rostnikov reached over, panting, turned off the radio, put his weights away, and went to the kitchen table.

The food was excellent. They drank the borscht slowly, dug into the chicken with gusto, drank the wine with approval. Then it came.

"Porfiry," Sarah said, playing with a piece of chicken on her plate. "What do you think about France?"

The question was startling since he had, in fact, just been thinking about France. Her blue eyes suddenly met his.

"I am not overly fond of the French," he said, pouring the last of the wine from the small bottle. "In their assumed superiority they have little tolerance for any other people. They find Russians particularly barbaric. I think it has something to do with Napoleon's inability to—"

"No," Sarah interrupted. "I mean what would you think about living in France. Or England, or Israel, or even America or Canada."

That was it, then, Rostnikov thought. The idea had remained unspoken for so long, but now it was out. Sarah was a Jew. She could apply for immigration. It would not be easy, but it could be done, and Porfiry, as her husband, could apply with her. The problem, as they both knew, was that as soon as they applied, they would become objects of abuse. Their lives would be made miserable. They might well lose their jobs and be given tasks of no responsibility or merit. Their son Iosef would suffer, and, worst of all, they probably would never be given permission to leave. But it was something Rostnikov had been considering seriously since his job had grown more political and since his knowledge had become a potential danger to the state.

"Sarah," Rostnikov sighed, "I'm a policeman. They would never let me go."

"You know people," she said. "People who could help us."

Whom did he know? Anna Timofeyeva? What influence did she have? And as a loyal Party member, what would she think of his wanting to leave, to desert the cause when she was giving her life to it?

"I don't know anyone who would be willing to help us," he said.

Their eyes met, and he could see something in hers that she had been careful to conceal before, if it had been there.

"Porfiry," she said. "We are more than fifty years old. It is worth trying."

Insanely, the name Isola came to mind. Isola, the city of Ed McBain, where the police behaved so differently from those in Moscow. Now, if he could go to Isola . . .

"Sarah," he said, "it cannot be."

She nodded, got up, and began to clear away the dishes. An observer might conclude from this that the matter was ended, but Rostnikov knew better. He knew that it had only begun and that Sarah was much more patient and even more intelligent than he was. Besides, Rostnikov had been more than toying with the idea for some time.

The knock at the door was gentle. They thought the sound was coming from across the hall. Then it was louder. Rostnikov grabbed the table and pushed himself up, feeling the tug of the conversation and the nip of the wine.

At first when he opened the door, he didn't recognize the man before him.

"Yes?" said Rostnikov, wiping his moist brow with the hem of his shirt.

"I'm from upstairs," said the thin Bulgarian.

"The toilet," Rostnikov suddenly remembered. He had dismantled the toilet early in the morning, and the Bulgarians had been waiting for his return.

"Ah," sighed Rostnikov, "I have consulted an expert, the chief plumber at the Metropole Hotel. I'll have it fixed in a few minutes. Never fear."

He pushed the Bulgarian gently into the hall.

"I'll just get my tools and be right there," he said softly, not wanting a neighbor to overhear and call the dreaded Samsanov.

Sarah looked up at him when he closed the door. In her eyes was the unspoken question, Would this happen in Paris or Montreal or Chicago?

Rostnikov shrugged, believing that it would, but thinking it unwise to raise the issue again.

"I'll be right back," he said. "This will take me no more than fifteen minutes."

It was, in fact, nearly two hours before Rostnikov returned. There had been unforeseen complications. The tools had been inadequate, and the book he had been using was far out of date. He had eventually managed to get the pipe repaired, but he feared that the repair was temporary.

"Toilet is now fixed," he told Sarah, who was sitting at the table writing a letter, probably to her sister or Iosef.

"That's good," she said, looking over the top of her glasses and smiling, her mind in Odessa or Kiev or San Diego.

Rostnikov was washing at the sink when the phone rang. Sarah answered it and held it out to him.

"I don't know who it is," she said with a shrug.

He crossed the room and took the phone. "Rostnikov," he said.

"In the morning," came the man's voice, "at precisely seven, you are to be at the office of Colonel Drozhkin."

Rostnikov said nothing.

"Do you understand?" came the voice.

Rostnikov recognized the man as Zhenya, Colonel Drozhkin's assistant.

"I understand," Rostnikov said evenly. "I will be there at seven."

They hung up, and Rostnikov turned to his wife. "Business," he said. "I have an appointment early in the morning."

That was all he said. He reread a mystery by Lawrence Block and went to bed wondering what the KGB wanted from him this time.

In the evening right after the incident with the gang of rapists, Sasha Tkach took a bus to the Rossyia Hotel. He went through the huge glass doors and across the vast lobby whose walls were covered with film posters and blowups of movie stars, mostly Bulgarians, and advanced to the desk. He gave the name of the woman he was seeking, Monique Freneau, identified himself, and waited while the clerk at the long desk looked up the name. He couldn't find it. Normally, the clerk would have given up, but this was a policeman with a determined look in his eyes, so the clerk tried the rosters for the other towers and eventually found the Frenchwoman's name.

The Hotel Rossyia is a sharp contrast to the Metropole. It is massive and new and official comments in tourist books and publicity call it "the Palace." Muscovites, looking up at the gigantic structure on the Moskva River, refer to it as "the box." The twelve-story hotel has thirty-two hundred rooms, nine restaurants, two of which can seat a thousand diners each, six bars, fifteen snack bars, and the world's largest ballroom. It also houses two movie theaters for eight hundred spectators and one larger cinema hall, the Zaryadye, which can comfortably accommodate three thousand people.

Sasha found Monique Freneau's room with no difficulty. He knocked, and the door opened on a woman who quite dazzled him. He was sure he had seen her before. She wore a thin pink blouse made of some silky material; her jeans were tight and certainly Western. But it was her face and hair . . . Yes, she looked like the French actress Brigitte Bardot, but Bardot must be older than this woman. Perhaps this was a younger sister.

"Yes?" the woman said in Russian.

Tkach didn't know that many young women in France capitalized on their resemblance to the famous star and adopted the Bardot look.

"You are Monique Freneau?" he said in French.

She smiled. Tkach wasn't sure whether she was pleased that he was speaking to her in her native language or amused because he was doing it so poorly. Either way, her smile made him uncomfortable. In fact, Monique Freneau made him quite uncomfortable as she gestured for him to enter the room, but gave him little space to get through the doorway without brushing against her.

He glanced around the room. It was far bigger than the apartment he and Maya shared with his mother.

"I am from the police," he said immediately.

"I'm surprised," she said, sitting in one of the two chairs in the room and crossing her legs. "I thought a requirement of nonuniformed Russian policemen was that they be over fifty, solid, sober, and shaped either like a lamppost or like an American mailbox."

Her description fit Rostnikov quite well, Tkach thought. He also was aware that the woman, who might be anywhere from twenty-five to forty, was looking at him with amusement and employing what must have been her formidable sexuality.

"I have, I am sorry to say, another appointment," Sasha lied. "So, I will have to ask you some questions rather quickly. You probably have much to do, too."

"No, not really," she said, putting a finger to her chin.

"You are a maker of films?" he asked, taking out his notebook.

"I am a producer of films," she said. "There is quite a difference. Actually, I am the assistant to a producer, and I'm representing him at the festival."

"I would have thought you were an actress," he said, and immediately regretted it.

"I was," she said. "But I found it more . . . rewarding to be the assistant to Pierre Maxitte. You've heard of him?"

"I'm afraid not," Tkach said seriously.

"You have a name," she added disarmingly.

"Inspector Tkach," he said. "On Monday—"

"A first name?" she cut in.

"Sasha," he said.

"That is a nice name," she mused. "Fun to say. Sasha. Sasha."

"Warren Harding Aubrey," Sasha threw in. It stopped her, but didn't seem to disturb or upset her.

"The writer?" she asked.

"I imagine there would be few with such a name," he said seriously, "though I must admit I know little about American names."

"Aubrey interviewed me a few days ago," she said.

"Monday," Sasha said. "What did you talk about?"

"Why?" she asked. "What has he done?"

"He has gotten himself killed," explained Tkach. "It may well be an accident, but we are trying to trace his movements up to the time of his death yesterday morning."

"Dead," she said, looking at Tkach more seriously.

"Quite dead," he said. "Why did he interview you?"

"About Pierre," she said. "The movie we're showing at the festival, *The Devil in the Wind*. I had the impression that it was not a serious interview, that he was looking for gossip, perhaps about Pierre. Who knows? He even hinted that he might look favorably on our film if I was friendly to him. You understand?"

"Yes," said Tkach, writing down far more than he needed in order to keep from looking at her. Now he thought perhaps he understood why Aubrey had referred to her as the frog bitch. But as a lead, this looked like a dead end.

"What was the essence of his interview?" he asked.

"The essence. Let me see." She tapped her even white teeth with a neat fingernail and seemed to be thinking. "He wanted to know if Pierre and I were lovers, if I had ever made any nude films, if we were thinking of bribing or trying to bribe judges. He was not a particularly nice man."

"Any other details of the interview? Did he seem . . ."

"Aroused?" she asked.

That was enough. Tkach closed his notebook and looked at her. She looked back. There was certainly intelligence in the brown eyes, intelligence and amusement and something else.

"I haven't been much help, have I?" she said, rising slowly.

"You've told me what was necessary."

"If you'd like to come back tonight after dinner and ask more questions," she said, taking a step toward him, "I'll be right here."

Now Tkach smiled, and his smile stopped her. The game-playing halted, for she had seen something that told her things had not gone as she had guided them. That smile was quite knowing and much older than the face of the good-looking young detective.

"I have to work tonight," he said, stepping past her. "But I may have more questions. And perhaps next time you will answer with the truth."

Without looking at her he crossed the room, opened the door, and stepped into the hall, closing the door behind him. At this point, he had no idea whether or not she had told the truth. He'd had no reason to be suspicious until he gave her the knowing smile he had been working on for four years. He thought of it as the Russian police smile, which says, I know what you are hiding. Tkach didn't know that it was the smile of all detectives from Tokyo to Calcutta to San Francisco to Moscow. He had seen her play her scene out, then had given her the knowing smile, and for an instant she had broken, showing that there was something more behind those eyes and that lovely facade. He had no idea what she might be hiding or why. He would simply give the information to Rostnikov and let him worry about it.

Meanwhile, Sasha knew of a store that supposedly had received a shipment of coffee. If he was lucky, and if he hurried, he could get there while there was still some left.

It would get him home late and cost more than he should really spend, but it would be a welcome treat for Maya and his mother.

The coffee was indeed there. The wait was long, and Sasha arrived home late but quite content at a few minutes after eight, precisely at the moment that the dark-eyed foreigner had put the third and final bomb in place behind the screen in the Zaryadye movie theater in the Hotel Rossyia.

SIX

THE THIN FILAMENT OF WIRE ATTACHED TO THE BOTTOM of the door to Emil Karpo's apartment was just as he had left it. An intruder, even if he or she located the strand, could not replace it at exactly the right point. No one, Karpo was sure, had ever broken into his apartment. No one, as far as he knew, had any reason to do so, but on the slight chance that it might happen someday, he religiously attached that filament each time he left his room.

Inside the room, Karpo turned on the light over his desk in the corner, removed his notebook from his pocket, and carefully copied his notes as he always did. He put the copied pages into a dark book, made additional notes for cross reference, and shelved the book with forty similar books. There was no such thing as a closed case for Karpo. If a criminal—an enemy of the state—was not caught, the MVD might forget about it, but for Karpo the case would remain active. He had twenty-five such active cases, some dating back sixteen years, and he devoted a specific time each month to each of those cases.

The case of the bookstore skewer took a precise thirty minutes of his time every two weeks. In 1968, on a Tuesday afternoon, in the midst of dozens of people, someone had driven a sharp saberlike object through a minor Party official who was browsing in the Moscow Book House, Dom Knigi. No one had seen the crime done. The following Tuesday, a reasonably well-known poet had been similarly skewered in the philately department of the Moscow Book House. Again, no one saw it happen. Karpo had worked for almost three months on the case, which his colleagues jokingly called the shish-kabob murders. Then he was ordered to go on to other things. But his spare time was his own, and his spare time existed only to serve the state. So, every other Tuesday afternoon, at precisely the time the murders had occurred, Karpo returned to the Moscow Book House, in the faint hope that the killer, who had not struck for almost a dozen years, might show up again. He looked especially hard at people carrying umbrellas or canes or anything that might hide a long, sharp instrument. Such dogged pursuit had, in fact, led eventually to the apprehension of eight criminals who would otherwise have gotten away with their crimes.

When the notebooks were in order, Karpo took a shower and ate a piece of bread and a potato, washing the food down with a large glass of Borzhomi, a mineral water that tasted a bit like iodine. By ten, after an hour of sleep made difficult by the constant ache in his left arm, he fixed the wire on his door and left his apartment. An hour later, about the time Rostnikov and his wife were getting to bed, Karpo emerged from the Novokuznekskaya metro station, walked slowly down the street to a huge Victorian mansion at number 10 Lavrushinsky Pereulok, went around to a small side door in the darkness, and let himself in with a key he'd had made.

Once inside the Tretyakov Gallery, Karpo, having visited the building many times in the daytime, moved softly in the shadows, avoiding the old guards, to a room on the second floor. There the walls were jammed with gilt-framed paintings of various sizes. Sliding around a small marble statue of a man with a spear, Karpo opened the door to a maintenance closet and eased inside. He had done this for the past five nights, knew the room well, and placed himself so that he could see out through a thin space where door and jamb failed to meet. As usual, he would stand there till nearly dawn, watching and waiting.

The building contains the world's largest collection of Russian paintings, certainly more than five thousand. More than one and a half million visitors each year look at the iconic paintings of Andrei Rublev or the massive nineteenth-century realist paintings of Ilya Repin or the hundreds of photolike social realist paintings done during Stalin's tenure, such as *Workers at the Feskoskaya Factory in Morensk*.

A week ago a director of the gallery had discovered that one of the oldest paintings in the collection was missing. This was Karpo's case, and he had advised the gallery director to say nothing. When another painting, of a different period and in a different room, was found missing two days later, Karpo had begun his closet vigil. If there was a pattern, and the pattern held, eventually the thief would enter this room during the night, and Karpo would be there to catch him. Throughout the night, guards came and went. The room was silent but for the scuttling of something, probably a mouse, just before dawn. One of the guards paused on his rounds for a long drink from a bottle hidden in his jacket, and then light came. There had been no theft, at least not in this room.

Karpo was undiscouraged. He would simply return again tomorrow and the next night and the next, as he returned to the Moscow Book House. He had enough time to slip out unseen, get back to his room, and catch an hour of sleep before returning to the current investigation. Karpo had no great interest in the murder of an American writer, especially one as decadent as Aubrey clearly had been, but it was his duty, and he would work on the case as diligently as he worked on any other.

As Karpo allowed himself to recline on his narrow bed at seven on Friday morning, trying to find a reasonably tolerable position for his arm, Porfiry Rostnikov was entering the huge pale yellow building at 22 Lubyanka Street. The KGB headquarters stands opposite the 36-foot statue of "Iron" Felix Dzerzhinsky, who organized the Cheka for Lenin. The Cheka went through many transformations and is now the KGB, "the sword of the Revolution." There are white curtains at the windows and shiny brass fittings on the door. Beyond the general offices and interrogation rooms are, as everyone knows, the cells.

The KGB has more than 110,000 members, including many of the most intelligent and highly motivated Russians. It seemed to be Rostnikov's fortune, however, to deal with but one of that number each time he entered this building. After a ten-minute wait, a stiff-backed man with dark, curly hair led Rostnikov down a corridor and up a short stairway. It was a repeat of his last visit, and Rostnikov did not look forward to it. The guide knocked at the unmarked door, and a familiar raspy voice behind it said, "Come."

Rostnikov entered alone and closed the door behind him. Yes, it was the same. Dark brown carpet, framed posters on the wall urging productivity and solidarity. Chairs with arms and dark nylon padded seats and an ancient, well-polished desk behind which sat Colonel Drozhkin, white hair, dark suit, black tie. Drozhkin examined Rostnikov critically and indicated with a gesture of his callused hand that the inspector could sit.

"Your son is back in Kiev," said Drozhkin, starting the game.

"Yes," said Rostnikov, gazing at his host without emotion.

"Good," said the colonel. "Afghanistan is not a safe place for a Russian. Our losses, I will tell you confidentially, have been high."

It was Drozhkin, Rostnikov knew, who had arranged to have Iosef sent to Afghanistan, and it was Drozhkin who, having gotten Rostnikov's full cooperation in covering up certain details about a politically sensitive case, allowed Iosef to return to Kiev with his unit. It was Drozhkin now who was making it quite clear that he could do the same thing again.

"There is," Drozhkin said, folding his hands in front of

him on the clean desk top, "a group of fanatics, capitalist terrorists who have sought on various occasions to embarrass the Soviet Union. This pitifully small group calls itself World Liberation. It has members from several countries. It seeks to drive us into conflict with the West. It claims in its literature that once we are at war with the Western powers, both sides will be destroyed, and World Liberation will be able to take over. We have infiltrated this group in the past. We thought we had destroyed them, but a few have survived. Some of them are now in Moscow."

There was nothing for Rostnikov to say as the gnarled colonel paused to allow him to speak. It was rare for a KGB official to reveal so much even to the police, and Rostnikov knew that much of it might not be exactly true. Rostnikov shifted his leg and nodded.

"Your dead American, Aubrey," Drozhkin went on, "was working on a story about this group, this World Liberation. We think that his death may be related to that story and the presence of those terrorists in Moscow."

"Why—" Rostnikov began, but Drozhkin cut him off, rising and waving a hand.

"We know where the core is," the colonel said, straightening a poster of a grim-faced woman holding a flag against a red background, "but we want them all. We will watch that core while you continue your investigation. We are especially concerned about possible terrorist acts. There are many Western and Third World people in Moscow for this film festival. Any act of terrorism would be most unfortunate."

"Most unfortunate," Rostnikov repeated, thinking, unfortunate for whom?

"This is your investigation," Drozhkin said, his back turned, his hands clasped behind him. "It is important that you not fail."

The situation was now quite clear to Rostnikov. Dealing with terrorists was the responsibility of the KGB. Drozhkin, a survivor of several decades of purges in the intelligence and security service, had been given a most touchy assignment, to find these terrorists before they acted. As he had done in the past, Drozhkin was covering his flank. If the terrorists acted, he would somehow blame it on Rostnikov and the MVD.

"I understand," said Rostnikov.

"We have been watching the known members of World Liberation who are presently in Moscow," Drozhkin went on. "In fact, they are in Moscow because we chose to let them come in."

"Moscow becomes the web of a spider," Rostnikov said and immediately regretted it.

"If you wish," agreed the colonel, fixing his eyes on the policeman. "I am not given to metaphor. Our watching has yielded little. If nothing comes from you in forty-eight hours, we will arrest those members we know. Your task is considerable, Comrade Inspector."

"Considerable," Rostnikov agreed blandly. "But we must face our daily challenges and responsibilities."

Drozhkin's mouth went tight for an instant and then relaxed. "I'll detain you no longer," he said. "You may return to your investigation . . . and your plumbing. And please give our best to your wife."

Ah, thought Rostnikov, rising, the final point goes to the KGB. Rostnikov was being watched even down to his little plumbing escapade. And what of the remark about Sarah, whom Drozhkin had never met? The most vulnerable aspect of Sarah was her Jewishness. Was Rostnikov's apartment bugged? Yes, he thought, it probably is, and the KGB knows that we have talked about applying for immigration. Drozhkin is making an oblique threat.

"It has been good to talk to you again," Drozhkin added.

Rostnikov paused at the door. "It is, as always, stimulating to talk to you, Comrade Colonel."

The guide was waiting in the hall to escort Rostnikov from the building. He moved quickly down the hall, making it difficult for the policeman to follow him, but Rostnikov took satisfaction in the conviction that he could surely lift the man above his head and hurl him through the colonel's door, should madness come.

All in all, Rostnikov decided, he had emerged reasonably well from the discussion. Granted, he now was in a dangerous situation, but that was part of life. He had discovered that Aubrey's death was probably part of a terrorist plot. Growing in him was the hope and near conviction that the people Aubrey had interviewed were connected to the murder—the Frenchwoman, the Englishman, and the German. He would push them, push them hard, but first he would speak to Mrs. Aubrey to see if she could shed any light on her husband's research on World Liberation.

The sunlight and fresh air came as a surprise to Rostnikov when he stepped back into Krov Street and crossed to the metro station in front of the Mayakovsky Museum. He dismissed the idea that he might be followed. It would be so laughably easy to keep track of him that the KGB would have no reason to follow, but the idea came nonetheless, and as he moved into the underground he considered checking. It would be easy to look back, scan the crowd, then go through the underpass, return, and watch to see which face doubled back with him. The person would be crafty, probably quite good, but Rostnikov was confident he could spot anyone following him. The problem was that the KGB would then know that he knew he was being followed. So, since it made no difference either way, Rostnikov fought back the urge to let the KGB know he was aware of their interest. Such devious thinking, thought Rostnikov, keeps the mind active.

Back at Petrovka, Rostnikov walked past the downstairs desk, grumbled something to the uniformed guard, and went up the stairs to his office. He nodded at the junior inspectors who shared desks in the outer office and went to his own cubbyhole, where he sat down at his desk, picked up the messages, and removed the small tape recorder from his pocket.

The message on top informed him that the poison which had killed Aubrey, the Japanese, and the two Russians was a bizarre extract, cultivated from bacteria that affect birds. This deadly extract causes psittacosis, a disease normally transmitted to birds and occasionally affecting human beings. The report did not puzzle Rostnikov. It confirmed his limited knowledge of small terrorist groups. Drama was very important to them. If you simply hit a victim with a bat and walk away, you generate little publicity. If you inject diseases, take hostages in public landmarks, hijack airplanes, bomb babies, the world looks at you with fear or disgust or awe. The important thing is that the world looks at you.

Yes, thought Rostnikov, and in a society like ours, the act would have to be so massive, so public, that it would be difficult or impossible to cover up. Now the only problem would be to decide what such a public display might be. Would they kidnap the president?

Rostnikov ran his finger along the scratch on his desk made last winter by a sickle, the murder weapon in the case that first brought Rostnikov in contact with Colonel Drozhkin.

In ten minutes, it would be nine o'clock, time for Tkach and Karpo to come to his office for a meeting. The ten minutes gave him just enough time to hide the tape of his conversation with Drozhkin, see Procurator Timofeyeva, and on his way shout to that blini-head Zelach to find Mrs. Aubrey.

When he entered Anna Timofeyeva's office two floors above, he was disturbed to see how pale she looked. She was definitely ill. She had told him to report as soon as he returned to Petrovka, but he found it difficult to concentrate on his account of the interchange and nuances of the meeting at KGB headquarters. He doubted if her office was bugged, but it might be.

She sipped her tea, nodding at crucial points, her breath heaving in and out.

"Anna," Rostnikov said, stopping in the middle of a sentence, "I must call an ambulance for you."

"No," she said gasping for air. "I have a pill. Give your report and leave. I'm very busy."

The look in her eyes filled Rostnikov with a deep and sudden sadness. She was frightened, and Rostnikov suspected that she was having a heart attack.

"Overwork," she said.

"I'm calling the police ambulance," he said, reaching for the phone.

"Porfiry," she gasped, pulling a brown bottle from her desk and extracting a small pill, which she put under her tongue, "they'll carry me out on a stretcher, past everyone. I . . . it would be a humiliation."

"I'll accompany you, Comrade," he said, taking the phone.

"I do not wish to show weakness," she said, gritting her teeth and willing the pain to go away, but it would not.

"Our bodies are weak," said Rostnikov, dialing. "There is only so much we can do about it. What we can do is face the inevitable with dignity."

Through the pain, Anna Timofeyeva smiled. "You are a comforting mongrel, Porfiry Petrovich," she said.

Rostnikov told the medical aides to hurry to the office, explaining that the procurator was probably suffering a heart seizure. He hung up, and turned to Anna Timofeyeva. He wanted to take her hand, but held back, knowing she would not want that. When Ivan Kolenko was knifed, Rostnikov had held the hand of his dying colleague, though the two had never been friends. But Kolenko was a man, and in this society where the sexes were supposedly equal, he did not have the burden of proving his strength as did Anna Timofeyeva.

They said little while they waited for the medical aides. He offered her some tea which she refused. They could hear the aides coming down the hall.

"Porfiry," she said, softly gasping, "I must ask you a favor. If they take me to the hospital, will you go to my apartment and take care of my cat? His name is Baku." The request took a great deal out of her.

"Of course," he said lightly. "I am very fond of cats." Rostnikov knew that he lied well. In truth, he detested cats almost as much as he hated dogs. No, it was those who insisted on keeping them whom he had always disliked. The animals themselves were the extension, the manifestation. For the first time, he saw in Anna Timofeyeva's face something of the need one might have for an animal.

They said no more on the subject, and she insisted on rising and lying on the stretcher. The two young men who came for her were properly respectful of her bulk and title. As they carried her out, she raised a hand and said, "No, Rostnikov. You stay here and continue the investigation. If I survive, you can see me at the hospital with a report."

Rostnikov smiled. This wasn't a posture, but the real procurator coming through. The meaning of her existence was in her job, and she was not going to let her own dysfunction hold back the apprehension of enemies of the State.

"I will report to you at the hospital," he said, stopping in the hall as the stretcher-carriers hurried away. Heads came out of offices. Murmurs were heard along the way, and Rostnikov lamented the fact that on the four flights down to the main floor Anna Timofeyeva would have to face the thing she so dreaded, the public display of her weakness.

"What happened?" demanded a senior procurator in a nearby office.

"Comrade Timofeyeva has had a heart attack," he answered.

The senior procurator, an old man with a bent back, immediately touched his own chest and backed away. "She will be all right," the old man said, retreating to his office. "She is quite strong."

Rostnikov nodded and went slowly back to his cubbyhole. Karpo and Tkach were squeezed inside opposite his desk. He sat down facing them.

He did not want to tell them about Comrade Timofeyeva, but he had to. Neither commented, and so he returned to business.

"Now we turn—" he began, but there was a knock at the door.

"Come in," he said, and Zelach stuck his head in. His face was pale.

He's going to tell us that Anna is dead, thought Rostnikov.

"Inspector," said Zelach. "I don't understand. I have found Mrs. Aubrey."

"That does not sound difficult to understand," Rostnikov said impatiently. "Send a car for her. I want to talk to her here."

"We can't," said Zelach, looking for help from the impassive Karpo and curious Tkach. "She's in Australia."

"How did she get to Australia?" Rostnikov asked, bewildered.

"She has been there for five years," explained Zelach. "They have been separated for five years. She is a photographer for a newspaper in Sydney."

"I see," said Rostnikov, and a wry smile came over his face.

The woman who had audaciously introduced herself as Aubrey's widow was an imposter. Things were a little clearer. He would have to find that dark-eyed woman and ask her some very important questions.

SEVEN

"So," said Rostnikov, fingering the scratch on his desk, "where is she?"

Zelach had quietly departed, closing the door behind him.

"Who is she?" answered Tkach.

"What is she?" added Karpo.

"We have no lack of questions," Rostnikov sighed. "We will begin with the usual routine—checking the hotels, circulating a description. Tkach, you get Zelach and someone else on it. Check Intourist for names of tourists of the right age and general description. We don't even know her nationality. I'm sure she was not Russian. She'll have changed her appearance. Hair may be short, blond or red, possibly curly. She may be wearing glasses. Most likely someone is harboring her. She took a chance posing as Mrs. Aubrey. Why?"

Tkach had no idea.

"She wanted to find out what Aubrey had discovered and what we knew about World Liberation," said Karpo. "To find out if we were a threat to her plans."

Rostnikov nodded. There was no smile now.

"Whatever she is planning, it has to be soon," Tkach

added. "She can't hide here indefinitely. The longer she waits, the more likely she is to be caught."

"So," said Rostnikov, looking in his top drawer for something to put in his mouth, a throat lozenge or piece of hard candy. There was nothing there. "While normal channels are being pursued, we continue our investigation. I will talk to the German. You, Tkach, talk to the Englishman. Call his hotel first and find out if he speaks Russian or French. Emil Karpo, you direct the search for the woman who posed as Myra Aubrey."

It was a dismissal, and the two men left Rostnikov looking glumly at his telephone. He finally picked it up, mumbled a curse, and dialed the number of the KGB. He had to pass on to Drozhkin the news about the imposter. It was several minutes before Drozhkin took the call. Rostnikov could tell that the conversation was being recorded. He heard no click and had no prior knowledge, but he assumed that all calls to the KGB would be recorded, and the tone of the conversation made him certain of it.

"Colonel Drozhkin," Rostnikov said, "I wish to report to you that the woman who claimed to be Mrs. Aubrey, the wife of the dead American, has been shown to be an imposter."

"I see," said Drozhkin slowly. "You actually talked to her, questioned her?"

"I did."

"And where is she now?" Drozhkin went on.

"We do not know," said Rostnikov.

"She, then, is your murderer," Drozhkin said.

"And very likely the key to whatever World Liberation plans to do in Moscow."

Drozhkin's pause was brief. There should have been no hesitation at all. Perhaps age was working against him.

"There is as yet no evidence to link our knowledge of that group with the murder of your American."

Yes, thought Rostnikov, *my* American. My murder. My problem. But one cannot save one's neck that easily. This conversation would do Drozhkin no good, but Rostnikov sensed that there might be something in it for him.

"I thought you should know, Comrade Colonel," he said.

"Yes. You are correct. Remember our discussion. I will do what needs to be done here."

Without a good-bye, Drozhkin hung up. Rostnikov felt the stirrings of an idea as he switched off the tape recorder and unplugged the microphone he had attached to the phone. He was in a very vulnerable position, but so was Drozhkin. Perhaps there was something to be gained from this. Time and ingenuity would tell. Now he would go feed Anna's cat.

Following Rostnikov's call to Colonel Drozhkin, a series of misunderstandings transpired that led to five deaths and a week of cleanup work for a party sent out by Central Repair Committee. The members of that party were never told what they were cleaning up after and none of them, considering the nature of the debris, really wanted to know.

It began when Drozhkin told his assistant to order the operatives watching an Arab named Fouad to be particularly alert for any contact he might have with a woman in her thirties, a woman with dark eyes. The same message relating to the other members of World Liberation was passed on to three other operatives. The operatives following the Frenchman named Robert, the woman named Seven, and the Arab named Ali continued their normal routine, simply adding the dark-eyed woman to their surveillance. Alexi Vukovo, the operative following Fouad, decided that he would need to stay much closer to his quarry if he was to determine whether or not a woman had dark eyes.

Vukovo was quite eager, quite intelligent, and ambitious to the point that it now caused him trouble. He wasn't incautious as he boarded a bus going down Lenin Avenue. He was simply not quite as careful as he should have been, and he did not take into account Fouad's animal-like sense of danger. A man who survives to the age of forty-four, having alienated the PLO, Black September, and the Israeli secret police, is someone to be reckoned with. Also among Fouad's enemies were the intelligence services of every major country of both East and West. The only nations that didn't seek him were the small ones that didn't know of his existence. He was a survivor. So, when the young man with the good clothes appeared both in the park and on the bus, Fouad decided to kill him. He did not put great thought into the decision. The man might simply have the misfortune born of coincidence. The bus was crowded and the traffic thick. Fouad looked out the window and jotted down on his hand the license number of a passing taxi: 53-65. It meant nothing, but Fouad was sure that he had aroused the attention of the well-dressed young man.

It was a bright, shiny day. Fouad wandered to the door, got off at the next stop, and crossed to a grassy ridge under a tree. A red flag a few feet away was flapping in the slight breeze, and a small boy began to cry as his mother dragged him toward the tall apartment buildings beyond the parkway. The boy wanted something, but Fouad's Russian was not good enough for him to determine what it was.

The well-dressed young man did not get off at the stop with Fouad. That was no surprise. The Arab leaned back against the tree, squinting into the sun as he watched the bus move down toward Lenin Hills Avenue. Then it stopped, and several people got off. One, Fouad was sure, was the young man. A group of six people scuttled between the traffic, which was moving slowly as always, and Fouad walked in the opposite direction, crossing to the grassy median strip behind a white-helmeted motorcyclist.

There was no doubt now. The young man was heading his way. One more check. Fouad crossed the road and paused near another tree, glancing back. Yes, the young man had seen him and was now crossing. Fouad was not worried, but thoughts were coming quickly. If he is following me, he thought, why is he not more concerned about our distance at this point? One answer, the most reasonable and disturbing one, was that the man did not need close contact because he or someone else could pick Fouad up somewhere else. Which meant that they might well know about Kalinin Street.

Fouad passed through the line of trees to the pedestrian walkway and began a steady but unhurried walk toward Kalinin Street. The walk was long, and with every step he was more sure of the danger. There was no phone in the apartment, and even if there were, it would be madness to use it. So when he got to Vorovsky Street, instead of continuing, Fouad turned into Malaya Molchanovka Street and paused in front of the old house where the poet Mikhail Lermontov once lived. Fouad had no idea of the cultural importance of the place; he chose it because he remembered that the side of the building was hidden from the street. He paused, pretended to be looking for someone, checked his watch, and moved to the side of the building. Alexi Vukovo appeared a few minutes later, and he, too, moved around the building. Twenty seconds later, Fouad reappeared on the street.

He walked slowly and deliberately down the narrow street that would take him directly onto Kalinin. Five minutes later, he was at the door to the apartment. This was just about the time that Vukovo's body was discovered by a hairdresser on his lunch hour. The members of World Liberation moved quickly, but the KGB, which had been watching the building, moved even faster. The death of Vukovo blew the operation. Drozhkin had no choice. He cursed the terrorists; he cursed his wife; he cursed Rostnikov, but he did so silently. On the surface he remained composed. He moved instantly to recover what he might from this failure. He told his assistant to bring in the terrorists immediately, and he made it clear that if they resisted, they were to be destroyed.

Shortly after one on that Friday afternoon, Robert, the Frenchman, stepped into the street carrying his belongings in a small sack. The first stutter of shots came before he was across the sidewalk, stitching a line across his chest.

Seven shut the door as Robert went down. She shouted into the street, "Death to the East and West!" but no one heard her over the roar of guns.

Fouad and Ali headed for the rear of the apartment where a small window opened on a side street. Neither expected it to be unguarded, but it was their only choice.

When the first burst of gunfire came from the apartment, Dmitri Kolomensk, a sergeant who had been on seven similar missions in his almost forty years, ordered his men to launch three grenades through the windows of the apartment.

Kolomensk thought he heard a woman scream something the instant before the first explosion. He wasn't sure, and he didn't care. This meant that he would have to prepare a tedious report and answer a series of questions put to him by Colonel Drozhkin. The hell with it, he thought, and ordered the men to launch more grenades through the apartment's back windows. The entire operation took no more than four minutes.

"At least the building's not burning," Kolomensk said. "Go in and see what there is."

The KGB agents found the bodies of four members of World Liberation, a variety of rubble, and the remnants of furniture. However, the sack that the Frenchman had dropped in the street proved to be a far more interesting discovery.

Kolomensk dropped the papers back into the sack, hurried to the waiting car, and told the driver to get back to Lubyanka as fast as he could.

The papers consisted of a series of black and white maps of Moscow with red circles penciled in at various locations. Kolomensk didn't stop to consider what they might mean. He saw them only as a potential buffer between himself and the wrath of Colonel Drozhkin.

In spite of the noise, no curious onlookers appeared for perhaps ten minutes. It was best in Moscow not to be too near trouble. One so easily became a part of it. But curiosity is a marvelously strong motivator, and they eventually began to trickle past, kept in control by gray-uniformed policemen.

"A homemade bomb," one man confided to a young

woman who nodded as they moved slowly down the street.

"Gas explosion," said a well-dressed man carrying a briefcase.

"Gas explosions are not accompanied by gunfire," said a woman behind him, who was taking in as much as she could.

Behind this small group of gawkers came a woman with short, straight brown hair and very dark eyes behind black-framed glasses. She did not gawk with the others. In fact, she seemed to be a secretary or clerk who wanted nothing but to get past this road impediment and go to work. She did not need to look. The smell was familiar.

Now she would have to activate the alternative plan, and she would have to do it far more quickly than she had planned and with far less reliable people, but there was no longer any choice. She did not consider abandoning the project. There were too many reasons to go ahead. First, she had to maintain her reputation. Second, she wanted to do it. This was what she lived for, and she did it better, perhaps, than anyone else in the world. She knew how to destroy, and destroy she would.

A taxi would have taken her to the Rossyia Hotel faster than the metro, but she preferred the crowds. Instead of heading for the hotel, she crossed to the white-walled Church of Saint Anne and looked over at the glass monster. There was a risk, but risks had to be taken and controlled. She crossed Razin Street and headed for one of the doors to the hotel. The lobby looked safe enough, but she took no chances. She moved quickly to the lobby of the first tower though she knew the person she wanted was in the central tower.

No one in the lobby paid any attention as she walked past a group of Americans talking about a movie they had just seen.

"But," said a thin, silver-haired man with a Yale accent, "must they make us pay by boring us?"

The dark-eyed one found the house phone and called the proper room.

"*Oui?*" came the voice of Monique Freneau.

"It's me." Monique Freneau said nothing, so she continued, "It will be necessary to make the purchase we discussed in France."

The pause was long, and the dark-eyed woman looked around the lobby. She could not afford to stay long.

"I cannot," said Monique in French.

"Tomorrow. Precisely at seven in the evening. There is nothing more to discuss."

"I'm sorry, but that will be impossible," Monique said, her voice breaking.

She had talked long enough. The phone might be tapped. The call could easily be traced to the lobby. The Frenchwoman's refusal to cooperate had not come as a surprise. There were those who claimed commitment but who could not carry out that claim. In fact, this had been true of all but a handful of people she had encountered. Either the German or the Englishman might have said the same thing, but the lesson had to be taught somewhere.

She hung up, and strode across the lobby toward the restaurant, pretending to look for something in her large cloth purse. In fact, she was watching the phone she had just left. If the police or the KGB appeared there, she would hurry into the dining room, join someone at dinner, and make up a story drawn from the thread of a dozen tales that had served her in similar situations in the past. But no one pounced on the phone.

It took her ten minutes to make her way carefully to the central tower and up the stairway to the right floor. It took her another minute to assure herself that Monique was alone in her room. It took only a knock to get Monique to open the door, and it took only a pair of blows with the fist to kill her. The dark-eyed woman stepped back into the hall, closed the door, and hurried away.

Word of the killing would have to reach the other two, and they would have to be made to understand what it meant. But even if they did their part, one-third of the task would remain undone. She would have to do that herself.

She would make two phone calls, and then she would simply hide, go back to the apartment of the student she had made it her business to meet. She would feign ecstasy at his touch and thus keep him busy for the remainder of that day and much of the next. He was relatively stupid, totally inept sexually, and probably harmless. If he did nothing to change her mind, she probably wouldn't have to kill him before she left.

Rostnikov left the room of the German, Wolfgang Bintz, at the Rossyia Hotel and went to the lobby, missing the dark-eyed woman by more than half an hour. A high-ranking assistant to the hotel manager stopped Rostnikov as he emerged from the elevator. He told the chief inspector that an urgent message had arrived at the desk: Rostnikov was to call his office at once.

Karpo's voice came as evenly and calmly as ever over the phone. "Inspector, there are several developments you should know about. A KGB inspector who was following one of the terrorists has been killed. Four members of World Liberation also have been killed in a KGB raid. And the Frenchwoman Tkach questioned yesterday has just been found dead there in the hotel."

Rostnikov sighed mightily. "Emil Karpo, even with all this killing, Moscow is one of the safest cities in the world. One of the *safest*. Can you imagine what it must be like to live in London or Tokyo or Rome . . . ?" Then his voice trailed off, for he was indeed beginning to imagine what those places might be like.

"Are you all right, Chief Inspector?" Karpo asked with something like concern.

"I am all right," Rostnikov replied, looking at the eavesdropping assistant manager, a porky man who hovered nearby pretending to read some mail. "Since I am here, I will go look at the body. Perhaps I will be lucky. Who knows? Perhaps I will make it all the way from the lobby to the room without discovering another body. How are you doing on finding the woman?"

"I am following procedure," said Karpo, relieved to get back to routine. "We checked the hotels and—"

"Do you have any leads at all?" Rostnikov threw in, glaring at the hotel assistant.

"Nothing yet," admitted Karpo.

Rostnikov grunted and hung up.

"Please get someone to take me to the hotel room of Monique Freneau, who has been murdered in your hotel," Rostnikov said maliciously. The man made a perfect target for Rostnikov's frustration.

"The hotel is not mine," the red-faced man said with a trained smile. "It belongs to the state. It is as much yours as mine, Comrade."

"Very well," said Rostnikov, letting out a long sigh. "Then let us proceed through *our* hotel while there are still guests alive to answer our questions."

The man smiled, unsure whether the policeman was slightly mad or trying to make some kind of joke. The all-purpose smile of the hotel official would cover either contingency, but in spite of his curiosity the assistant manager decided to get away from this strange, limping barrel of a man as soon as possible.

Had Rostnikov, at that moment, gone back to the German's room and listened at the door, he would have heard something that would have saved much time and at least one life, but he did not hear Wolfgang Bintz answer the ringing phone with a very tentative "*Guten tag*?"

EIGHT

THE INTERVIEW WITH THE GERMAN DIRECTOR, WOLF-
gang Bintz, had not gone quite as Rostnikov had anticipated. Bintz had been sitting in a chair in the center of the
room when a dark young woman from Intourist led the
chief inspector in. She looked quite calm, but the calm-
ness, Rostnikov could see, was as thin as the first film of
ice on the Moskva River. A very slight pressure would
crack it.

"Chief Inspector Rostnikov," he had introduced himself.

"Ludmilla Konvisser," the young woman said in a busi-
nesslike way. "I am from Intourist and will translate for
you as needed. This is Herr Bintz."

Bintz's robe was partly open to reveal a gold chain and
crucifix lying against the wiry gray hairs of his chest. His
hair was gray and bushy and his eyes gray and riveting.
His face was clean shaven and pleasant, but what struck
Rostnikov was the man's massive bulk.

"*Do'briy d'en*," said the German seriously without rising.

"*Guten tag*," replied Rostnikov as Bintz waved a massive hand at the chair opposite him.

Since they had both exhausted their vocabulary in the
other's language, they looked at Ludmilla Konvisser. Bintz

was accustomed to translators and spoke quickly in German.

"Herr Bintz," she translated for Rostnikov, "wants to know if you speak any language besides Russian."

"English," said Rostnikov, taking the chair across from Bintz.

"Good," replied Bintz in English, "then we need not a translator."

In German he said something to the young woman. Rostnikov was sure it was a dismissal. She turned almost apologetically to Rostnikov and was about to speak when he said, "It's all right. We'll be done in less than an hour."

With that, Ludmilla picked up her blue bag, said something in German, and left the room.

"You are a policeman," Bintz said, examining Rostnikov.

"Yes," agreed Rostnikov. "I'm a policeman."

Bintz grunted and continued to examine him.

"What do they call you? You have a special name. An affection name?"

Rostnikov was puzzled.

"My name is Porfiry Petrovich Rostnikov."

"No, no," sighed Bintz, impatiently clapping his hands together. "I am called Der Grosser in German, the big one."

"Washtub," said Rostnikov understanding. "I am called Washtub."

Bintz smiled.

"This is a good name?"

"It is not a bad name," agreed Rostnikov, beginning to like the huge man with the dancing gray eyes. "I would like to ask you a few questions."

"You are hungry?" came Bintz's answer.

"I . . ."

Bintz gave an enormous grunt, pushed himself out of the chair, and lumbered across the small room to the dresser. His robe slipped open, revealing a mountain of stomach and a small pair of shorts. Bintz absently retied his robe, plunged his hand into a travel bag, and came out with something. Then he turned to Rostnikov.

"You try," he said, lumbering back to Rostnikov and handing him a sausage and a knife. Rostnikov accepted the offering and cut himself a small piece. Bintz gave an exasperated sigh and cut a more generous piece for himself and another for Rostnikov. Then he watched Rostnikov intently as he took a bite.

"Good?" he asked.

"Very good," agreed Rostnikov, biting into the larger piece of sausage. Rostnikov's reaction brought a look of satisfaction to the German's face. He took his seat again and leaned forward. "We are bugged?" he asked. His voice was gravelly and resonant.

"I don't know," said Rostnikov.

"I know," Bintz said, finishing the last of his sausage and pointing to his chest. "We are bugged. That is expected. You have seen my movies?"

"I'm sorry," said Rostnikov shifting slightly. "I have not seen them."

"I do not think they show my pictures in Russia," Bintz said, nodding. "Only at the film festival, and only ones they think are socialist. I make socialist westerns, socialist horror movies, socialist historical movies. In this festival, they are showing my *Bullets of Bonn*."

"I would like to see it," said Rostnikov. "But for now, I have a few questions."

"Excuse me," said Bintz, folding his hands on his belly and giving his full attention to Rostnikov.

"Warren Harding Aubrey," said Rostnikov, looking directly into the man's gray eyes. Bintz's face did not change. His mouth moved into a small pout, but he said nothing. Rostnikov repeated, "Warren Harding Aubrey."

"I meet him," Bintz whispered. "His German is not bad. His manner is not good."

"Why did he interview you on Tuesday?" Rostnikov went on.

Bintz looked around the room slowly. Rostnikov wondered if he was in search of food.

"Aubrey is a . . . I don't know the words, one who likes to write bad words, make jokes. On top he is smiles and friends, but behind one sees the derision. Is that the right word, derision?"

"Yes." Rostnikov nodded. "And he only asked you about the movies?"

"No," growled Bintz. "He asks about Herzog. They all ask about Herzog. And he asks why I am in Moscow."

"Why are you in Moscow?" Rostnikov asked.

"To show my movie and"—he winked—"look around. I plan a big horror picture set in Moscow. I look, go back to Berlin, build Red Square. In English, we will call it either *Werewolf in the Kremlin* or *Red Nights in Red Square*." Warming to the subject, Bintz got to his feet and began to act out the scene he described. "Imagine, a German werewolf, maybe French if we get Belmondo. The moon is above. He leaps to top of the Lenin Mausoleum, fighting off attack of soldiers, howling at the Kremlin. You know who he wants?"

Bintz was standing on top of the chair now, and Rostnikov was sure it was going to break and send the German director through the floor of the Rossyia Hotel.

"Who?" asked Rostnikov.

"Andropov," Bintz shouted. "We have an actor, Hungarian, looks just like your Andropov. You like the idea, huh? Political allegory, better than Herzog."

Bintz managed to get down from the chair, but not before the right arm flew off and hurtled into a far corner. Both Rostnikov and Bintz stopped to watch the wooden arm skitter across the floor. Then Bintz spoke.

"Aubrey made jokes with his eyes," he said, easing himself into the one-armed chair.

"And that's all you talk of?" said Rostnikov.

"All," said Bintz.

"Herr Bintz," Rostnikov pushed on, "have you ever heard of the organization World Liberation?"

Yes, no doubt about it, Bintz winced. He was an actor of the first order, but that wince came too spontaneously to hide.

"It is familiar," he said, putting his clasped hands to his mouth.

"Terrorists," said Rostnikov. "Aubrey was writing a story about them. So why did he interview you?"

"Because . . . I no know. Not about terrorists."

"You have terrorists in Germany," said Rostnikov.

"I make no movies with terrorists," said Bintz, his hands still to his lips, his head shaking a vigorous no. "If they don't like your movie, they put your head in bag and shoot off your knees. Werewolves are safe."

"I agree," said Rostnikov.

"Why you want to know about Aubrey?" Bintz said, cocking his head.

"He's dead. Murdered. We think it might have been done by World Liberation."

"I make movies," said Bintz, his gaze even, his mouth straight, determined, his statement almost a non sequitur.

"I catch criminals," said Rostnikov, his gaze even, his mouth straight, determined.

"You have acted?" Bintz asked.

Rostnikov shrugged.

"To be a Russian is to act, yes?" supplied Bintz, leaning forward.

Rostnikov tilted his head slightly to indicate that Bintz was not off the mark.

"You would be good in *Werewolf in the Kremlin*," Bintz said, warming to the idea. "You could play yourself, detective, chasing the German werewolf. It appeals?"

"I catch real killers," Rostnikov said. "What do you know of World Liberation?"

Bintz's eyes looked toward heaven in exasperation at this Russian who would not let loose of an idea.

"Nothing," he said. "Nothing, nothing, nothing, nothing, nothing. No thing."

Which, Rostnikov was now sure, meant that Wolfgang Bintz had something on his mind, and it was related to World Liberation.

Rostnikov rose, and asked, "How long are you to remain in Moscow?"

"Feature competition ends Tuesday next," said Bintz. "*Bullets of Bonn* shows tomorrow night. I will win nothing. So I will go home two days. Food in Moscow is not good, not like Germany, not like Italy, not even like New York."

Bintz now looked quite sad, but Rostnikov didn't know just what he was sad about. Was it the poor chances of his film winning an award? The mention of World Liberation? The quality of food in Moscow?

"We will have to talk again," Rostnikov said, going to the door. Bintz shrugged and looked up, but not at Rostnikov. His eyes found the flight bag that contained the sausage.

Bintz's phone did not ring until a minute or two after Rostnikov left. The voice of the woman on the other end was familiar, a voice Bintz had hoped never to hear again, but there it was, like the voice of an actor who had been told he can't have the role but who keeps coming back in the hope that all the other performers have met with disaster.

"Our friend from Paris had an accident," she said in German. Bintz said nothing. "A terrible accident," she went on.

"Accident," repeated Bintz.

"Yes," said the woman's voice sadly. "An emergency came up, but instead of taking care of it, she tried to get someone else to do it, and met with an accident. I thought you would like to know. I'm sure you would know what to do in an emergency. I suppose there are even times when you could step in for another actor."

Bintz said nothing but looked at the door through which the policeman had left. The phone call was dangerous, insane. The room might well be bugged, probably was if he had read the Russian policeman correctly. This call was madness, and what the woman was asking of him was madness.

Twice, before the terrorism had begun in earnest, Wolfgang Bintz had hosted fund-raising parties for World Liberation, had pledged that his films would be devoted to showing the basic rot of the nations on both sides of the East–West struggle. He had given money and, in a fit of good fellowship, had pledged his help. Good Lord, he'd never expected them to ask him for any help other than money, yet now he was being told to commit an act of terrorism. Had they really killed Monique? He would find out for sure soon enough, but he also knew that the woman on the other end did not lie. He had never met her, had only heard her voice once in the dark. In fact, he didn't think she was a member of World Liberation, only an outside expert. Robert and Seven had insisted that he meet her and talk to her. They had made him part of their backup plan because he was going to be in Moscow during the film festival.

At that point, he had considered telling Robert to cart himself off, that World Liberation had become an embarrassment. The train bombing in Iraq, the shooting of the Japanese cabinet minister. But it was too late now. These people were mad. He should have seen that.

"You understand?" came the voice. "You know what to do?"

Bintz said yes and hung up the phone. He wandered across the room, tried to bend to pick up the arm of the chair from the floor, found, as he expected, that he could not. As he straightened, he discovered that he was in front of a mirror. His robe had come open again, and he examined his massive chest and belly.

It was a joke, a better joke than any of those his films were known for. A three-hundred-pound German who could speak no Russian was now supposed to join the terrorists and destroy one of the most famous landmarks in Moscow.

He imagined himself running away from the explosion. The image was impossible. He cast Klaus Kinski as himself running away, and he could imagine the scene, but a look in the mirror reminded him that this was no movie and that he would not be directing the scene. She was directing it. And afterward, was there any chance he would get away? Would that washtub policeman with the wise eyes come after him? Would he have to hide out in dirty rooms? Wolfgang Bintz? The last time he had hidden was during World War II when he was a boy in Berlin. Then he had been thin and fast.

He tried to pull his stomach in, but it did nothing more than shift a bit. And then he began to chuckle. And the chuckle turned to a laugh, and the laugh went out of control till there were tears in his eyes. When Ludmilla came through the door she found the massive director choking and laughing, bright red in the face, his right hand on his chest.

"Sit," she cried, rushing to him. "Herr Bintz, sit, please. I'll get a doctor."

He shook his head and kept choking and laughing. She put her arm around him and got his right arm over her shoulder, trying to hold him up as she struggled toward the bed. She had never felt weight like this before and couldn't erase the horrible image of this huge man on top of her in an act of sex or violence.

Why, she thought, did I get him? Does Stasya really dislike me so much that he gave me this one? Am I going to keep getting these problems until I give in to him? And what then? Is it worth it?

"I'm all right," Bintz said, easing himself onto the bed.

"Are you sure?" Ludmilla said, leaning toward him with a look of real concern. If he died while she was responsible for him, it would not look good on her record.

"Yes," he said sitting back, the bed sagging beneath him. "I need only a little rest. You can leave me. But make a reservation at a good restaurant for seven, and be back in time to get me there, please."

She gave him a final look of concern and turned to leave.

So, thought Bintz as the door closed, blowing up a swimming pool might not be the strangest thing I've ever done.

The dark-eyed woman called the Englishman, James Willery, before the police visited him.

James Willery had friends and acquaintances all over the world, for he was internationally known in certain circles. Those circles, granted, were not densely populated, but they were far-reaching. Their membership consisted of the most avant of the avant-garde filmmakers of the world, who referred to themselves variously as the underground, the new structuralists, and the experimentalists. James Willery's films were definitely not for the masses. In fact, it had been difficult to determine which category his film should be entered in for the festival. Although it was ninety minutes long, it had no real story line and so did not fit into the feature film category as defined by the committee. In fact, Willery's film didn't have any people in it. This led the committee to consider putting *To the Left* in the animated film category. But someone pointed out that the film had no animation. *To the Left* was a single shot taken with video equipment and later transferred to film. In that shot, the camera moved to the left on a tripod. The camera was set up in the ape house of the Lincoln Park Zoo in Chicago and, for ninety minutes, made slow and fast 360-degree turns. The only sounds were the occasional hoots of the gorillas. The highlight of the film came when one curious gorilla came forward to examine the spinning camera. The viewers, however, glimpsed only a fleeting image of a hulking black figure with bared teeth.

When the film was described to the committee, one member suggested that it be entered either as a documentary or as a popular science film. The only thing they could all agree on was that it was not a young people's film.

Oleg Makhach suggested they refuse to accept the film, but that was not possible. It had already been accepted on the basis of Willery's international reputation as a radical socialist filmmaker. Besides, the film was subtitled, *Homage to Eisenstein*.

It was finally decided that the film would be shown as a special feature. When informed of this, the very tall, very gaunt Willery, with his Edwardian jacket and faded jeans, adjusted his dark glasses, gave a pleased smile and said, "Super."

James Willery had friends. He also had inherited a bit of money. His father had been an earl, but better than that, he had owned a great deal of land in Essex. James Willery had sold it soon after his father's death and used the money to make films and support a variety of causes that appealed to his sense of the absurdity of the world. World Liberation had been one such cause.

When the call came, he was lying on the floor in the room of Alexander Platnov, a student at the Moscow Film School who had agreed to put Willery up and had long since regretted it. Platnov had no phone in his small room; the call came in to the floor office of the Party member who served as dormitory supervisor.

The Party member, a man of dark looks who made it clear that he did not like to be disturbed, stood and listened to Willery's end of the conversation.

"Hello," said Willery cheerfully, casting an even-toothed smile at the dormitory superintendent, who didn't respond.

"Mr. Willery," came the woman's voice, "there has been an accident."

"An accident," said Willery. "Sorry to hear it."

"To a Frenchwoman at the Rossyia Hotel. Her name was Monique Freneau."

"Was?" said Willery, the smile disappearing.

"She had an accident," said the woman, "which means she cannot make the movie tomorrow night. You will have to go in her place."

"Me?" said Willery.

"You know what I'm talking about."

"Yes, but—"

"Miss Freneau had an accident because she felt she was unable to make the screening. An unfortunate series of events. It could never happen again. But then again, who would have thought it would happen to Miss Freneau? You will make the screening, won't you?"

Willery glanced at the supervisor, but he was wearing dark glasses, so the supervisor could not see the panic in his eyes as they darted back and forth, looking for a way out that wasn't there.

"I'll make the screening," he said.

"Sunday night. You know the time," said the woman. "And you know where to pick up the ticket."

"But—" he began. The phone went dead.

Willery hung up and looked down at the supervisor. The look he got back was not vastly different from the one the gorilla had given him when he set up the camera in that zoo in Chicago.

"Thanks," said Willery, his mouth moving into an automatic smile. He had a wide, sincere smile and a very good laugh, after which he would inevitably say, "Priceless," but he doubted if that smile and laugh would come back soon.

Willery left the room and walked back down the corridor to Alexander Platnov's room. The door was open. He walked in and, ignoring Platnov, went over to the small mirror on the wall. He looked at his face and wondered if he could do it. Unlike Bintz, James Willery had no impulse to laugh. He felt no hysteria, no panic, just a supreme curiosity. He, who had never engaged in an act of violence, never struck another human being, was going to destroy an entire theater full of people, and for a cause he didn't really understand.

Apparently they had gotten to Monique Freneau, and he had no doubt that they could find him, too, if he refused to cooperate. Could he get away after his act of terrorism without the Russians catching him? What would they do to him if they did catch him? Whatever it was, he was sure he would confess before they even started.

It was a toss-up as to whom he was more afraid of, the woman on the phone or the Russian police. He was still looking at his face in the mirror, marveling at its composure, when someone knocked on the door. Behind him he heard Alexander get up from his studies, cross the room, and open the door. Behind him he heard the voice say, "I'm Inspector Tkach of the MVD. I would like to talk to Mr. James Willery."

Willery's command of Russian was not much of a command. It was more of gentle plea. He had understood the word "inspector" and the name Tkach, but the rest escaped him.

Then Alexander Platnov introduced Willery to the young policeman. After an unsuccessful attempt to converse in Russian, they decided to speak French, a language neither was terribly comfortable with, but which they could control.

Tkach wondered whether the Englishman was incredibly nervous or whether he behaved this way all the time. A glance at the Russian student told Tkach nothing. Was talking to a policeman sufficient to start this thin Englishman's pale hands trembling? Was there something else making him nervous? Tkach decided to push. As far as he was concerned, he had failed in his interrogation of Monique Freneau. He felt that he could have gotten more out of her if he had handled the questioning another way. If he could have spoken to her in Russian, he would have done better. Now he and this strange Englishman were on neutral ground in French. Tkach would not let this one get away.

To establish his direction he politely but firmly asked Platnov to leave the room. Willery looked as if he might protest, but Tkach turned a cold eye on him, trying to imitate Karpo. Platnov left the room with a sullen scowl, Willery withdrew his resistance, and Tkach moved forward to advance his control of the situation.

Tkach pointed to the chair Platnov had vacated, and Willery dutifully sat down with the detective standing over him. Tkach would have liked to open his collar, loosen his tie, even pace around, but he stood looking down at the Englishman, whose face held a fixed smile betrayed by a few drops of sweat on his brow.

"Mr. Willery," Tkach began, referring to his notebook as if he had a series of important questions written there, "you were interviewed on Tuesday by an American journalist, Mr. Aubrey, were you not?"

"Yes," said Willery. "Not the most cheerful person. Don't know why he singled me out."

"What did he talk to you about?" Tkach went on, acting as if he could see through Willery's tinted glasses.

"My career, my films. He said he was doing a series on different directions of film in different countries, and he wanted me as an example. I had the distinct impression that he was going to ridicule me. My films are, after all, not terribly accessible to the average film-goer, and the ignorant can easily cast stones."

"I have not seen any of your films," said Tkach humorlessly.

"Fantastic," bleated Willery. "My latest film, *To the Left*, is being screened tonight, at the Zaryadye. I'll give you a pair of tickets."

Willery had stood up and was nervously searching his jacket pocket. He found the tickets, peeled off two, and handed them to Tkach, who took them. To accept a gift might destroy his command of the situation, but the temptation was too great. Free tickets to an international movie for himself and Maya. He considered asking for one for his mother, and Willery responded as if he had read Tkach's mind.

"Would you like another?" he said warmly.

"Yes," said Tkach. "I would appreciate it."

And Willery peeled off another. Tkach now had the impression that he could ask for dozens of tickets and the nervous Englishman would keep supplying them. What Tkach did not know was that word of mouth on *To the Left* was far from favorable. The theater would not be as jammed as it was for most screenings during the festival.

Tkach pocketed the tickets and again motioned for Willery to sit, which he did with an almost boyish enthusiasm, a kind of overeagerness to cooperate that made Tkach all the more suspicious. The detective pushed a wisp of straight hair from his eyes and pressed on.

"Mr. Aubrey has been murdered," Tkach said.

"Sorry to hear that," replied Willery, who showed not the slightest trace of sorrow, though something like concern did come into his eyes.

"And a French producer named Monique Freneau has

also been murdered," Tkach pressed on. "You knew her?"

Tkach had no doubt now. Willery was in a state of great agitation, which he tried to cover with his broad smile.

"Name is a bit familiar," he said, biting his lower lip as if trying to recall, "but . . . I'm sorry."

"And," Tkach said stepping closer to Willery, "I suppose you have never heard of World Liberation?"

"I . . . well . . . perhaps," Willery said, adjusting his dark glasses, which needed no adjustment. "I meet so many people in so many different organizations all over the world."

It is time, Tkach thought. It was worth the chance. He could always fall back if he failed, but he figured that the Englishman was too far off balance to mount a decent counterattack.

"Mr. Willery," Tkach sighed, imitating Porfiry Petrovich's tone, "we have clear evidence that you are well acquainted with members of the organization known as World Liberation. We also know that Mr. Aubrey interviewed you because of your connection to that terrorist organization and that you are in Moscow because of your affiliation with them." Though Tkach knew none of this he snapped his notebook shut and squinted at the man before him. It would have helped if his face were harder, but it seemed to be doing the job.

"Good Lord," Willery cried. "I've talked to . . . I mean I've met a few of them in—I think it was Berlin . . . but Aubrey never asked about World Liberation. As for me being here because . . . that's absurd. My film was accepted, invited. Look, I want to cooperate with the police, but you've got this all wrong."

Tkach said, "I am just a policeman investigating a series of murders. There are people in another branch of our government who might be less sympathetic in dealing with you. Do you follow?"

"I . . . yes," gulped Willery, looking to the door for help that would not come.

"That branch of the government located a small band of World Liberation members in Moscow this morning,"

Tkach said, "and eliminated them as all terrorists or violent subversives who threaten our nation are eliminated."

Tkach had put as much fervor as he could into this statement though he felt little of the zeal. Karpo would have meant it, but Tkach prided himself on his acting, and now he was playing the role of the dedicated Marxist police officer. He did not know that every new disclosure of the death of someone involved with World Liberation was another persuasive argument for Willery to do what the woman on the phone had told him to do. Willery's very life was at stake. The most the MVD or KGB could do to him was prison, he reasoned, possibly with a bit of psychological or even physical torture. He could probably survive that; he might even beat the accusation with sufficient pressure from the British government.

"That is a reasonable position to take," Willery finally said with a dry throat, not feeling at all cunning.

"Enough," said Tkach. "You know what I need and want. We do not want any more dead people."

"Meaning me?" Willery said, touching his thin chest.

Tkach nodded in sad agreement.

"I have nothing to do with World Liberation," Willery said with a laugh. "This is absurd. I make films. No one is going to kill a filmmaker, an artist."

"I hope not," said Tkach, putting his notebook into his pocket. "I should hate to be the one to have to examine your body, especially if it looked anything like that of Monique Freneau. She had been . . . but you do not need to know about that. I've taken enough of your time. I thank you for the tickets."

Tkach walked slowly to the door. Behind him, Willery said, "Wait."

Tkach turned and faced the man who still sat in the chair, his long jean-covered legs outstretched, his bespectacled eyes searching the ceiling for help.

"Yes?" asked Tkach, feigning boredom and looking at his watch.

"What makes you think I'm involved with these World Liberation people?" Willery got out, but Tkach felt sure that was not why the Englishman had called him back.

Tkach smiled sympathetically and shook his head as if at the ignorance of a foreigner who did not realize the extent of the resources of the MVD.

"A friend of yours, or someone you thought was a friend, told us everything. The meetings. Everything."

A professional or even a calm, intelligent amateur would realize that a policeman would never give away such information if it was true, but Willery, while intelligent, was far from calm, and he was clearly not a professional. This struck Tkach. Willery was no terrorist, though they might use him. Tkach was convinced that he was essentially harmless.

Tkach would discover that he was quite wrong.

"Anything else you wish to say?" he asked Willery.

The Englishman's answer was a wordless shake of the head that suggested there was much to be told. Tkach told Willery that someone would be back to talk to him at greater length. Then he left, closing the door behind him.

In the hall, Alexander Platnov stood waiting to get back into his room. He scowled at the detective, who paused eye to eye with the student. Tkach looked down at the young man's shirt and sweater, his dark trousers, and assessed him as earnest and slightly belligerent.

"How long have you known the Englishman?" he said.

Platnov shrugged indifferently, indicating he could not remember. Tkach responded by telling Platnov to put his books in his room and accompany the detective to Petrovka where he might be more inclined to cooperate. Tkach had no intention of taking the student back to Petrovka. The threat was usually enough to get people to speak. Platnov was no exception.

"I've known him four days," he said quietly, turning away from Tkach as if bored, trying to retain his dignity in defeat.

"Why is he staying with you?"

A pair of young men passed by on the stairway, glancing at them. Tkach looked squarely at them, and they went on.

"I am interested in film, and I read a piece about him in a British journal. I wrote to him and invited him to stay with me when I heard his film was to be shown at the festival."

"And?" Tkach said, closing the space between them to a narrow gap. "Whom has he talked to? Who has called him? What does he talk of?"

"I don't know," Platnov almost whined, trying to avoid Tkach's eyes. "He is a bore. I don't understand him most of the time, and he keeps talking about expanded structures, vibrating spaces, collapses of time and space. He eats too much and won't let me study. He wants attention all the time."

"So you've met none of his friends?"

"He doesn't know anyone here," Platnov said. "He was interviewed by some American journalist. I was glad to have him out of my life for a few hours. He talked only to the people on the festival committee, a few of the students here, and the woman."

"Woman? Who was she?" Tkach said, trying to hide his excitement.

"Who knows?" Platnov answered. "A foreigner, I think. They went for a short walk a few days ago. I don't think he was happy to see her."

"What did she look like?" Tkach asked, looking back at the closed door and trying to decide if he should make another assault on Willery with this new information or take it to Rostnikov.

"A woman," sighed Platnov. "She wasn't ugly, but not pretty either. Too old for me, too intense, too. I don't know. Dark woman with dark eyes. Much too serious. She did manage to shut up the Englishman for a few hours."

"Go," said Tkach, "but do not tell Willery we have spoken. You understand?"

"I'm going to go back in there and put my head in my books," said Platnov, easing past the detective. "I want no further conversations with him."

Tkach let the young man pass. He would not confront Willery now, but would meet with Rostnikov. He had learned a great deal, but he was not at all sure what it might mean.

Once in the street, he removed the three tickets from his pocket, checked his watch, and hoped that Rostnikov would not keep him working on the case so long that he would miss the movie. He walked slowly down Karl Marx Prospekt, splurged by buying ice cream from a street vendor, and headed for Petrovka.

NINE

"**S**O," ROSTNIKOV BEGAN AFTER VIGOROUSLY WIPING his nose with a large gray handkerchief, "what have we?" He looked across his desk at Karpo and Tkach, not caring who spoke first.

Tkach began by reviewing his meeting with Willery. Rostnikov told him to stay with Willery, pursue the matter, and assign a watch on him.

They devoted fifteen minutes to discussing the murder of Monique Freneau.

"Foreigners are dying at an alarming rate in Moscow," Rostnikov observed. "It is an embarrassment, and we must put an end to it. Catching a murderer is very satisfying." His right eyebrow went up. "But you would not know of this satisfaction yet, Sasha and Emil."

Neither junior spoke.

"So, Emil Karpo," Rostnikov finally said after rubbing his callused fingers over the scratch on his desk. "What do we have on this dark-eyed woman of mystery?"

"She exists," Karpo said.

"Yes," agreed Rostnikov. "We both saw her at the Metropole, but where is she now and what is she up to? Does she have anyone helping her? How can she hide? Where?"

"I think," said Karpo, passing Rostnikov a folder, "she

means to plant bombs in key places in Moscow, if she has
not already done so."

Karpo was at the apartment on Kalinin Street less than
one hour after the KGB attacked it. Had he been ten minutes earlier he might have spotted the dark-eyed woman
across the street. Granted she was well disguised, but
Karpo was a man obsessed, and disguises are often insuffi-
cient in the face of obsession.

There were two uniformed MVD men at the door of the
building with orders to keep everyone out. Their orders did
not apply to an inspector, however, particularly not to Inspector Karpo, the Vampire, who was familiar to them.
Neither uniformed man could even formulate a challenge
in his mind let alone voice it to Karpo, who showed his
identification and marched past them.

The KGB investigators were going through the rubble,
turning over tables, examining cupboards. There were
three of them. A dour man with graying temples, who
wore a light gray suit and looked like a movie star, was
clearly in charge. The other two were efficient drones. The
dour man glanced over at Karpo, annoyed, and made a
mistake of which Karpo did not disabuse him.

"What are you waiting for?" said the man, reaching into
his jacket pocket for a cigarette. "Start in the other room."

Karpo went into the room and closed the bullet-riddled
door partway to give himself some privacy. He could hear
the man shouting orders to look here and there, check this
and that.

The room Karpo found himself in was very small,
hardly more than a closet. His impulse was to tear through
the chest of drawers, to search the clothes that hung on
hangers, to lift the well-worn little rug. But a systematic
search would take time, and in that time the KGB men
might learn that Karpo was not one of their own. Instead,
he stood silently looking. If there was anything worth finding, it would almost certainly be hidden. The terrorists
would probably have avoided the most obvious hiding
places. There would be no notes taped to the bottoms of

drawers, no loose floorboards. He was not even sure what he was searching for, but he needed a link, a link to the dark-eyed woman who had made both him and Rostnikov look foolish. That confident woman, he was sure, was a threat to what he believed in and lived for, and he felt that something drew them together. He sensed that she might very well be every bit as dedicated to her beliefs as he was to his. She was far too formidable to be allowed to walk the streets of Moscow.

The bulge in the wallpaper was very slight. Actually, there were places all around the room where the wallpaper bulged. It was very old, very worn, but this bulge was above eye level and hidden by a wooden shelf. In front of it was a pile of books, apparently stacked quite haphazardly, but that was what caught his attention—the books. The apartment—as bullet-torn as it was, as picked through as it was becoming—still gave signs of having been sparse and neat. It had a quasi-military aura, except for that random pile of books. It was almost laughable, though Karpo never laughed. These World Liberation people, for all their fanatic courage, were playing a game. They weren't professional. He was sure the woman was professional, but not these others, the dead ones. He shook his head slightly in disgust as he climbed up on the little desk. His movements were awkward, since he could use only one arm. His left arm still hurt sometimes, and he used it only when he needed to convince others that he had two good arms.

Atop the desk he could see that he was right. He peeled back the wallpaper behind the books, revealing a depression in the plaster. A series of numbers had been written on the plaster. Karpo read and then reread them. He closed his eyes and repeated the numbers until he was certain he had memorized them.

He replaced the wallpaper and had just climbed down when the dour-faced KGB man burst through the door.

"Who are you?" he demanded angrily.

Calmly, Karpo removed his identification and showed it to the officer, who waved it away.

"The guards at the door made a mistake," he said, his

eyes scanning Karpo, "no one but KGB is to enter here for now. You will have to leave."

"As you say," Karpo agreed.

"One of my men will have to search you to be sure you have taken nothing," the man challenged.

"As you say," Karpo agreed.

The examination took three minutes, conducted by one of the men who had been going through the rubble in the other room. Karpo thought it was a good examination and was quite pleased with their efficiency.

"I shall speak to your superiors about this, Comrade Karpo," the man said, throwing his cigarette into a corner.

"Of course," said Karpo. Perhaps he should have given the numbers to the KGB man, but that, Karpo knew, would mean that he could not pursue the lead, and he was involved in a murder investigation. This man was not in his immediate chain of command. The decision to turn the number over would have to be Rostnikov's. It didn't matter; judging from the thoroughness of their body search, the KGB men would soon find the number without any help from him.

Karpo was escorted from the building. Both MVD guards avoided looking at him and stood at strict attention as he left. He didn't look at them either. His mind was already working on the numbers and what they might mean. An idea had already begun to form. Interpreting the numbers would require no great imagination. This was not some inventive code. He was sure that, like the terrorists who conceived it, it was something naive.

Instead of returning to Petrovka, Karpo went back to his apartment where he sat at his own small desk and wrote the numbers on a sheet of paper. It took him less than twenty minutes to figure it out.

The first number was 87. The second was 2. The third was 65. The last number was 81. The 81 was, perhaps, the current year. The other numbers referred to something easily obtained, checked, used. But why numbers? The conclusion was startling even for Karpo. The numbers had not simply been hidden there. They had been left there to be found, perhaps by the police. The crudeness of the hiding place was not the act of a naive terrorist, as he had thought, but of someone who feared, perhaps even expected, betrayal. It was supposed to look like someone's idea of a good hiding place.

So, thought Karpo, whom did the terrorists fear would betray them? The answer was obvious: the dark-eyed woman. This series of numbers might well lead him to her. If the numbers were a clue to her whereabouts, it would not be too hard to follow. And then it came to Karpo.

He reached for his phone book. Few in Moscow own such books, but for a police officer it was an important tool. He turned to page 87, found the second column and ran his finger down to the sixty-fifth entry.

Thirty minutes later, he stood in front of the door to an apartment near the Sadova Samotchnaya, the Stalin-built ring road known as Sad Sam Street. He kept his right hand on his gun and knocked with his left. There was no answer, but he had expected none. If he understood the woman, there was no chance that she would still be there. She would anticipate the possibility of betrayal. If the World Liberation cadre knew she was here, she would make it her business not to be here if things went wrong, as they most certainly had.

Opening the door was no problem. The corridor was dark, but the lock was old and easily opened. No neighbor stuck a curious head out. It was early, and most people were at work.

The sight of the dark room caught Karpo off guard, for while the layout was different, the furnishings were startlingly like his own. It was like a mockery of his own convictions.

The room officially belonged to S. Y. Ivonova. Karpo had learned that S. Y. Ivonova was an engineer on assignment in the Urals, but someone had been using Ivonova's room, with or without consent. The visitor had made the room his or her own. Karpo was sure it was the woman.

He did not know how long it would take the KGB to find the numbers and figure them out, but he felt that he must have at least an hour or two. He had no intention of taking any chances, however. He would be out in fifteen minutes. As it turned out, luck was with him. Whoever had been here had not picked up his or her belongings and might come back, but Karpo was confident that the woman had fled, knowing danger was near, for another hiding place without taking the risk of returning to this one. Whether she simply did not trust the people who knew of this room or whether something else had happened did not matter. She was gone.

It took Karpo no more than three minutes to find what he was looking for. There was so little in the room that it was easy.

He found the sheets of paper exactly where he himself would have put them, tucked into a book on a shelf that held several dozen books. He carried the sheets carefully in a newspaper so he would not obscure any fingerprints, though he now respected the woman enough to believe she would have wiped everything clean each time she left the little room. But she had made a mistake. She had not memorized these sheets. He had no idea why, but now he had a lead.

Three hours later, after being sure that there were no prints on the paper and having made his own copies, he handed them across the desk to Chief Inspector Rostnikov in a neatly numbered departmental folder.

The first sheet in the folder was a map of Moscow with fifteen small circles in ink. Most of the circles were in the center of the city, a few were to the north or east or west. There was nothing in the south. In the same ink at the bottom was scrawled, in English, "Choose one."

"You've examined this?" said Rostnikov, rubbing his head.

"I have," said Karpo.

Rostnikov handed the sheet to Tkach.

"And?" Rostnikov prodded.

"I don't know yet, but I am—" began Karpo.

"The film festival," Tkach said, staring at the map.

"These are the locations of the theaters showing entries."

Rostnikov reached over impatiently and took the map back. It told him nothing, so he returned it to Tkach. "What theaters are they?" he asked.

"I don't know them all," said Tkach. "I'll find out. But this one is the State Central Concert Hall. This is the Young Pioneer Palace on Lenin Hills, where the children's films are shown. Here is the Rossyia, the Zaryadye, the Udarnik, the Mir. The others I don't know for certain."

"'Choose one,'" Rostnikov groaned. He looked at Karpo who remained calm.

In addition to the ache in his arm, Karpo felt a migraine coming on. He should excuse himself and take a pill, but he knew he would not do so. He would work through the pain, welcome it even, and prove that he could function in spite of the weakness of the flesh.

"She means to bomb one of these theaters," said Karpo, "or release a gas inside it or shoot a great many people."

Rostnikov nodded in agreement. It was logical, but something disturbed him. "She is so smart, so careful, so clever," he said, looking at his two assistants, "and yet she leaves this. Can you account for it?"

"She mocks us," said Karpo. "She is confident that she will succeed and we will fail. It is her pride."

"Maybe she simply made a mistake," said Tkach. "She didn't know we would find her room, and she simply didn't have time to clear it out."

"And maybe," sighed Rostnikov, "she wishes to be caught."

His eyes went to the two men, but neither responded. Tkach squirmed slightly. Such psychological conjecture was officially frowned upon, but Porfiry Petrovich was given to such thinking and marveled at the twists and turns and the devious self-destructiveness of the human mind.

"She wants to succeed, as Emil says, and fail at the same time," Rostnikov mused.

"Then she is mad," said Tkach.

"No," said Rostnikov, "she is human. Let us hope that we are quick enough and clever enough to take advantage of her perverse desire to be caught before her will to succeed does indeed result in her success."

"That will not happen," Karpo said, with such conviction that the other two stared at him. There had been more emotion in that response than either of them had ever heard from Karpo.

The ringing of the phone interrupted the moment, and Rostnikov picked it up.

"We are most busy," he told the officer taking calls.

"It is Colonel Drozhkin," the young man answered.

Rostnikov sighed. "Put him through."

He looked across the desk at Karpo and Tkach and made a decision. He reached into a drawer, pulled out a tiny tape recorder, and attached a small suction cup to the receiver, under the curious eyes of the other men. Then he turned on the unit and took the call.

"Inspector," came Drozhkin's serpentine voice. He spoke slowly and evenly and with more than the hint of threat.

"Yes, Colonel," Rostnikov replied calmly.

"One of your people violated security this morning," said the colonel. "An Inspector Emil Karpo."

"He is here in the office with me," said Rostnikov.

Tkach, not knowing whom the call was from or about, looked up, trying to control the ever present below-the-surface fear of the unseen authority. Karpo gave no reaction.

"We have reason to believe that he discovered something vital to the investigation of World Liberation activities and potential terrorism," said Drozhkin.

Drozhkin was not letting on whether the KGB had found the numbers and made its way to the apartment, and Rostnikov would be most careful not to give any information away.

"He was following my orders, Colonel," said Rostnikov. "He found nothing of great importance. Your men did not give him time to search. Had he discovered anything, we would have informed you immediately."

It was clear now to Karpo who the subject of the conversation was, but it was not clear to him why Rostnikov was lying to the KGB. Rostnikov was far too clever to be caught in a lie, and yet here he was taking a chance that could endanger his career.

Drozhkin's pause lasted so long that Rostnikov thought he had hung up quietly or the connection had been broken.

"You are treading down a dangerous path, Inspector," he said finally.

"It is the nature of existence to recognize and face random disaster that might come our way," said Rostnikov. "We are but the servants of the state and must not let our individuality stand in the way of the good of the Soviet people."

"Irony is a dangerous weapon," hissed Drozhkin. "It has no handle. You hold it by the blade, and with one slip you can become its victim."

"Irony is based on an understanding between two people," Rostnikov countered, bewildering Tkach, who could not imagine the other end of this bizarre conversation. "If someone perceives irony, he does so on the assumption that the person presenting that irony intended it to be so read. For myself, Comrade Colonel, I lack the wit and education to indulge in irony."

"When this investigation is at an end, Comrade Inspector, you and I shall have a talk." There was no mistaking the threat now, but that was just what Rostnikov wanted.

"I always look forward to meeting with you, Comrade Colonel," he said.

"You have made progress on the case?" Drozhkin went on.

"A little," admitted Rostnikov.

"For your sake, let us hope you make a great deal of progress. There can be only one or two World Liberation members left in Moscow, and they are your murderers," said Drozhkin.

"Yes," agreed Rostnikov. "That seems likely. I will keep you informed, Colonel."

They hung up, and Rostnikov turned off the tape recorder and dropped the tape into his pocket. Then he took the second sheet of paper from the folder Karpo had brought. It was another map of Moscow, and it needed no interpretation. The names of national monuments were circled, and the tomb of Lenin in the heart of Red Square was clearly marked.

"In time, I will turn these maps over to Colonel Drozhkin of the KGB," Rostnikov said. "He will, I hope, provide guards for every location circled on both maps. Meanwhile, Tkach, you will be responsible for watching the Englishman, Willery. I will stay with the German, and you, Karpo, will continue your pursuit of this woman. Thanks to the KGB, she has been deprived of her terrorist connections. She has resorted to recruiting amateurs, and they are, as we know, most unpredictable. Tkach, you can work with Kirslov in shifts. Questions?"

Both Karpo and Tkach had many questions, but neither dared ask them. They got up and left the office quietly. When they were gone, Rostnikov pulled out the tape and looked at it, thinking a moment, then returned it to his pocket and got up. He had to move quickly.

On the sixth floor, he made copies of the two maps. He then walked directly to the office of Anna Timofeyeva. If someone stopped him, he would say that the procurator had asked him to get some papers from her office and bring them to her at the hospital, which was true. No one stopped him. A clerk pushing a cartful of folders ignored him. It took him only a few minutes, with the portrait of Lenin staring down at him from behind Anna Timofeyeva's desk to get what he wanted and leave. If someone stopped and searched him now, he would be hard put to find an explanation, but he had already worked out a story that might stand up. However, there was very little chance that a chief inspector would be questioned inside Petrovka.

He was back in his office within three minutes and out the front door only shortly after that, his worn briefcase bumping against his thigh. By now Drozhkin most certainly had someone watching him. That didn't matter. When the time came, he would lose the follower, but it wasn't time yet. The Volga was waiting at the curb. The driver was unfamiliar, and Rostnikov decided he was probably KGB, though he wore a police uniform.

He ordered the driver to wait outside Procurator Timofeyeva's apartment, got out of the car, and went into the building carrying his briefcase.

In spite of her high position, Anna Timofeyeva lived in a small one-room apartment in an old one-story concrete building that had originally been built as a barracks for an artillery unit. When the site was abandoned after ground-to-air missiles were developed, the barracks on the Moskva River were converted into small apartments with a communal kitchen that had once served the unit stationed within its walls.

Rostnikov entered the apartment with the key she had given him. The cat on the bed arched its back and hissed.

"I've come to feed you, animal," Rostnikov said gently, reaching for the can of food. "Straighten your back. I know you have no claws."

The cat put down its back and watched the heavy man shuffle across the room, get the familiar can opener, and open the can. The smell lured Baku off the bed and across the room. Rostnikov grunted as he got to one knee and offered the animal the open can of fish and a fresh cup of water. He changed the newspaper in the wooden box in the corner and then, without the slightest feeling of guilt, went through Anna Timofeyeva's belongings. In a dresser drawer, he found a note stating that if she died her instruction book on outstanding cases was in the top drawer of her office desk. The note also requested that, in the event of her death, the cat be given to Rostnikov.

Rostnikov looked at the orange cat. He felt nothing for the animal but quite a bit for Anna Timofeyeva.

"Animal," he said, and the cat paused in its eating to look up at him with yellow eyes, "we may have to be comrades for a time. We shall have to practice mutual tolerance. I will make the effort, and I expect the same from you."

The cat went back to eating, and Rostnikov failed to find anything in the apartment that would be of use to him. Anna Timofeyeva kept her official business in her office and her private life, which was almost nonexistent, in her room.

From her bed in the hospital, Anna Timofeyeva watched the woman across from her. There were only four women in her room, a remarkably small number, so the hospital knew she was a relatively important official. They had allowed her no papers or work and had told her little about her condition.

The nurses were efficient but unenthusiastic. The doctors were respectful but volunteered very little. After the pain had stopped and they had ceased scurrying around attaching machines to her and shouting at one another, she had concluded that, at least for the immediate future, she was going to live. The heart attack had been fairly mild, but it was not her first. The doctors had no plans to operate on her and no plans to release her. They would simply watch her, and when her recovery was sufficient, if it ever was, they would release her. She suspected that she would not be long in the hospital. Beds were scarce, and the staff could do little for her.

A doctor would make the obligatory visit, she was sure, and tell her that she must stop working and relax. She would acknowledge the warning and terminate the conversation as soon as possible. She would also return to her work the moment her health permitted her to do so. There was nothing else she wanted to do.

So, for the moment, she watched the woman across the room, a very fat woman who seemed to be telling herself a silent story. The woman sometimes looked sad and at other times smiled, revealing very few teeth. Anna Timofeyeva wondered what the woman could be thinking.

"Comrade Procurator." Rostnikov's voice came through her reverie, and she turned to him.

"Porfiry Petrovich," she said, trying to sound gruff.

He looked, as always, solid, with something dancing behind his eyes. Today, however, the light dancing back there was particularly bright. Not many would have noticed, but she had made it her business to read the faces and minds of those who worked with her.

"I have taken the liberty of examining the files on pending cases," he said, "and I have taken care of your cat."

She nodded in acknowledgment, and Rostnikov changed the subject.

"You are better," he said.

"It appears that I will survive," she said. The woman across the aisle laughed. Both Rostnikov and Timofeyeva looked at her, but she seemed to be responding to voices in her own mind. The other beds were empty. Their occupants were having X-rays . . . or operations; Anna couldn't remember which.

The pause now was awkward. She was not given to small talk, and her helplessness was an embarrassment for both of them.

"How is the investigation progressing?" she asked.

Rostnikov shrugged and shifted his briefcase from his right hand to his left.

"It progresses," he said, reluctant to go into details.

"Good," she said.

The pause this time was even more awkward.

"Can I bring you anything?" he said.

"I will be home in a few days and back to work soon."

Rostnikov reached into his briefcase, pulled out a book, and handed it to her.

"Something I had at home," he said.

It was a book on the history and collections of museums in Moscow. He had thought for some time about what kind of book she might like and had settled on this, though he had been tempted to bring her a novel. He was sure that Anna Timofeyeva had not read a novel for several decades.

"I will study it," she said, putting it next to her. "What are you planning, Rostnikov?"

"Me, planning?" he said, looking around the room. "Nothing."

"Be careful," she said, closing her eyes. "Whatever it is, be careful."

"I will be as careful as I can," he said, but he was

thinking that there were times when one must take a chance.

When he looked down at her, she was snoring gently.

The woman across the way looked at Rostnikov as he stepped away from the bed. Her eyes met his, and she too seemed to know his innermost secrets. She smiled. He hid a shudder and left as quickly as he could.

TEN

"I DON'T LIKE MOVIES," SAID LYDIA TKACH AS SHE SAT down in the Zaryadye cinema hall in the Hotel Rossyia. Most of the theater's three thousand seats were full, and since Lydia Tkach was almost deaf and had spoken very loudly, many of those present were aware of her sentiments. Sasha gave an apologetic look to the well-dressed man sitting next to his mother and shrugged at Maya, who smiled sympathetically, having grown used to her mother-in-law.

Lydia was a proud woman of sixty-five. During the day, she worked in the Ministry of Information Building, filing papers and telling anyone who would listen that her son was a high-ranking government official. Lydia was not a popular woman in the Ministry of Information Building. People avoided her because she drew attention to herself with her loud conversation. This tended to make her more lonely and crotchety, which in turn made her turn on her captive audience at home, her son and daughter-in-law.

Sasha had more than once urged her to get a hearing aid, but Lydia had stoutly refused, insisting that there was nothing wrong with her hearing. Nor, she insisted, was there anything wrong with her common sense, which was why she disliked most movies.

"Mother," Sasha said in a normal voice, which he had little hope his mother would hear, "please."

He handed her the headphones attached to her seat and urged her to try them. Maya put hers on and played with the switch. The translation would be given in six languages on six separate channels. Nothing came through on the headset, so Maya put it down.

"I understand this movie has no words," Maya said to her mother-in-law, mouthing each word carefully. Lydia nodded, trying to get comfortable in her seat and staring down a woman in front of her who turned to indicate that she would allow none of this chatter to continue after the film began.

Sasha was pleased that everything had worked out so well. Willery sat in the front of the theater, wearing a jacket and tie, looking about nervously. In spite of the jacket and tie, he still wore faded jeans. Tkach knew that Kirslov was at the door of the theater to pick up Willery after the performance. The program notes Tkach had been given made the film sound suitable for his mother. It was, he discovered, silent. There was no need for her to hear anything. *To the Left* was also dedicated to the great silent film director Eisenstein so it might tell a story his mother would like. In addition, it was made in America, so they could see a glimpse of that elusive country.

"It's about America," Maya told her mother-in-law, leaning close to the woman's ear. Sasha and Maya had flanked Lydia for their own protection as well as hers.

"I don't like movies," Lydia answered emphatically.

With this second assurance, a small titter of laughter erupted from some young people who looked like students sitting to the far right. Sasha urged the second hand of his watch to move more quickly. He longed for darkness. Then Willery, responding to Lydia's second declaration, looked in her direction, spotted Tkach, and gave a sickly smile.

"It will start in a minute," Sasha said, sinking deeply into his seat and pointing to his watch. His mother looked down at the watch and pursed her lips.

"I hope it's funny," she said. "If it's funny, it will be all right. I've had enough tragedy."

Then mercifully the lights began to go down.

"Isn't it in color?" said Lydia as the film began. Shushing sounds came from nearby, but Lydia was right, the film was in black and white, and Sasha was disappointed.

The audience soon discovered that *To the Left* was not silent. In fact, as the titles appeared in white against black, faint animal noises and the chattering of birds emerged from the speakers.

Then the film began in earnest, and Tkach could see vertical bars on the screen. A prison, he thought, a political prison, but what was that moving black hulk in the corner of the cell? Before he could make it out, the camera began to move, at first to the left, just far enough to put the black hulk off the screen. The chattering sound continued, and as the camera began to move faster, the sound grew louder.

The audience sat in rapt attention for almost ten minutes. Experimental beginning, Sasha thought. And then, in the twelfth minute, he began to lose faith. Luckily, Lydia had remained quiet. Sasha and Maya both glanced at her fearfully from time to time, but her eyes remained riveted to the screen.

A quarter of an hour into the film Lydia said in her loud voice, "Monkey. That's a monkey in the corner."

People called out for her to be quiet, but one man said, "She's right. It *is* monkeys."

The audience fell silent once more, and the camera increased its spin to the left. Those who were fleet of eye could see the lumbering figure move forward.

"A gorilla," said Lydia Tkach with satisfaction, for while her hearing was failing, her eyesight rivaled that of an Olympic marksman.

"Gorilla . . . gorilla," came the echo of agreeing voices in the theater.

Forty minutes into the film, however, people were extremely restless.

"What is this?" came a voice from back in the theater.

"A gorilla," said Lydia Tkach smugly.

The gorilla cries on the sound track had risen in volume, and one hour into the film, the majority of the audience was in open revolt.

"Is this a joke?" someone shouted.

"Shut up," came a young woman's voice.

In front of the theater, Willery stood looking back at his tormentors and defenders, a frail dark outline. Tkach could make out his flickering form. Very few in the audience knew who he was. If he keeps quiet, Tkach thought, he may escape without bodily injury.

People began to leave, the better-dressed patrons first. With fifteen minutes of film to go, the screen was simply a blur as the camera spun around and the shrill blast of gorilla cries filled the theater.

Sasha glanced at his mother, who was watching the screen with a smile on her face.

"Shall we leave?" Maya asked, looking back toward the sound of what appeared to be a fight in the rear.

Lydia gestured for her daughter-in-law to sit still.

By the time the film ended and the lights came on, there were less than two hundred people left in the theater. Four young men and a woman stood up and applauded furiously, shouting "Bravo!" and looking defiantly at those who did not join them. Willery glanced back at his supporters with a thin smile.

Tkach had a headache. The sound and the spinning image had affected him like a drug. His first impulse was to apologize to his wife and mother, but Maya simply agreed with him and Lydia actually looked elated.

"Not as bad as I thought," she said, leading the way up the aisle, ignoring the clusters of still arguing moviegoers.

Tkach didn't bother to look back at Willery, and that was unfortunate for at that moment Willery was looking around the nearly empty theater, lifting his dark glasses and scanning the walls and seats. Tkach, if he had seen him, would have wondered what he was looking for, and almost certainly he would have concluded that Willery was looking for something connected with the map of festival theaters Karpo had given to Rostnikov. Tkach might even have concluded that Willery was looking for a hidden bomb, which is exactly what the filmmaker was doing.

Feeling misunderstood, angry, and hostile, James Willery was thinking that it might not be such a bad idea to blow up this theater while some of the people who had just ridiculed his film were still in it. James Willery had a marvelous imagination, and he could quite clearly imagine the writhing bodies, the screams, the burned survivors fleeing blindly.

The cluster of students remained after everyone else had gone. The ushers came in and told them to clear out because the next feature would be starting soon. Willery considered beating a hasty retreat behind the screen, but the students had already begun moving toward him down the aisle.

It would do his ego some good, Willery thought, to have a few drinks with some people who would reassure him about his creation. After all, this Russian audience was not as sophisticated as those in London, Paris, New York, or San Francisco. Yes, a few drinks with these students would help him forget the audience. And the young woman in the group did not look bad at all. Maybe she would even help him forget for a while the bomb that was hidden somewhere in this theater and that he would detonate the following night.

The dark-eyed woman smiled at the young man next to her and nodded in appreciation at his assessment of the film he had seen a few hours ago. She had pleaded a headache, and now she was feigning interest in his infantile explanation of film, audience, and filmmaker.

He had forgotten that it was she who had urged him to see *To the Left* and arranged for him to get the tickets. In fact, she'd done it so skillfully that he'd thought it was his idea. She reached over in the bed and put her hand on his pale leg. She wondered how he would react if she squeezed him like a vise until he begged for release. Instead, she pretended that what he said was not only interesting but profound.

"And you had a drink with him?" she encouraged.

"He is brilliant," said the young man, looking at her with drunken dancing eyes. "His grasp of the need for destruction of structure is so pure, so clear. No wonder he is rejected and scorned."

"And," she said, letting her hand move away when she realized he was too drunk to respond, "he seemed in a good mood even after what happened?"

"Distracted, perhaps, but brave. He was laughing," said the young man with admiration. "They all sat there feeling so superior, neo-capitalists every one, and they couldn't face a true act of artistic revolution. He laughed at them. He has an inner strength, that man."

He will need it, she thought as the young man's eyes closed and he fell asleep repeating "that man."

She got up, then turned off the light, and climbed back into the narrow bed. She pushed the young man over, and he grunted petulantly.

The links were weak, perhaps, she thought. One or both might even break, but the job would be done. Of that she was quite sure.

She was asleep, as always, within minutes, a light sleep always on the edge of cautious consciousness. She had learned to sleep this way from the one who had taught her, who was now dead. She told herself that it was the sleep of the professional. She did not acknowledge that it was also the sleep of one who fears dreams.

From time to time, in spite of her training, she did fall into deep sleep for a few minutes, and the dream did come, the dream of circles within circles that turned to a spiral of wire on which she was skewered. She twisted downward on that spiral toward the ever narrowing center hidden in darkness, below which she would fall off the wire and plummet into the void.

She ground her teeth furiously, awakening herself. She sat up breathing deeply; it seemed she had a weight on her chest. The void surrounded her. She willed it away.

Beside her, she heard him snoring. It was reassuring for an instant, and then she hated having felt any reassurance in his presence. She got out of bed and went to the window, wishing it were Sunday.

Rostnikov's mouth was inches from Sarah's ear as they lay in darkness well after midnight.

"It will be," he said so softly that even the most sensitive microphone could not pick it up.

She turned to look at his stubbly, dark face with its knowing smile. She smiled back. He had managed to carry them this far, she thought; perhaps he could do it. There was much about it she didn't like, but if he could do it, it would be beyond what she had ever really expected.

If he failed, however, she knew quite well that neither of them would see another Moscow winter.

Osip Stock lived near Druzhbin, not far from the Moscow Ring Road, which encircles the city, marking its perimeter beyond which it is exceedingly difficult to travel without private transportation. Osip Stock had no private transportation.

Osip was almost thirty years old and looked rather like a tubercular bird. In spite of his dry appearance, with his thin chest and a hacking cough from too much smoking, Osip was a passionate man. In his free time he would take to the roads near his home, winter or summer, and in his precious running shoes, one of his few extravagances, take flight, losing himself in distance, not knowing how far he ran, returning sometimes hours later. Osip was well aware that his primary reason for running was to escape from the three-room apartment he shared with his parents, his aunt Sophie, and his cousin Svetlana, a grotesque creature.

But Osip had a plan to end this lifestyle, which was the reason he arose so early this day. He was up by seven in the evening. He slept alone in the bed during the day. Usually when he arose, his parents were ready for sleep, and would take over the bed, occasionally changing the sheet. Aunt Sophie and Svetlana slept in the large room, which was not so large, in which they shared meals, conversation, battles, and comforts.

"You are up so early," said his mother. Cousin Svetlana made her familiar gurgling sound and agreed that he was indeed up early. Osip grinned, showing his silver teeth, and searched for his cigarettes. He couldn't immediately find them and nearly panicked. But his mother, to head off his grumbling, joined the search and found half a packet.

Lighting up, Osip leaned back in his chair at the wooden table, adjusted the buttons on his uniform, and drank some coffee to wash down the chunk of bread that was his meal. There was more food, but Osip was not much of an eater.

"Why are you looking so happy?" asked his mother, a red-cheeked little woman.

"Why?" he answered, grinning more broadly. "Because it is a fine evening. I have a good job and a secret."

"A secret?" asked his mother, looking at Aunt Sophie and Cousin Svetlana for an explanation. They had none. Svetlana made her gurgling sound again.

"Nothing important," said Osip, standing up and adjusting his jacket. "We must have some privacy if only on the open road and in our own heads."

"It would be better if when you talked you made sense," his mother said, again looking at Sophie. This time Sophie nodded in agreement. Svetlana seemed to be dozing.

Osip looked at all of them with great tolerance. Soon he would be rid of them. Soon he would be a man of means, a respected man with his own apartment, far from this. Privacy. Oh, how he longed for it.

His mother seemed about to pursue the subject of his secrecy, but he said, "I'm off," and grabbing the small sack that contained his midnight meal, he hurried out the door. In the dark corridor, his father approached, moving slowly and wearily, returning from his job on a road repair crew.

Father and son grunted at each other as they passed, and Osip hurried out into the light. He wanted to run or at least jog to the metro station, but the sweat would ruin his uniform. So he walked slowly, planning. There weren't many people going to the heart of town at that hour, so there were plenty of seats when he got to the metro.

It was almost nine when he got off at the Novokuznek-skaya metro station and headed for number 10 Lavru-shinsky Pereulok, a quiet side street across the Moskva River not far from the Kremlin. When he arrived, he paused in front of the low metal fence with the fancy repeated design of circles and pointed stars and stared at the building beyond. Yes, it was something from an old fairy tale, this gingerbread building, complete with its second-story frieze of Saint George slaying the dragon. He looked up at Saint George and smiled.

He had taken the job at the Tretyakov Gallery more than five years ago. His main reason then was the privacy. He would be alone for many hours in the mansion, though other guards would be wandering about on their rounds. But soon after he took the job he began to grow interested in the thousands of sculptures, drawings, watercolors, and engravings that covered the walls and filled the rooms.

More than four thousand people visited the gallery every day, plunking down thirty kopecks each and waiting in long lines, but Osip paid nothing and had the rooms to himself. He could pause and carry on a conversation with Kiprensky's portrait of Pushkin or sit on the bench, his feet planted firmly on the inlaid wooden floor, and lecture to Rublev's larger-than-life nine-hundred-year-old saints.

Tonight, however, would be special. It had all been arranged. It would be his last trip through the gallery, and he would say good-bye to almost all of his iconic acquaintances. Osip checked in at the side door, trying to control his grin as he said hello to old Victor and put his sack on the ledge in the small guards' room.

"Quiet so far," said old Victor, looking up from the chessboard over which he sat slumped for hours. It was what Victor always said. Osip would miss that. He wondered what old Victor would be saying about him tomorrow.

In ten minutes, Osip began his rounds. In the past four years, he had slowly, carefully, and systematically stolen eighty-five paintings from these walls, carefully replacing them with others of about the same size and shape from various storage rooms of the collection.

The thefts, in fact, had been discovered only recently, and only a few of them, because of a complaint from a Belgian art student who could not locate a small canvas by Ilya Repin. He had been most careful since then and had cooperated fully and enthusiastically with the police investigators, who found that Osip Stock lived most frugally, did not have the paintings hidden in his home, and seemed most eager to find the missing artworks. He was confident that he was very low on the list of suspects, but after tonight he would be quite well known and very far away.

None of the thefts had been his idea. Well, a few of the later ones were at his suggestion. He had been recruited by the Dutchman, who had invited him for a drink. It had seemed that the two had met accidentally, but it did not take long for Osip to figure out that it had been well planned. Van der Vale had dined and befriended Osip for three weeks before he brought up the possibility of taking some paintings. Osip had been most receptive, and the partnership had begun.

Osip would remove a painting from the wall, hide the frame, wrap the canvas around his body, replace the stolen painting with a similar one from the storage rooms, and walk out. He would meet van der Vale in an alley not far from the gallery where they would make the transfer.

The agreement was that van der Vale would bank Osip's money in Amsterdam and, when the right moment came, would supply Osip with a forged German passport and a ticket to Zurich. Tonight was the right time. Osip would take the most valuable painting available. At first they had tried to figure out a way to take the Rublev *Trinity* or Dionisii's icon of the Metropolitan Alexis, for which Osip had particular affection, but getting the wood blocks out would have been impossible. They settled on a series of eighteenth-century paintings which, when wrapped around Osip, would make him a bit stocky, but not enough for any of the guards to notice. By the time the theft was discovered in the morning, if it was, Stock would already be in

Zurich. He had been preparing for this for almost five years, right down to learning enough German to carry him past the airport inspectors if necessary.

Osip was most patient. He made his rounds, chatted with the other two guards, ate with them and encouraged them to hold a mini chess tournament. Each guard would patrol while the other two played. Osip got in the first game and lost. He couldn't have beaten Victor no matter how hard he tried, but he did not want to win. When Vasily sat down to play what Osip knew would be a long game, Osip ambled slowly out of the room. Once out of sight, he moved quickly down the hall and up the stairs. Within ten minutes, he had removed the six canvases and piled their frames in a closet. He juggled the remaining paintings around to cover the loss, knowing that it would not take a careful inspection the next day to discover the theft.

By the time he was finished, Osip was sweating heavily, something he had not counted on, but there was no help for it. He had to move quickly. The chess game should go on for an hour, but what if Vasily made a stupid move?

He had wrapped the small canvases around his waist and tied them neatly to his chest. He felt a bit awkward, but reasonably confident that he could carry it off. He was buttoning the final button on his jacket just as Vasily stepped into the room.

"Victor won," he announced as if there had been any doubt of the outcome. "What's wrong with you?"

"Me?" said Osip. "Nothing."

"You are sweating and walking strangely," said Vasily.

"Maybe I'm ill," admitted Osip. "I've been feeling strange since I ate."

"You ate something bad," Vasily said wisely, his words echoing off the ancient figures that looked down at them. "Maybe you should go home."

"Maybe," Osip said, reaching for a cigarette. "I'll go talk to Victor."

It was even better than he had thought. He could get out even earlier. The Dutchman would be waiting. He always arrived early and checked the alleyway to be sure it was safe. Maybe Osip could get an even greater head start, catch an earlier flight, and get out of Russia even faster. It was worth discussing with the Dutchman.

Victor agreed that Osip looked terrible, but then, he thought that Osip always looked terrible. Tonight he looked a little stiff and was sweating through his uniform.

"Go home, Stock," he said, flushed with his double chess victory. "We'll take care."

Osip feigned reluctance but accepted finally, moved slowly to the door and stepped out into the star-filled night. He took a deep breath and, after a final look back at the gallery, started down the street. Five minutes later, he entered the alley and waited. Ten minutes later, the little Dutchman, whose name was not van der Vale and who was not Dutch, decided it was safe to enter the alley. He followed the glowing tip of Stock's cigarette and moved forward cautiously.

"Stock?" he said in accented Russian.

"Yes."

"You are early," said the Dutchman, looking around. "Is something wrong?"

"No," whispered Stock, moving forward, where he could make out the slight form. "I said I was sick and got away early. You have the clothes for me and the suitcase?"

"Yes," said the Dutchman, thinking that it would have been much better if this fool had gone through the night on the job. Perhaps it did not matter. He did not, in fact, have clothes for Stock, nor did he have a suitcase or a passport. The Dutchman planned to take the remaining paintings and bludgeon Osip Stock to death with the metal bar he now held behind his back. In spite of his open face and slight body, the Dutchman had done such things before. "The paintings, quick."

Stock removed his jacket and shirt and peeled off the paintings. In his haste he had hidden the bottom painting, a landscape, so that the paint pressed against his sweaty chest. A good deal of paint stuck to his skin when he peeled the canvas off.

If they inspect me at the airport, Osip thought, the evidence of my guilt will be painted in reverse on my body. He thought about where he might wash.

"Enough."

Stock thought the voice was the Dutchman's, who in turn thought it was Stock. They were both wrong. It was the voice of Emil Karpo who now stepped out into the starlight, a tall outline with a hand outstretched, holding a gun.

"Police," he explained evenly. "You will raise your hands slowly and lie on the ground, face down."

Osip let out a small whimper and looked at the Dutchman. The Dutchman looked around quickly, and seeing no escape, he brought his hands up. In his right there glittered the bar of metal. Stock took in the metal bar.

"You were going to kill me," he said slowly.

The Dutchman, who knew more about the Soviet system of justice than Osip Stock did, was beyond concern. He was thinking of the prison years ahead, but Osip was a man who had been betrayed and whose dream had been shattered. He threw down the paintings and, ignoring Karpo's gun, lunged at the Dutchman.

"Stop," shouted Karpo, but Stock was not to be stopped. The Dutchman swung the bar and caught the advancing madman on the shoulder, but Osip had his hands around the smaller man's throat. The metal bar went skittering across the pavement, clanking and sending up sparks.

"Stop," Karpo repeated, stepping forward. With but one good arm, he doubted if he could separate the two and knew that if he came too close he ran the risk of losing his gun. "I am going to shoot," he said over the grunting of Osip and the gurgling of the Dutchman.

Karpo aimed a few feet from the struggling pair, who had rolled over on the paintings. The bullet hit the head of an eighteenth-century saint but did nothing to discourage Stock. Karpo aimed the second bullet at Stock's legs. But it was dark, and the thieves were moving. Even as good a shot as Emil Karpo could be forgiven for what happened. The bullet struck the Dutchman on the left side of his chest and made a path through his heart before lodging in his lung. There was a convulsion, and the man died, but Osip Stock kept strangling him. As long as he kept his attention on the little man, he would not have to think about what was coming next.

"He is dead," said Karpo, stepping forward to stand next to Stock. "You madman. He is dead."

It took a substantial clout with the gun to make Osip stop and look about. It took another clout to make him react.

"Now get up and pick up those paintings," Karpo said. The kneeling Stock looked up at this angel of death, then down at the Dutchman. Anger turned to fear, which turned to panic. Stock rose, looked at the gun pointed at him, glanced around the alley, and took off at a sprint. Karpo considered chasing him, but he was running at a breakneck pace, his jacket flying open, his thin, birdlike chest heaving.

Karpo raised his gun, but when he had Stock's back firmly in sight he changed his mind. He knelt to be sure the Dutchman was dead and listened to Stock's clattering footsteps receding in the darkness.

From a public phone nearby, Karpo called for an ambulance. Then he called the gallery and told one of the guards to come for the paintings. His third call set up a general alarm to pick up Osip Stock. Then he returned to the alley to wait with the body. He would have to make out a report, but he would worry about that later. The fact that he had shot a parasite did not bother him, though he considered that he might have handled the situation better.

For Karpo it was a case closed, a job done. Even as he leaned against the wall within feet of the dead man, his mind was back on the woman with the dark eyes. It was almost like love, this hatred he felt for her, but either way it spurred him on. If he could think like her, he might be able to figure out her next move. As he waited for the ambulance, he closed his eyes and went over the case from his first sight of the woman to his discovery of the maps.

Just before the ambulance arrived at 3:15 A.M. an idea came.

By the time Osip Stock was picked up at 4:47, he had run almost ten miles. The police had found him not far from his home. He was exhausted and not terribly coherent. Karpo did not know that Stock had been picked up till nine the next morning, because he had left word that he was not to be disturbed. He had a plan to work out, and it would require his full concentration.

ELEVEN

DISCOURAGING, ROSTNIKOV THOUGHT, MOST DISCOURaging. The room was crowded with people. It was normally a basketball court, but at present it was being used as a warm-up room for those competing in the Sokolniki Recreation Park's annual weight-lifting competition for men and women over fifty. The contestants warmed up in here and then competed in another building. Four people competed at a time early in the competition, and as the lifting continued, this was decreased to two, and at last the finalists competed individually before a substantial audience.

In the past, Rostnikov had seen only the finalists. He did not realize how many people in Moscow over the age of fifty considered themselves weight lifters. There were several hundred, and it was discouraging. The room was filled with people doing situps and pushups, running in place, turning red in the face from their efforts. It was madness. Some of the contestants looked too old to compete in anything. Others looked far younger than fifty.

Feeling awkward, he moved to a corner and flexed his muscles. Normally he warmed up by simply lifting. He had a terrorist killer to catch, a dangerous plan to execute. How long could he wait here to be called? Yes, it was Saturday, and most of the people here did not have to work, but for him this was a working day.

"Breathe," said a robust woman doing situps next to him. "You don't want to hyperventilate. Breathe deep."

This discouraged Rostnikov even more. He must look like a novice if this woman was giving him advice. Many of the people in the gymnasium were wearing sweat suits like his. Others wore fancy European running suits in blue or red. A good number were in shorts and shirts emblazoned with the names of the cooperatives or factories they represented. Rostnikov's sweat suit was gray and baggy.

"Breathe," insisted the robust woman, coming up from a situp.

"I *am* breathing," Rostnikov replied. Off in a corner, someone dropped a weight with a terrible clang and cursed. A man with an enormous belly and a bald head came past and paused to look down at Rostnikov as if he were inferior competition. Around his neck the man had draped a blue towel, which he held with both hands and used to flex the muscles in his hairy arms. Rostnikov suddenly felt like apologizing and heading for the exit, but it was too late for that, and this might well be his last chance to compete.

Names were called. Weight totals were posted solemnly on a blackboard to indicate leaders. Losers trooped in silently, some angry with themselves. The bald man, as it turned out, was an early loser. He stomped past Rostnikov and threw his towel at the wall. It hit with a sweat-soaked splat. People around pretended not to notice.

And then Rostnikov was called. The robust woman who, he was sure, had warmed herself up into total exhaustion, wished him luck and reminded him to breathe. He promised to do so.

"Name," said a man in a white shirt, dark tie, and thick glasses. He held a clipboard and did not look back at Rostnikov as he led the way. Rostnikov, dragging his bad leg, had trouble keeping up with him.

"Rostnikov, Porfiry Petrovich," the chief inspector called ahead, following the man through the crowd and out of the building.

"That is right," said the man, heading for the next building.

"I thought it might be," said Rostnikov.

The man stopped and turned to the detective, his clipboard clutched to his chest. "This is a most serious competition," he said. "We take it seriously."

"As do I," said Rostnikov, wondering if the man was using an editorial "we," or whether "we" referred to the state, or to everyone competing except Rostnikov.

The man examined Rostnikov and found nothing impressive in the washtub with the oversized gray sweat suit.

As a participant rather than a spectator, Rostnikov's first view of the auditorium was a revelation. The sense of being looked over and criticized was overwhelming. He followed the man with the glasses like a lost child latching onto the nearest adult.

There was little formality. When he got to mat number three, a no-nonsense woman checked his name again and pointed with a pencil for him to move to the weight that sat waiting. No one told him how much it weighed. Things were moving too quickly. The morning was too hot, and there were too many people to eliminate. A pair of bored, muscular young spotters with tight white shirts moved to either side of Rostnikov as he stood behind the bar and looked at the woman who held the stopwatch.

"Time," she said.

Rostnikov took a deep breath, bent awkwardly with his bad leg braced. He had taped the leg to give it a bit more stability, but he knew he could not count on it for help. He looked down at the bar but not the weights. You will rise and become one with me, he commanded the bar.

Rostnikov had not practiced the snatch very often. It was too difficult to do with his leg, to bring the weight from the floor to a locked overhead position in one smooth move. In addition, when he practiced in his apartment, he was afraid of sending the weights through the floor onto the heads of the Vonoviches below.

Rostnikov grabbed the weight. Though this was not his event he would try not to embarrass himself. Up, he commanded, up as one, and he imagined Alexiev or young Anatoli Pisarenko flinging the metal overhead with that beauty of motion that demonstrated a man's control over his own body.

He bent his good knee and moved his other leg to a firmer position and lifted. Up, up, up, he commanded, but he was lucky to get the weight as far as his chest. Fearing that time was running out, he paused only a fraction of a second, then pressed the weight upward and held it. It was heavy, but tolerable. He looked over at the woman and the man with the glasses for the sign that he could drop the weight and end the embarrassment of having failed, but there was something strange about their faces. Both had mouths open and the woman was not looking at her watch. Several people from the other mats had moved over quickly to look at him, and there was a buzz of words he could not make out. The weight above his head began to sway, and he was afraid he would drop it.

Rostnikov pleaded with the woman with his eyes, and finally she nodded to indicate that the lift was complete. He dropped the weight as easily as he could and pulled his bad leg back out of the way as the bar bounced against the mat as if alive. The two spotters bent over to stop it, and Rostnikov straightened up, a slight ache in his back. It was at this point that he realized the cluster of people around his mat were applauding.

"Why did you do that?" asked the man with glasses, a look of awe on his face.

"It was too heavy for me to snatch," Rostnikov answered, bewildered.

"You weren't supposed to snatch it," said the man. "That was the weight for the dead lift. It was more than three hundred pounds. You were just supposed to lift it off the mat. No one has ever cleaned and jerked that much in this competition."

Rostnikov's eyes widened. So he was doing all right after all. Then again, he knew that Alexiev and Pisarenko and a handful of Americans, Poles, East Germans, and Bulgarians could clean and jerk almost 600 pounds.

Then things began to move quickly. Rostnikov developed a retinue led by the man with glasses, who became his guardian through the competition.

"Did you breathe?" asked the woman back in the warm-up building when Rostnikov returned between events. She sat cross-legged, red-faced, rubbing her cheek.

"I breathed," he said.

"I forgot," she said, getting to her knees and reaching for a blue bag. "Good luck." And she was off.

With the help of the man with glasses, Rostnikov found out not only what the weights were but how he stood in the competition as the morning moved to afternoon. For the final rounds of each event, there was but one mat, and things moved more quickly.

Rostnikov's snatch proved to be his weakest event, and there was even a moment of consultation among the judges when they had to decide if his awkward thrust counted.

One of the judges stepped forward, a young man with enormous shoulders and white-blond hair.

"How did your leg get like that?" the young man asked.

"The war," Rostnikov explained. "Battle of Rostov."

The young man nodded, looked at his pad of paper, bit his lower lip, and returned to the other two judges. They consulted briefly and announced that Rostnikov's lift, good enough for third place, would stand.

In the dead lift, however, there was no problem or question. His 560 pounds won easily as did his 300 pounds for the clean and jerk. His totals for the three events were enough to give Rostnikov the championship.

"I knew it," said the man with glasses, taking Rostnikov's sleeve and leading him back to the platform to receive his awards. "I knew we could do it."

Then applause, and lights. Rostnikov blinked back the sweat and wiped his face with his sleeve. He knew he should smile, but the serious look would not leave his face. He held one arm up to acknowledge the applause. It was too much like a dream, and the most amazing part of the dream was Alexiev. Rostnikov could see him now, but it was a strange Alexiev wearing a suit. He had never thought of Alexiev wearing a suit, only the shorts and light shirt or blue sweatshirt, but it was Alexiev, and he was applauding —applauding for Rostnikov. It was a moment to savor. Rostnikov tried to shake himself out of the dream and enjoy the moment, but his mind would not respond. He walked as if in a heavy fog.

When the moment came to accept the silver trophy, Rostnikov solemnly shook Alexiev's massive hand. He wanted to say something, but it seemed too little to say, "You inspired me" or "This is the great moment of my life." So, cursing himself, Rostnikov said, "Thank you."

"If you were twenty years younger," Alexiev said clapping his shoulder, his dark face just as serious as Rostnikov's, "you'd be giving Anatoli and the East Germans worries."

And then Rostnikov smiled. And in that smile came the idea of abandoning his plan. But before the thought was fully formed, while Alexiev still grasped his hand and Rostnikov clutched his trophy to his chest, he saw Sarah in the crowd. He had not expected her to come, for he'd never told her how much this competition meant to him. But she was there, her hair pinned back, a broad smile on her face matching his own, and his resolve returned. He held out the trophy for her to see, and she cocked her head as she often did, feigning deep concentration. Then she nodded and laughed, and Rostnikov laughed.

When he finally escaped from the man with glasses and the reporters from the weight-lifting magazine, who took his picture, and from the other contestants, who congratulated him, Rostnikov changed into his trousers and a clean shirt.

"You did very well, Porfiry Petrovich," Sarah said, touching his arm as they walked outside. Rostnikov had wrapped the trophy in his sweatshirt, not wanting to draw attention as he went home.

"It was a good feeling," he admitted.

"Are you sure you want to go ahead with it?" she said. A trio of soldiers passed them, one bearing a resemblance to their own Iosef.

"I'm sure," said Rostnikov. "And I must stop to make a call. Would you like an ice cream?"

Sarah found an ice cream vendor while he entered a phone booth and dropped some coins into the slot. He attached the tape recorder to the phone, shifting the trophy. It took a few minutes to reach Drozhkin at Lubyanka. It was Saturday, but the colonel was at his desk, just as Rostnikov had assumed he would be.

"What is it, Rostnikov?" he said impatiently.

Good, thought Rostnikov, the pressure from above is on him. Now it was a question of correctly gauging the size of the man's ego. A wrong guess at this point would destroy Rostnikov's plan.

"Colonel," he said, "I suggest that you arrest and detain the German Bintz and the Englishman Willery. I believe they are involved in the plan to assist World Liberation by committing terrorist acts."

"Inspector," Drozhkin hissed, "have you taken leave of your senses? This is a telephone conversation."

"I understand," said Rostnikov, "but the situation is urgent."

"My respect for your abilities has diminished, Inspector," sighed Drozhkin, showing signs of impatience. "We will watch these men. You will be responsible for watching them also. We will wait for them to make some move. They are foreign nationals. We cannot simply arrest them."

"But they might get away," Rostnikov persisted.

"Inspector," said Drozhkin with barely concealed fury, "if they give any sign of their involvement, they will not get away. I suggest you get about your business, and let me get back to mine. I did not waste my morning and much of my afternoon playing games in the park."

With that reminder that the KGB was watching him, Drozhkin hung up. Rostnikov removed the rubber cup from the phone, put it in his bag, and went in search of Sarah.

Though Rostnikov did not know it, others besides the KGB were aware of his participation in the competition.

Sasha Tkach had heard about it from Dmitri Gregorich in the records office. Gregorich heard about it from a switchboard operator at Petrovka who happened to overhear Rostnikov when he registered for the competition months earlier. Tkach had planned to witness Rostnikov's efforts since he was well aware of his superior's strength, but circumstances do not always favor the well-intentioned.

Instead of watching the weight-lifting competition, Tkach sat in People's Court, Leninskii District, City of Moscow. The courtroom was small, old, stuffy, and crowded. There was a single bare light bulb, aided by July sunlight spilling through the two double-paned windows. The judge, a man with a sharp, pinched face that would never quite look shaved, put a finger behind his neck to loosen his slightly frayed collar, then sat down at the battered desk.

"Misha Vernoska, Boris Panyushkin, Alexi Arenko, Sergi Sarnoff," said the judge in a weedy voice that bespoke too many cigarettes, "do you understand the charges against you?"

The four young men who had tried to kill Sasha Tkach and had very nearly killed several women, looked at one another, particularly at Sarnoff, to decide their collective answer. They had been cleaned up, properly dressed, and talked to by a member of the procurator's office who was not obliged to defend them, simply to tell them what the situation was and what they should be prepared for.

"Come, come," said the judge, tapping a yellow pencil against the desk top. "What is so hard to understand? You are accused of rape, theft, and attempted murder."

"Comrade Judge," said Sarnoff, glancing over at Tkach, who sat on a wooden chair nearby waiting to testify. "We understand."

"And," the judge went on, "do you admit guilt as charged?"

Sarnoff looked at the other defendants and glanced over at Marina Restovya, the third victim, who still showed signs of the beating they had given her. It seemed incredible to Tkach that the four thugs had not anticipated that question.

"We did some of those things," Sarnoff said, sullenly looking down so that his dark hair fell forward over his eyes. He threw his head back and looked at the judge. "But not all of those things."

"Will you tell us which you did and which you did not do?" the judge asked with a sigh that indicated that he did not intend to believe anything the young man said.

"We didn't try to kill anybody," Sarnoff said defiantly, glancing at Tkach. Sasha tried to engage the young man's dark eyes, but Sarnoff turned away.

"Admirable," the judge said sarcastically and let out a hacking cough. "So all you did was beat and rape women who were no longer young."

"Yes, Comrade Judge," Sarnoff said, enjoying his moment in center stage. "That's all."

"Then you robbed them," the judge added, looking down at the long yellow sheet in front of him and checking something with the pencil.

"Yes," agreed Sarnoff, "but we were not always responsible."

"The women forced you to do it?"

"No, but they didn't—"

"Stop," said the judge, raising his pencil. "Just tell us what you think of what you have done."

"We are sorry it happened," Sarnoff said with what he must have taken to be smile of contrition.

"You are all sorry," the judge said.

"Yes," the others answered together.

"Have any of you ever been arrested before?" the judge asked.

"Not that we can remember," Sarnoff answered for them.

"A forgettable thing, being arrested," the judge agreed. "Could happen to anyone. Why should you remember it? Let's see, Vernoska, age twenty-five, arrested for illegal profiteering, fighting in the metro. Do you remember now, Vernoska? It comes back to you?"

The young man who had confronted Tkach in the elevator and who now had a wide strip of tape over his nose, which Tkach had broken, looked up and spoke.

"I remember," he said quietly.

"Good," said the judge. "Arenko—theft, vandalism. Panyushkin, what is this, no arrests?"

"The police once took my knife in a store," said the youngest member of the group.

"Sorry," said the judge, making a note of this. "We wish you to have all the credit you deserve. And now, Sarnoff, your lack of memory is hard to understand in view of the frequency of your dealings with the police. Illegal sale of goods, making indecent suggestions to a little girl. Yes, I can see how you would forget such things. Let us have the witnesses."

Three of the women testified, followed by Tkach, who was greeted by applause from the small gathering of relatives of the victims when he described Rostnikov's decimation of the gang.

"We object," cried Sarnoff, looking back at a young woman who sat near the door and was giving him a sour look.

"You object to having been humiliated?" said the judge.

"It didn't happen that way," insisted Sarnoff.

"I'll decide which way it happened," said the judge.

Normally, the detective who has made the arrest does not appear at the trial, and the judge simply reads a statement written by the detective. The detective's deposition is normally a repetition of the charges with any comments about the defendant's background or character that the police wish to make. In this case, however, Tkach was actually a party to one of the charges, that of attempted murder, and so was called on to testify though there had been little doubt from the moment of arrest what the conclusion would be.

"So," the judge said, after Tkach had finished his testimony, "does anyone have any questions, anything to say? Is everything clear? No? Good, the defendants can have the last word."

"Comrade Judge," said Sarnoff, launching into a speech he had obviously rehearsed, "we have done a terrible thing. We are not worthy of Soviet citizenship, but we have learned from your wisdom, and we now see that what we did was wrong. We wish to accept our punishment and as soon as possible return to useful jobs to demonstrate our commitment to the state and the future." Sarnoff paused and got prodded from behind gently by the one called Arenko.

"Oh, yes," Sarnoff added. "We beg the court to be merciful."

"That's all?" the judge said. "Good. I'll be back with the verdict in a little while."

An armed police officer stepped forward as the judge rose and moved to the little dark closet that served as his chambers. While the judge wrote out his verdict and decision and smoked four black cigarettes, the defendants conferred, argued, and ignored as best they could their relatives and their victims.

Tkach sat down next to Marina Restovya who, now that the swelling in her face had gone down a bit, looked even more like an older version of his Maya.

"Will they be executed?" she whispered to Tkach.

"Not for a crime such as this," he answered, "but I'm confident the punishment will be severe." The death sentence, Tkach knew, was generally reserved for murder and political heresy.

The judge returned in about twenty minutes, sat down, and motioned for silence. By now the already stuffy room was stifling with twenty sweating bodies and poor ventilation.

"In the name of the Russian Federated Socialist Republic," began the judge wearily, "it is found that the defendants committed the acts charged in the indictment, crimes specified in the criminal code. In determining punishment, the court has taken into consideration the past record of arrests of three of the defendants, the clear hypocrisy of their contrition, and the disgusting nature of their acts. The sentence is ten years of corrective labor with deprivation of freedom in a penal institution to be decided upon by the state."

It was about what Tkach had expected. Everyone in the courtroom knew that ten years meant ten years, that this meant Siberia, that in ten years the men would age thirty years, and that at least one and possibly more of them would not survive. Tkach looked at Marina Restovya, who nodded solemnly in approval of the verdict. A woman of about fifty began to weep softly and was comforted by a gritty man her own age in worker's clothes.

"Is the sentence clear to you defendants?"

"It is clear," said Sarnoff, his voice breaking.

"Good," said the judge rising.

The defendants were ushered out by the armed police officers and a few minutes of shuffling cleared the courtroom except for the judge, Tkach, and the court secretary.

The judge lit a cigarette and coughed.

"If I could," said the judge to Tkach, "I'd have them executed as an example."

"Yes," said Tkach, thinking that examples, from his experience, didn't seem to have much effect on the behavior of such young men.

"Ludmilla," the judge said to the secretary, "a copy of the trial report for the police."

With that, the judge turned his back, coughed again, and returned to his little office. Ludmilla brushed past Sasha and went into the corridor.

All in all, Tkach thought, Soviet justice was swift and clear, which was just the way he and most of the police wanted it.

TWELVE

WOLFGANG BINTZ HAD NOT ALWAYS BEEN A FAT MAN. He had been thin as a young man, but then his boyhood and very early manhood had coincided with the decline and fall of Berlin, during which almost everyone was thin. If one was not thin at the end of the war, one had much to explain.

Bintz had vivid recollections of his agile former self. One particularly vivid memory was of running down a narrow street off the Wilhelmstrasse in 1945 after he and Bruno Wolfe had killed a Russian soldier. It was at night. The soldier was looking in a bakery window, and Bruno hit him with a metal bar. Wolfgang had always assumed the Russian died. He had not stopped to check, nor had there been any published report of the murder.

It was the running Bintz remembered. They ran for miles, the city blurring to their right and left, through bombed-out streets.

Then, when the war was over, Wolfgang got a speaking part in a movie. He enjoyed the work. And he enjoyed the eating. He ate and ate and soon became a fat young man. Subconsciously, he was storing food away in case another time of starvation should descend on Germany.

With the fat had come an aversion to moving quickly or

walking far. He let his camera move for him. His films were full of movement and action. They were the execution of his imagination. In them, he relived that run through the streets of Berlin after the attack on the Russian soldier.

And now he was being called on to run again, or at least walk a long distance. The run might come later. He left the hotel at three o'clock Saturday afternoon after telling the girl from Intourist that he wanted to walk around and see Moscow on his own. It was not at all what he wanted to do, but she was glad to be relieved of responsibility and let him go without protest.

Bintz had a map and a vague idea of how to get where he was going. He found Sverdlov Square, looked around at the Hotel Metropole and the stretch of wall that dates back to the sixteenth century. He found 25th October Street and made his way along the walls of broken brick. Near the old Stock Exchange, he turned in Rybny Pereulok, or Fish Lane, which was little more than an alley. This took him to Razin Street with its row of government office buildings. He then found the Znamensky Monastery and, as directed, stood before it. He knew that he was a few hundred yards from the Hotel Rossyia and that he could have gotten to this spot in less time. In truth, he had been tempted to neglect the precautions, to save having to walk, but he had overcome that desire and now stood, the crowd moving past him, pretending to examine the seventeenth-century building in which he had no interest. He did imagine a werewolf atop the roof growling down in defiance at a troop of armed Russian soldiers, the moon behind him.

He almost managed to lose himself in the vision of the werewolf leaping down, the camera on a massive boom rising over him. His right hand began to rise inadvertently to simulate the smooth animal movement and, as it did so, he felt something against his side.

It was a familiar feeling, and Bintz almost shouted in German that his pocket had been picked, but he had nothing in the side pocket of his pants. His hand slapped down and now felt something small, about twice the size of a pfennig and much heavier.

Bintz looked at the figures passing by in both directions, but no one was looking at him. He had no idea which of them had dropped the object into his pocket. He turned back to the monastery without seeing it and let his hand slide into the pocket to touch the solid metal object. He knew what it was, and he knew that a step had now been taken that would make it difficult for him to back out of this.

He cursed his own stupidity. He cursed the woman who had arranged this. He cursed World Liberation and almost cursed his mother for bringing him into a world where such a thing could happen. Then, growling at a young man who bumped into him, Bintz began the walk back to his hotel in as direct a line as possible.

Not far down the street at number 18, a man in a dark short-sleeved shirt seemed to be taking a picture of the museum that had once been the birthplace of the Romanovs. Actually, he was considering whether to report the odd behavior of the German to Chief Inspector Rostnikov. The policeman was under the impression that all Germans were a bit odd. This fat man had waddled for almost a mile past dozens of historic buildings, stopped and stared at the old monastery, and then suddenly acted as if he had been shot in the thigh.

Germans, the policeman thought, were not to be trusted. He decided to report the man's behavior to Rostnikov immediately as he had been ordered to, even if he could make no sense of it.

In the crowd, far ahead of the detective and Bintz, the dark-eyed woman hurried toward her next appointment. It was all very dangerous, but she had no choice. She felt exhilarated.

Within fifteen minutes she was inside a department store on the New Arbat standing beside two women who were examining dolls. The dolls had blond curly hair and had been made in Hungary, imitations of their American counterparts.

"So much money," complained the younger of the two women, biting her lower lip.

"What else is there to do with the money?" her companion said. "It's her birthday."

The dark-eyed one glanced across the store and picked up one of the dolls. She saw the person she was seeking, and doubt struck her. He was quite conspicuous, clearly foreign. He craned his neck and looked around the store. If he was being followed, his tail would certainly recognize this as an assignation. She wondered if she could count on him and decided she could not. He did not even pretend to look at the goods on the wooden tables but scanned the crowd anxiously.

The dark-eyed woman trailed along with the two women customers, turning her head as if taking part in their conversation. They could have been three young mothers on a shopping trip, as they moved past the tall foreigner, who looked down to check his watch. At that moment, the dark-eyed one reached over and dropped the object from her palm into his pocket. Taking a step forward, she touched the sleeve of one of the two young women and said, her voice polite, "Do you know if there is a sale on fabrics today?"

A passerby would have thought, looking in their direction, that the three women knew each other. This, in fact, was just what James Willery thought. He had felt nothing enter his pocket and did not know the object was there.

"I know of no sale," said one of the two women.

"Nor I," said the other.

The dark-eyed woman with the glasses thanked them, kept up the conversation briefly as they walked along, and then veered off in another direction toward a door. Only when she reached the door did she glance back at the tall Englishman who continued to look nervously around. Either he was a fine actor or he had no idea that the detonator was now in his pocket. He would find it, she was sure, when he reached for some change. That concerned her less than the bored-looking man four counters away who was pretending to examine a plastic suitcase. The man's hands were on the suitcase, but his eyes were on the Englishman.

It didn't matter. She had done what she could. It really didn't matter at all if the Englishman was caught, but she hoped he would complete his assignment before that happened. Chance, while kept to a minimum, could work either for or against her. Her only hope was to control events as much as she could, have as many options for action as possible, and hope that the odds were in her favor. She had learned that the odds were usually in favor of the person who initiated action. It was far safer to act than to react.

She walked slowly from the store into the late afternoon crowds and turned in the direction of the apartment. One more night, she thought. Just one more.

Rostnikov had washed, shared a drink with Sarah from the bottle of Mukuzani No. 4 wine they had been saving, and now sat at the table looking at his trophy. Plenty of late afternoon sun came through the windows, so they had not turned on any lights.

"Shall we call Iosef?" he asked.

"We can try," Sarah said, looking up from the book she was trying to read. "He would like to know about the trophy."

The look they exchanged made it clear that there was more they would like to tell their son, but that, for the present at least, it would have to remain unsaid.

"I probably can't get a call through to Kiev," he said.

"If you don't try, you'll never know."

There was no arguing with that logic. Rostnikov had already put together the packet he had been working on, had already wrapped it into a small bundle and taped it. It would be bulky in his pants pocket but it would fit. He had considered hiding it, but there was no point in that. There was no safe place. He would simply carry it in his pocket.

"I'll try to place a call," he said, starting to get up.

Before he could take a step, there was a knock at the door. Rostnikov and his wife looked at each other. Her eyes peered over the tops of her round glasses. The knock was urgent and authoritative. Rostnikov himself often knocked just that way.

He gestured to her and held up a hand before crossing the room and reaching for the door. He resisted the urge to touch the packet in his pocket. If he did so now, he might do it without thinking later. He opened the door and found himself facing Samsanov, the building manager, a thin, sad-faced creature.

"I must talk to you, Comrade Rostnikov," he said seriously.

"Talk," growled Rostnikov.

"Can I come in?" said Samsanov, nodding toward the interior of the apartment.

Rostnikov backed up to let the thin man enter and closed the door behind him. Samsanov nodded at Sarah, looked around the room and back at Rostnikov. The building manager wore a dark, worn suit and white shirt with no tie. His neck was speckled with gray hairs and made him look rather like a sorry chicken.

"You fixed the toilet and disturbed the Bulgarians," Samsanov said, his eyes narrowing.

Rostnikov could see that the man had been drinking, perhaps building himself up for this moment.

"I did," said Rostnikov, "and let me remind you that I am a chief inspector of the MVD and that I have given you certain tokens of good faith for you to do something about the toilet and that you failed to do so."

Samsanov raised a placating hand as Rostnikov had hoped he would. The ploy was to start an offensive before he could be attacked.

"I have not come to complain," Samsanov said. "I've come to see if we can reach an understanding."

"Understanding?" asked Rostnikov, moving toward the building manager and looking over at Sarah.

"You seem to be good at repairing the plumbing. You know something about it," said Samsanov softly. "People who need such repairs are willing to pay to bypass the normal procedure. I thought that you and I might—"

"That we might make a profit by illegally doing plumbing repairs," Rostnikov said.

Samsanov looked at the door and back at Sarah.

"I'm not talking about illegal profits," he said soothingly. "I'm talking about helping people."

Samsanov clearly had no idea that the apartment was bugged, had not been part of it. The KGB could have used him but had chosen not to. Rostnikov's near certainty about the apartment being bugged had been confirmed the night before when he found one of the devices and marveled at how incredibly small they had become.

The KGB was almost certainly uninterested in the petty profiteering of a building manager, but Rostnikov was amused at the possibility of telling Samsanov that he was proposing a punishable offense and that his proposal was being recorded by the KGB.

"Out," said Rostnikov. "I have a good mind to arrest you."

In truth, Rostnikov was not at all offended by Samsanov's proposal. He was rather flattered, but he enjoyed acting out the scene for Sarah, who smiled, and for whoever was listening.

"I didn't mean—" Samsanov said, moving toward the door.

"You meant," said Rostnikov, opening the door. "Out."

"Remember," Samsanov said, trying to regain control as Rostnikov gripped his arm and urged him into the hall. "You violated the order of the committee."

"I will be most happy to address the committee on the subject," said Rostnikov, making no effort to keep his voice down. "In fact I would welcome it. Please let me know when it will be." He shut the door firmly on Samsanov.

Karpo was up by five on Sunday morning. The streets were almost empty, and the sky was still dark. It was his favorite time of the day, and he enjoyed the long walk to Petrovka Street.

Even at the noisiest of times, Moscow was comparatively quiet; the noise level was comparable to that of Sau-mur, France, or Waterloo, Iowa, rather than that of New York, Rome, Tokyo, or London. Part of this was due to the smaller number of automobiles, but part was due to the relative quiet of Muscovites. From time to time foreigners have attributed this quiet atmosphere to the fear of the peo-ple in a totalitarian state, but they have only to read ac-counts of Moscow streets before the current century to know that this is not true. No, while Muscovites can be given to hearty laughter and heated argument and even madness, they are essentially a private people. They drive their emotions inward where they build, rather than out-ward where they dissipate. And Russians are fatalistic. If a person is run over by a car, it is terrible, horrible, but no more than one can expect.

This tendency to keep things inside is perhaps to a large degree also responsible for the heavy consumption of alco-hol in Moscow. The emotions have to be diluted, tem-pered, and released, or they might explode. Karpo had seen such explosions many times. He accepted it as the human condition. Every once in a while a human being, an imperfect mechanism at best, would malfunction, and clog up the machinery of the state. Such flaws had to be re-paired or removed. They simply couldn't be tolerated. Karpo saw himself as an expert in the maintenance of the commonweal.

As he walked, Karpo's left arm began to throb slightly from the movement. He had several options. He could take one of the pills, which might affect his alertness and would do only a little to ease the pain. He could seek public trans-portation, a rather difficult thing to find so early on a Sun-day morning. Moscow was the center of a godless state, but the concept of the Sabbath was so much a part of the Russian psyche that the government had eased its rules on Sunday and had gradually allowed it to become a day of rest. Karpo could have called Petrovka and had them send a car for him. After all, he was on official business, but to ask for a car would be an indication of weakness, and that would never do. He chose instead to accept the pain and walk on. He would think through the pain.

By six he was at his desk. The long, narrow room was not yet full, but Kleseko and Zelach were at their desks, and in the corner fat Nostavo was eating a piece of dark bread and talking to a uniformed officer, who stood nearby acknowledging the sage advice he was getting. Eating at one's desk was forbidden, but many inspectors did so. The practice offended Karpo, who regarded any infraction of the rules as a threat to the entire structure. Lenin had said the same thing most clearly, and had led a most ascetic life. If one is willing to break a small rule, how will he know whether the next rule is also a small one when he breaks it? Soon the line between small and large is a blur and the individual becomes a detriment to the state. But Karpo did not report such offenses. There were too many of them. There were too many bribes, too many inspectors who took advantage of their privilege.

Zelach looked over at him, and Karpo nodded in recognition. Then Zelach looked away. Karpo picked up the phone and dialed.

"Kostnitsov, laboratory," came the voice after a long wait.

"Karpo."

"So, I'm here," said Kostnitsov. "The sun is coming out over the Kremlin Wall, my wife is turning over for another few hours' sleep, and my daughter is who the hell knows where."

"Do you have the report ready?" said Karpo.

"Would I be in my laboratory now if I had no report? Would I have gotten myself up in darkness, cut an acre of my chin shaving in a daze, traveled without food to say I had nothing?"

"I do not know you well enough to answer such questions," said Karpo.

"I'm talking human nature, not Boris Kostnitsov. Sometimes, Inspector Karpo, I despair of you. Come on up to my office. That is the least you can do. No, wait, the least you could do in addition to coming to my office is to bring me some tea."

With that, Kostnitsov hung up. The assistant director of the MVD laboratory had no fear or awe of Karpo, no respect for his reputation. Others shied away from the Vampire and limited their contacts with him, but Kostnitsov had always treated him as he treated others, with no respect at all.

In a rather strange and inexplicable way, Karpo liked the man. So, as he would for no other—with the possible exception of Porfiry Petrovich Rostnikov, who would never ask—Karpo made his way to the darkened cafeteria, boiled some water, and made a cup of tea. Then he took the elevator to the lower level, which housed the laboratory.

There was no name on the door, only a number. Knocking was awkward. Karpo shifted the hot cup to his left hand, which he could only raise to his waist. He knocked with his right.

"Come in," shouted Kostnitsov. "Come in, Karpo. Why are you knocking? I told you to come down. What do you think I'm doing in here? Performing lewd acts with laboratory specimens?"

Karpo opened the door, walked across the hard tile floor, and placed the cup on the walnut desk in front of Kostnitsov. Kostnitsov was somewhere in his fifties, medium height, a little belly, straight white hair, and a red face more the result of his Georgian heritage than of his intake of alcohol, which was moderate. He wore a blue lab jacket and was holding a gray envelope.

"Sit," he told Karpo and reached for the tea, which he drank in a single gulp. "Not enough sugar. How am I to get through this morning without dextrose?"

"I don't know," said Karpo, taking a seat across from the desk.

Kostnitsov sucked in his cheeks and examined Karpo.

"Has anyone ever told you you are a most humorless man?" he asked.

"Four times," Karpo replied. "You have a report ready for me."

"And an image to protect," Kostnitsov said with a glower. "You'll have to tolerate my eccentricity. It is all I have to keep me going in this mausoleum. You know what I really wanted to be in this life?"

"No."

"A soccer coach. Here is your report. Do you want me to summarize it for you?"

"Yes."

"Death was definitely caused by an irradiated liquid dosage of psittacosis bacilli," said Kostnitsov, looking at the report. "An unnecessarily flamboyant method for murder. The means available to someone to commit murder by poison without resorting to exotic potions smuggled into the country is almost infinite. Your murderer is a showoff. He is—"

"She," corrected Karpo.

"She was signing her crime with a flourish," said Kostnitsov.

"Where could she get this psittacosis material?" Karpo asked, commanding his arm not to throb.

Kostnitsov's grin was broad and manic, revealing rather poorly-cared-for teeth.

"Only one place as far as I can tell," he said, tapping the report before him. "The Suttcliffe Pharmaceutical Company in a place called Trenton, New Jersey. How she stole it or why is beyond my knowledge, but, as far as I know, Suttcliffe is where Dr. Y. T. Yui is working. He is the foremost authority on the disease which, incidentally, normally affects parakeets, parrots, and other jungle birds. It can be passed on to man, but this happens rarely. Of course you must understand that the strain which killed your Mr. Aubrey and the other three gentlemen was carefully nurtured for this destructive purpose. Suttcliffe is well known for its private work on biological warfare."

"I see," said Karpo when Kostnitsov paused to scan the report for other pertinent information.

"Has this charming woman used the poison since the murders at the Metropole?"

"I think not," said Karpo. No, he doubted she would

use it again. He understood her more with each bit of information. She considered herself a professional, perhaps even an artist in terrorism. Once she had used a method, she would not repeat it—at least not without introducing some striking variation.

"Karpo," Kostnitsov said, handing the report to him, "that concoction appears to be amazingly virulent. I would guess that even if an expert in virology had been at his side the moment your victim took it, he could have done nothing to save him."

"And if she is still carrying this or has given it to someone else to use—" Karpo began.

"Anyone ingesting it," said Kostnitsov, examining the plastic cup for remnants of tea, "will be absolutely safe. I bred a culture of the bacilli taken from the stomach of the Japanese. Its life is incredibly short, four days at most. You or I could drink a cup full of her leftover psittacosis bacilli and suffer nothing worse than a bad taste in the mouth. Unless there are other side effects, though none would be—"

"Wait," Karpo said. "Would it be possible from your study of the bacilli and the samples taken from the body to determine when it was created?"

"When the culture was created?" asked Kostnitsov with a puzzled look, which turned to one of enlightenment. "Of course, yes. You are a clever devil, Karpo. Five days ago, six at the most."

"And," said Karpo thinking aloud, "since it was cultured in the United States—"

"Could have been recultured elsewhere," jumped in Kostnitsov, "or perhaps someone else is working on psittacosis. Perhaps even someone in the Soviet Union. The KGB would know."

"But if it was taken from New Jersey and brought to the Soviet Union," Karpo persisted, "the person who carried it would have to have arrived in Moscow on Wednesday, since the flight from New York takes a full day, with stopover and time difference, and then customs checks here."

Kostnitsov nodded. "Thin, thin," he said.

"Logical?" asked Karpo.

"Worth trying," agreed Kostnitsov.

Karpo got up with his file and nodded at Kostnitsov. "You've been most helpful," he said.

"I most certainly have," Kostnitsov agreed. "Don't forget the empty cup."

Back at his desk, Karpo glanced at fat Nostavo and the uniformed policeman, who was still nodding. A new inspector, whom Karpo did not recognize, was seated at a desk across the narrow aisle. He was humming something that sounded vaguely French. Karpo had no ear for music and no interest in it. Right now he was interested only in flights from New York.

He called Intourist and was told that he could have a list of all passengers who had arrived on Wednesday and Thursday.

"Can I have a list of females between the ages of thirty and forty-five only, both Soviet nationals and foreigners?"

"Yes, but it will be long, perhaps two or three hundred names," said the man from Intourist.

"I will come and get the list," said Karpo. "Where will it be?"

"The Intourist Office, sixteen Karl Marx Prospekt."

So far, it had been easy. Most Soviet institutions worked with painful slowness and indifference. Intourist, however, was a model of efficiency because it was on display to foreign visitors. Its efficiency carried over into its dealings with Soviet officials, including the police.

By eight, Karpo was back at his desk. By noon, he had managed to locate many of the people whose names were on the list. Since tourists have to register, it was much easier to find them than it might have been in any other country. The indifference of hotel managers hampered him, though, as did the veiled hostility of a few younger people who answered the phones in homes and apartments.

But it was coming. With patience and determination, of which he had much, he was confident that by early evening he would have the name the woman was using. He might also, with luck, have a photograph of her.

Karpo considered calling Rostnikov and asking for help, but he had a hunch that time was now precious. He also admitted to himself that he did not want help. He wanted to do this by himself.

She woke from a deep sleep with a teeth-clenched cry. Never could she recall falling so deeply into sleep. It had taken an effort as great as breaking to the surface of a deep pool to come out of the dream, and when she was out and awake, the dream was gone.

"What is it?" asked the young man, blinking at seeing the woman as he had never seen her before.

She couldn't stop a look of hatred from flickering across her face, though she did avert her dark eyes in the first dull patches of morning light and reach for her watch. It was six o'clock, but even now that she was awake, the feeling of something, someone, closing in and smothering her wouldn't go away.

The young man's arm went around her.

"It's just a nightmare," he said with a superior little laugh.

She held back the impulse to push him away, this weak creature who strutted his frail masculinity. She even toyed with the idea of killing him on the spot, but he might be useful for the rest of the day, and she didn't want to be on the move again, not until it was necessary.

"I'll be fine," she forced herself to say.

"Women," he chuckled and rolled over to his side after giving her a pat on the shoulder. He was sure that whatever he had seen on her face, that mask of stone, had been an illusion from his own dreams. He was asleep almost instantly.

She was well aware that the Russians claimed to have achieved equality of the sexes, but she was equally aware that it was a hollow claim, that women were rarely given anything but token positions of importance, that, in fact, women were expected to work at full-time jobs and to be responsible for homemaking as well, while men complained and continued to run things, just as they had done

in the past. It was the same everywhere. What she had, she
had taken by her own intellect and strength. She had long
since decided not to take part in the world of men like this
one next to her. But her motivation was not a feminist one.
No, she felt far above and outside such considerations.
Any "ism" was an illusion created by individuals or groups
to give false meaning and direction to essentially meaning-
less lives. All that counted was one's image of oneself, not
what others saw. One lived only to have the satisfaction of
achievement and control. It was a game she would lose,
but she would not play by false rules. She would create her
own rules. •

She got up as quietly as she could. He stirred behind her
but did not wake. She bent over her flight bag, unlocked it
and found the small aspirin bottle. Silently, she removed
two tablets, which were not aspirin, from the bottom of the
bottle and tucked them into the pocket of her shirt. When
the proper moment arrived later in the day, she would dis-
solve the pills in a beverage and be sure he drank it all. The
dosage would probably not kill him, but would make him
ill and dazed and keep him out of her way. If he was going
to be killed, this one, she wanted to do it with her own
hands. She wanted him to know what she was doing.

Thinking about the day and the night helped ease the
feeling of liquid weight. She moved to the window, pushed
the grubby curtain aside, and looked out at the city. Somewhere they were looking for her, that barrel of an inspector
and the lean monk of a detective she had deceived at the
Metropole.

The feeling that ran through her now was not fear, but a
sensation of inevitability. Thinking about the lean one had
brought on that feeling. Perhaps it had been part of her
nightmare.

The phone call they'd placed to Iosef came through at
six on Sunday morning. Rostnikov heard it but dimly,
wondering if it was the bells of some imagined church.
Sarah roused herself quickly and picked up the telephone.

"It's Iosef," she said, poking Rostnikov, who grunted

and let go of the dream image of a large bottle of Czech pilsner beer.

"Up, I'm getting up," he said and reached out for the phone.

"When I'm done," she said, slapping his hand away.

Rostnikov sat up, scratched his stomach, and held one hand to his ear as he pointed to the corner where he had discovered the tiny microphone. Sarah nodded.

Rostnikov heard Sarah ask Iosef how he was, what he was doing. She told him about Rostnikov's weight-lifting trophy.

When he saw the tear in the corner of her eye, Rostnikov reached for the phone. Sarah pulled back, then sighed deeply and gave it to him.

"Iosef," he said.

"Father," replied Iosef in a voice almost forgotten in the past year. The familiar tones jolted Rostnikov's emotions. He looked at Sarah and closed his eyes. "Yes, you are well?"

"I'm well," said Iosef. "Congratulations on your trophy."

"It's a fine trophy," said Rostnikov, looking across the room to where it stood on a table near the cabinet that contained the weights. "Iosef, we would like to see you. It has been a long time. Have you applied for leave?"

"Difficult," he said. "Those of us who have been—"

"I know," Rostnikov stepped in. It didn't have to be spoken. Those who had been to Afghanistan were being kept under tight security, at least for the present. "Perhaps things will change. You are well?"

"You just asked that," Iosef laughed. "I'm well. Are you catching criminals?"

"No criminal is safe with Rostnikov in Moscow." He laughed, too.

Sarah reached for the phone back, but he turned away to continue the conversation.

What there was to say couldn't be said on the phone.

"Was there anything special?" Iosef asked after a brief pause.

"Special? No, nothing special. We just hadn't heard your voice for some time," Rostnikov went on. "The film festival is going on here. Lots of visitors, a carnival. You remember."

"I remember," said Iosef. "Do you remember when you took me to my first movie? Jane Powell."

"Yes." Rostnikov remembered. "She was almost as good as Deanna Durbin."

"I have to go now," said Iosef cheerily. "The officer in charge has just told me my time is up. So, good-bye and take care."

"And you, too," said Rostnikov. "Say good-bye to your mother."

He handed the phone to Sarah who managed not to sob as she said good-bye. She listened to something Iosef said and then hung up.

They looked at each other for a few seconds in silence.

"I forgot to tell him Illya asked about him," Sarah said looking at the phone.

"Put it in a letter," he said, standing up. He looked around the room for his pants, though he always put them in the same place, draped over a wooden chair in the corner.

"You can go back to sleep for a while, Porfiry Petrovich," Sarah said, sitting on the bed and looking up at him.

"No, I have work to do," he said, lifting his pants from the chair and sitting down as he wondered what time his German would get out of bed to begin what might be the most important day of both their lives.

After Iosef Rostnikov hung up the phone, he walked slowly and correctly to the door of the small squad room without facing the lieutenant who sat behind the desk a few feet away. The officer, Galinarov, had listened openly and intently to Iosef's side of the conversation with his hands folded in front of him. He had been instructed to do so, but he would have listened anyway because he did not like Rostnikov.

Iosef looked far more like his mother's side of the family than his father's which, in the mind of Galinarov who knew the histories of every man under his command, made the younger Rostnikov a Jew. Galinarov had nothing in particular against the Jews, just as he had nothing against the Mongols and Tatars who were forming a larger and larger percentage of the militia. That worried Galinarov and others above him. There had always been a rather high percentage of Jews in the Russian army, going back to the days of the czars. The reason was simple: Jews could not buy their way out, and it was believed that an important function of the army was to control and contain the Jews.

During the rule of the czars, soldiers would go to the Jewish villages once a year to round up their quota of boys twelve and older. The boys would serve for a period of five to forty years. The longer they served, the more likely they were either to die or to accept Christ, though the Jews had proved stubborn, and deaths had always outnumbered conversions among Hebrew soldiers.

Since the Revolution, the goal of the military was no longer to convert the Jewish conscripts to Christianity or even to communism, since the majority of the Jews seemed to embrace socialism with the great hope that it would ease their lot in life. No, the roots of the army's hostility to the Jews were deeply anchored in the Russian psyche, nurtured by suspicion of Jewish separateness and intellectualism.

"Rostnikov," said Galinarov as the young corporal reached the door.

"Yes, Comrade," Rostnikov answered without turning, which was a mild but obvious insult.

"Turn around," said Galinarov.

Iosef turned around and faced the officer, who was almost exactly a year younger than he was.

"Calls to this station by relatives are, as you know, discouraged except in emergencies," said Galinarov, tapping his fingertips together.

"I know, Comrade," Iosef said.

"And?" prompted Galinarov.

"Nothing further," Iosef said. "I did not tell my parents to call. I have informed them of the order. You can, of course, call them yourself and so inform them. You can reach my father at home now or at his office tomorrow. His number is—"

"I know he is a policeman," said Galinarov through his teeth.

"A chief inspector," Iosef amplified, adding a gentle smile.

"Are you trying to impress me with your family's position?" Galinarov said, standing. He was in full uniform, his collar buttoned, clean and shaved as always.

"No, Comrade," said Iosef. "I was simply providing you with adequate information with which you could make a decision on the proper course of action."

"You have a tendency to say more than is good for you, Rostnikov."

Iosef nodded. "A habit I acquired from my father," he explained.

"A racial quality," Galinarov prodded.

"Perhaps, Comrade," Iosef said agreeably. "But it is my mother who is discreet, and she is the one who is Jewish. My father comes from a long line of Russian Christian peasants, like your father."

"You will not get very far in this army, Rostnikov," Galinarov said, tapping his fingers nervously on the desk top.

"I do not expect to, Comrade. My goal is to do my job, serve my time with honor, and return to civilian life where I can make my contribution to the state."

"You don't really know how difficult things can be for you, Rostnikov," Galinarov went on.

"They were quite difficult in Afghanistan during the winter," Rostnikov responded. "The man you replaced was killed there, as you know. I realize that you have not had the privilege of serving in combat for the nation, but—"

Galinarov moved from the desk in three boot-clapping steps and faced Rostnikov, his nose inches from that of his subordinate.

"To say that you will regret this conversation is an understatement to match Napoleon's comment that he would destroy Russia in two weeks."

Galinarov's breath was surprisingly minty, to cover the smell of Madeira wine, which everyone knew was the lieutenant's constant companion. Rostnikov was also quite sure that Napoleon had said nothing of the kind. It was a typical Soviet ploy. People were forever quoting Lenin, much of the time with a great deal of creativity, knowing that even scholars had a difficult time identifying quotations from the mass of Lenin's writing and speeches.

Rostnikov couldn't resist joining the game.

"I believe it was Hitler who said that," he said as innocently as he could, though he had no idea if Hitler had said any such thing.

"Get out," Galinarov said, a faint tic quivering above his right eye.

Rostnikov turned and left as smartly as he could. He knew that Galinarov was sorely tempted to test him physically, but both Rostnikov and Galinarov knew that Iosef was stronger, faster, and a good deal smarter. And that was part of the problem, along with the fact that Rostnikov found it very difficult to conceal his superiority.

In the hallway with the door shut behind him, Iosef looked at his hands, which were quite steady. He had to admit that he really enjoyed such confrontations. He had been honed on them over meals at home and had learned to consider such verbal jousting not only a fact of Soviet life but one of its intellectual joys. Actually, Galinarov could make his life at the barracks near Kiev quite miserable and would probably do so, but soon Iosef would inherit the secret rock, the rock that was always passed to the man with the shortest time remaining in service. The short-timers' rock, painted red and quite smooth, would rest in the pocket of the fortunate holder, to be passed ceremoniously to the next man when it was time for the holder to go.

The procedure had been part of Rostnikov's company for years, and it had been a lighthearted ritual until the return from Afghanistan. The expedition had brought the men—those who survived—close together.

As he returned to his barracks room where Misha and

Rolf were waiting for him with a chess game, Iosef had two concurrent thoughts. First, he thought it might be interesting to be a policeman as his father was and spend much of the time confronting people as he had confronted Galinarov. He had never seriously considered that before, and though he was trained as a mechanical engineer, he wondered if his father could make some arrangement for him to join the MVD. The second thought was less specific but troublesome: What, in fact, *had* prompted his parents to call him?

THIRTEEN

James Willery sat silently on the floor, his legs crossed, staring at the wall. Several students came to look in on him and discuss the controversy that had arisen after the screening of *To the Left*. One of them managed to get a grunt out of him shortly before two o'clock. Half an hour later Alexander Platnov, who was rather enjoying the silence, felt obliged to offer his guest something to eat. Willery rejected the soup but accepted a piece of coarse white bread, which he ate slowly and silently.

"What's wrong with him?" asked a young woman with long dark hair when Platnov went out in the hall to use the toilet.

"I don't know." Platnov shrugged, quite happy to talk to the woman who, until now, had acted as if Platnov was not a member of the human race. "He was in India a few years ago. I think he may be meditating."

The young woman looked toward the room. "He is a very profound filmmaker," she said.

He is, thought Alexander Platnov, an ass. However, he said, "Yes, yes, he is. And I've learned much from him in the last few days."

The woman, who was named Katya, looked at him seriously with intense gray eyes.

"I'd very much like to know what he has shared with you, Comrade," she said.

"When he leaves," Platnov said, "I'll be most happy to share his thoughts with you."

Willery's thoughts at the moment would have interested the two very much, but not for aesthetic reasons. He was trying to work himself up to a sufficient level of courage—or numbness—to blow up a building. After his walk the previous day, he had gone from despair to euphoria when the woman failed to contact him. He allowed himself to imagine that she had changed her mind, been caught, or met with an accident.

A good two hours after returning to the student residence, while he was discussing the possibility of getting between two thoughts with a young woman he had met at the screening of his film, his hand bumped against his side, and he felt the hard object in his pocket. Without thinking, he pulled it out to look at. It was about the size of a small tape cassette, very black and shiny with a black plastic button in the center.

"What is that?" the young woman had asked.

"This?" said Willery, looking at the object in terror.

She laughed. "Are you making fun of me?"

"No," he said. "This is an invention."

"What does it do?"

"It is a remote control switch for starting a hidden camera," he said.

"I see," said the young woman with a wicked smile, "and you have such a camera in this room. Let me push the button and start it."

She had reached for the black piece in his hand, and he had leaped back, ramming into a desk.

"No," he said sharply, and shoved the thing back into his pocket.

It had then taken him five minutes and several promises to get the young woman to leave. He had to think, he had told her. Inspiration came on him like that, between two thoughts.

Since she had already decided that part of her fascination with him was his Western eccentricity, she accepted his need to be alone, though she wasn't at all sure she accepted his reason. As soon as she had left, Willery had headed for the bed and had hidden in sleep in a near fetal position till the next morning. His snoring kept Alexander Platnov up most of the night, but Platnov kept telling himself that the madman would be gone in a day or two. Willery had already been informed unofficially that he had no chance to win a prize in any competition.

In the morning, Willery had accepted coffee and a sandwich and taken his seat on the floor, looking at the wall. Once in a while he adjusted his dark glasses, but otherwise he was completely still.

Willery had come to several conclusions. First, he did not have to get too close to the hotel and the theater when he pressed the button. It would almost surely work from some distance, but what distance? He had been told that when the moment came he was to be across the street, no more than fifty yards away, but maybe it would work from farther away. He could try, couldn't he? If it didn't work, he could simply move in a little closer. The best thing about this was that he would not have to see what happened inside the theater when he pressed the button. The worst thing was that he could easily imagine what would happen. He had seen the damage done by IRA bombings in London. He had wanted to make a movie about terrorism, but one visit to the site of a bombing had changed his mind. That was how he had met Robert from World Liberation.

He had no misgivings about blowing up the theater. In fact, he was quite happy about that part because it was the same theater where two nights before the audience had ridiculed his film. Yes, that very ridicule made him an aesthetic martyr. He would tell the Western reporters, especially his friend Elsie Brougham who worked for the *Guardian*, about the vulgarity of the Russian movie-goers. But still, there would be some justice in imploding that overdone excuse for a movie theater. If only there would be no people in or near it—or if he could carefully select the people who would be inside. He could come up with a nice list, starting with the pock-faced little turd from the Moscow Film Festival Committee who had tried to get him to withdraw his film and had smirked at him every time Willery tried to explain what his film was about.

He looked down at his watch and discovered that it was almost four o'clock. He groaned. In one hour, just one hour, he had to do it. He really had no thought of not doing it. They had killed Monique, and they would surely kill him. The Russians, even if they caught him . . . One more hour.

When Willery groaned, Platnov put down his book and turned to see what was happening. In the past few hours the student had developed a bit more tolerance for his guest, since he might well prove to be the bridge to Katya.

"What is wrong?" he asked.

"I've got to go," whispered Willery.

"Where?" asked Alexander Platnov.

"Out," said Willery, getting up on cramped legs. "But I'll be back."

"Of course," Platnov said, now looking with some puzzlement at his guest. Had the man obtained drugs? It would not surprise Platnov. Whatever it was, Willery was going out and had not invited Platnov to go with him. The man from the Moscow Film Festival office had said that Platnov should stay with his guest at all times, but it was Sunday afternoon, and every man had his limits of tolerance. Both Marx and Dostoevsky had made that quite clear.

"I'll be back," Willery repeated, going to the door.

I'm sure you will, said Platnov to himself, wondering if he should go just to keep the man from wandering into a passing motorbus. "Would you like me to come with you?"

"No," Willery snapped, and then, with a weak smile, he repeated, "no," quite softly, and went out the door.

Platnov shook his head and turned back to his book. It was about computer technology for heavy machinery factories, and he hated it.

In a halfhearted attempt to get lost, Willery wandered about the city. To Sasha Tkach, who was following him, it looked at times like an amateur's attempt to lose anyone who might be on his trail, but if so, it was so incredibly inept that the man appeared to be feebleminded, a possibility that Tkach, having seen *To the Left*, considered briefly. Willery took no public transportation, went through no buildings, but simply wandered, sometimes winding up where he had been before. It was also possible that he was simply trying to determine if someone was following him, but if so he was doing an amazingly good job of not being caught looking back.

No, Tkach decided, the Englishman was simply some kind of fool who disrupted the lives of policemen who would much rather be home with their families. When this thought came to Tkach, he smiled. A passing old couple saw his smile and smiled back.

That morning as he ate breakfast at their small table, Maya had told him and his mother that she was pregnant. It had struck Sasha like a hammer to the heart. His first response, strangely enough, was a feeling similar to the one he had last winter when he shot the young thief in the liquor store. He wanted the child very much. He had thought about it a lot and discussed it many times with Maya.

Then, as Maya shouted the news to his mother who had failed to hear the announcement, Sasha recognized that feeling in his chest. He didn't give it a name but knew it had something to do with responsibility. Who had said . . . Yes, Rostnikov had said that for everything good, one has to pay a price, shoulder a responsibility. And then Rostnikov had added that for everything bad one also pays a price and shoulders the responsibility.

He had wanted to stay home with Maya. He'd considered asking Zelach to do a double shift of tailing Willery, or calling Rostnikov and asking his permission to stay home. Sasha wanted to give the news of the coming child to the Washtub, but he thought better of it. Willery was his responsibility. And so he went out and took over from Zelach just as Willery came out of the apartment building shortly before four and began his seemingly drunken wandering about the city.

Shortly before five o'clock, Willery's wandering seemed to become more purposeful. He headed north, hesitated to gain his bearings, and then made his way to the river. Tkach closed the distance between them. There were plenty of people on the streets, most of them coming or going from nearby Red Square; and Willery, as had been made quite clear to Tkach, was not aware of or interested in the possibility that he might be followed.

When they passed the Kremlovskaya Embankment, which runs along the Kremlin Wall, Willery's pace slowed. Through the crowd, Tkach could see the man furrow his brow over his dark glasses and look at his watch. For almost the entire trek, Willery's hand had been moving restlessly in his right pocket. The hand went rigid as they came in sight of the Rossyia Hotel. Willery crossed the street and stood next to Saint Anne's Church, but he was not there to admire the beautiful fifteenth-century building. Instead, he looked over at the hotel. Because of Willery's dark glasses, Tkach could not tell if he was looking at the State Concert Hall or the Zaryadye Cinema. Tkach's guess was that he had simply come to relive the agony of his film screening in the theater.

Certainly there was nothing happening in the theater at the moment. A huge sign indicated that the next screening would be in an hour. A few people were waiting for the doors to open, but there was no crowd. Tkach made his way closer to Willery as it became evident that the man was not going to move.

Tkach had expected to see a pensive look on Willery's face when he got close, but it was not easy to read what he saw. From a distance of about twenty feet Willery looked frightened and determined. His thin lips were tight, as he looked at the people passing by or examining the small church. His eyes ran past Tkach, who turned his back to ask a passerby for the time. Four minutes to five.

Tkach walked across the street toward the theater, his back to Willery, and made his way to a cluster of men and women who were having an animated discussion of montage. He tried to look as if he was hurrying to join them. Moving behind the group of people, he smiled and asked the leader of the discussion what time it was.

"A minute or so to five," the man said with irritation, and returned to his discussion of montage.

At this point Tkach looked again at Willery, who seemed to be staring back at him though he showed no sign of recognition. It was then that Tkach had an uneasy feeling. The Englishman was not looking at him but at the Zaryadye Movie Theater. He seemed to be expecting something. As he watched, his mouth dropped open and his hand plunged into his pocket. His look was so intense that Tkach turned to the theater to see what there was to look at.

The montage man was in a state of near apoplexy in his argument when the explosion came. It was not a massive, ear-splitting sound, but the boom of a giant stomping on an enormous paper bag. The boom was followed within a breath by the shower of glass.

Tkach had been facing the theater when the first sound came. He turned and threw himself face down on the pavement, covering his head just as the rain of glass exploded behind him.

Something skittered across his back and over his arm like a sharp-clawed animal, and then he heard a tinkling and crackling like a fragile hail. He kept his head down till the sound stopped, and then he looked up.

Sitting in front of him was the montage man, a look of total bewilderment on his bloody face. At his side stood a woman in a blue dress holding her arm, which oozed blood at an alarming rate. Tkach rose, trembling, and looked around. The half-dozen or so people in the immediate vicinity of the theater were in the stage that precedes panic. They were numb; they had no idea what had happened or why. Tkach stepped over a torn movie poster that had been blown to the street and looked at Willery, who stood agape with something in his hand.

"Willery," Tkach shouted, for now he knew that somehow, for some reason, this lunatic Englishman had set off an explosion in the theater. Tkach had hoped that his shout would paralyze Willery. Even if it did not, he knew he could catch the Englishman. What Sasha Tkach had not counted on was his own injury.

A sharp pain coursed from his shoulder down his back to his buttocks as he pushed past the dazed people. The pain was not nearly as intense as his fear that he had been mortally wounded. The irony of discovering one was to be a father on the day one was killed came to him in a sob and froze him in place.

His eyes were still on Willery, who now spotted Tkach, and suddenly seemed to recognize him. Instead of running, he began furiously pressing his thumb against the small black object in his hand as if it might make this apparition of the policeman go away.

Tkach twisted around to check his back. He couldn't see down to his buttocks, but he could tell that he had received a long straight cut that had gone through his clothes and charted a path as if drawn with a ruler. It was ugly, but Tkach was fairly certain it wasn't severe.

"Willery," he called again, growing angry now at this man who had almost killed him on the day he had learned that his child Misha was to be born.

Willery saw only a figure who seemed vaguely familiar, and the figure was coming at him, looking determined and furious and calling his name. The man seemed to have emerged from the explosion—a miracle. So Willery had pushed the button again in the hope that another explosion would come and take this man away. The button had no effect, so Willery threw the little box at the man who was advancing on him. He had originally meant to wipe it clean of any fingerprints and heave it in the river, but that was forgotten.

The small box clattered to the ground in front of Tkach, stopping him just in time to prevent his being hit by a small, brown Pobeda automobile whose driver had lost control as his right front tire was punctured by a shard of glass.

Tkach instinctively put his arms to his head in the belief that the object thrown at him might explode. When there was no explosion, and the Pobeda skidded by, Tkach bent and picked up the object. Bending caused him some pain, but even in the madness of the panic-stricken screaming behind him and the skidding, crashing car to his left, he knew he had to get that little box.

"Willery!" he shouted, resuming his determined pursuit.

This time Willery turned and ran. How did it come to this? he asked himself, weeping inside, as he ran without knowing where. I'm a goddamn filmmaker. He wanted to turn to see if the wild man was chasing him, but he didn't dare. He had done some running in school, but that was almost fifteen years ago. But fear and adrenaline prodded him forward, as he pushed past groups of people who were moving against him in the direction of the explosion.

"Stop that man!" shouted Tkach, but no one stopped the thin man with the dark glasses and jeans. His little Edwardian jacket billowed behind him as he dashed madly down Marx Prospekt.

Then a woman stepped in front of him and grabbed Willery's arm, almost spinning him to the ground. She was enormous and insistent.

"What was that noise?" she demanded with authority.

"I don't know what you're talking about, you Russian cow. Let me go!" he cried in English, glancing back at Tkach, who was no more than thirty yards behind.

Not understanding what he said, which was fortunate for him, she pushed him away with disapproval and stalked onward. Willery stumbled, righted himself, and plunged forward.

"Stop him!" Tkach was panting and unsure whether he should continue to expend energy shouting or preserve his strength for the pursuit of the surprisingly swift-footed Englishman. No one stopped Willery. The determined woman reached out to grab Tkach, hoping to get some coherent information about what was going on. Tkach dodged past her, though her hand brushed his shoulder and came away smeared with blood.

Later Tkach would estimate that the chase covered about a mile. In reality, it was only half of that. Tkach feared that Willery would never get tired, but as he passed the Central Exhibition Hall and entered 50th Anniversary of the October Revolution Square he found himself facing a pair of youths wearing caps and silly grins, arms linked, and clearly having drunk more than was reasonable on a Sunday afternoon. Willery tried to dash around them, but the young men, in trying to get out of his way, moved in the same direction as his charge. He hit them full speed, breaking their arm link and sending him into a triple somersault from which he rose like a circus performer. His face was bruised and he seemed to have lost his sense of direction completely. Just then a car pulled up next to him, and two men jumped out. They were very large, sober, dark men, and one was carrying a machine gun.

Exhausted and bleeding, Tkach stopped a dozen yards from the car. People all around were watching, but no one stepped forward as one of the men grabbed Willery by the arm and shoved him roughly into the back seat of the car, then pushed the door closed and turned the gun on Tkach.

There was no doubt in Tkach's mind who these men were. Their look, their size, their command of the situation told him they were KGB.

"He's mine," panted Tkach, feeling that his kill was getting out of his hands and being taken by predators, vultures. He was the one who had done the tracking and chasing. If he'd had his wits about him, Sasha Tkach would never have questioned the authority of the KGB, but there was a touch of hysteria in his tone now.

The KGB man with the gun said nothing, but simply shook his head firmly and motioned with the gun for Tkach to back off. Willery was hidden inside by the dark windows of the car. Tkach wanted to say something more. He opened his mouth, but the man with the gun shook his head again, silencing him. The man opened the front door and got in, carefully watching Tkach. Then he closed the door, and the black Moscovich turned slowly and drove away.

Passersby who had stopped to watch the show now

moved on past the young man with the wounded back, who stood in silent frustration and fury.

How many times can one fail? Tkach asked himself as he walked slowly back in the direction of the explosion. He would have to call Rostnikov and tell him not only that Willery had succeeded in committing an act of terrorism, but also that he had been wrenched from Tkach by the KGB. It was, at best, a sorry effort.

Then a young woman stepped forward and suggested that he see a doctor and Tkach looked down and saw a boy of about three holding the woman's hand. The boy seemed frightened, and he lifted his thumb to his mouth.

Tkach gave the child a pained grin. There was something to salvage in the day. He thanked the child's mother and moved on, thinking that it was absolutely impossible to make any sense out of the ways of the world. He completely forgot, for the moment, the small black object in his pocket.

She had not witnessed the explosion or Tkach's pursuit of Willery, because the explosion had taken place one hour too early. For some reason that unreliable English dolt had detonated the bomb at five instead of six as she had instructed him.

She was almost half a mile away when she heard the blast and looked at her watch. She had intended to remain a safe distance away until the explosion came, but this had been much too early. At five o'clock there would be no one in the damned theater. What kind of act of terrorism is it to destroy an empty theater? Had this been some attempt at cleverness on Willery's part? She didn't think so, for she had recognized fear in his voice and had gauged his character with confidence the two times she had observed him. He had simply fouled up, which meant that at some point, if the police or KGB did not dispose of him, she would be obligated to do it herself.

As she headed back toward the apartment, a babushka tied firmly on her head and her glasses set firmly on her nose, she was not concerned about the whereabouts of

James Willery. Even if they had him he knew nothing. She had been most careful about that. They could threaten him, torture him, do what they wished, he would have practically nothing to tell them that they did not already know.

One thing did bother her though. The police knew that Aubrey had interviewed the Englishman, the German, and the Frenchwoman. They had told her this. Now, the Frenchwoman was dead, and if the Englishman did not get away, they might guess that he was part of a conspiracy of terror.

She had plenty of time to get to the next site. She had originally allowed herself one hour and had told the German to detonate his bomb at seven. She would make use of the hour by preparing for her own action, which now seemed even more essential, and taking care of the young man whom she had left in a drugged sleep. She had decided to get rid of him in such a way that the police would know it was indeed she who had done this. She wanted to rub their defeat and stupidity in their faces as she had done to the police in five other countries. But her desire to show that pursuing vampire that she was not afraid led her to carelessness, for she decided to use the last of the small vial of liquid with which she had eliminated Warren Harding Aubrey. She decided to murder the arrogant young man with what she did not realize was a dose of dead and quite harmless psittacosis bacilli.

When Tkach finally got to the phone at the hospital after being treated for his cuts, he called Rostnikov's apartment only to discover that the chief inspector had been out the whole afternoon.

He then called Petrovka, but Rostnikov was not there either. He talked to Emil Karpo.

"Karpo," he said, "the Englishman, Willery, set off a bomb at the Zaryadye. No one was killed, a few injuries, the KGB got him. Find Rostnikov and tell him."

Karpo hung up the phone and pushed aside the papers he had been working on.

"She is making mistakes," he said softly to himself and

glanced down at the notes he had taken. Tkach's call had confirmed what Karpo had already concluded. This was the day that everything would happen.

Louise Rich of Trenton, New Jersey, had a reservation for a flight out of Sheremetyevo International Airport at midnight. Karpo had no doubt at all that Louise Rich was the dark-eyed woman. He had eliminated all other possibilities and confirmed his conclusion by discovering that Louise Rich was not in her room at the National Hotel and had not been seen there for several days, though she did call in to assure the hotel that she was well and staying with friends. She even gave her friends' name and number. Karpo had checked on one of the numbers, and the woman who answered knew no one named Louise Rich.

Of course, her name was not Louise Rich, but she might try to use the reservation. She would be careful and would make sure no one followed her, but it was an escape route. American tourists were not bothered much by customs, and in Madrid, her destination, American tourists were even less likely to be inspected carefully.

She was making mistakes, but would she make enough for him to catch her or stop her from committing whatever acts of terrorism she still had planned? She was his responsibility. He took a pill to dull the pain in his arm. He was not in agony, but he could afford no distractions. He had to think like her. No, think *ahead* of her.

Karpo did not give a thought to the German. Bintz was the chief inspector's responsibility, and Rostnikov was one of the few people—perhaps the only one—whom Karpo felt was truly competent.

Karpo's task was to find the dark-eyed woman within the next few hours.

FOURTEEN

Rostnikov was well aware that he was being followed by a KGB man. This afternoon Rostnikov made an effort for the first time to discover who the agent trailing him might be. Normally that would have been easy to determine, but he had to do it without making the agent suspicious. On the way to the Rossyia Hotel, he walked along the river embankment and, just before he came to the Lenin State Library, he mounted the stone stairs leading up from the embankment. He moved very slowly. His leg really gave him no choice, and he paused to lean against the metal railing at the top as if to catch his breath. At that point he saw the white Chaika sedan parked near the traffic light below him. The front door was open, and a man was looking back at him through the rear window. Of course Rostnikov could not be entirely sure, but it was enough. He took one step back and then, letting out a deep sigh, turned back to the fence and bent over to rub his thigh. It was then that he saw the man get out of the car. He was of average height, hatless, and almost bald. He was very quick. He seemed to spot Rostnikov without looking up, and instead of crossing to the steps, he moved along the embankment in the opposite direction.

There was someone else in the car who did not get out,

but Rostnikov was less concerned about that. They would only switch street men if they were reasonably sure Rostnikov had spotted him. It was almost certain that the two men knew he was a police inspector and not an enemy of the state, but the KGB was assembling a dossier on him so as to be able to apply political pressure later on. They would be most effective, but they would not suspect him of anything unusual.

Later, he knew he would have to discover the identity of the KGB men who were watching the German, Bintz.

As Rostnikov stood before the desk of the general manager of the Rossyia Hotel, he concluded that the task he had set for himself would not be quite as easy as he had expected.

He had hoped the director would be harried and of average competence, but as it turned out, the man was quite shrewd. He easily juggled the frequent calls on his forty-button telephone without losing track of the discussion.

The office was large, with wood paneling and a green carpet. It contained a conference table, a desk, and a closed-circuit television system with monitors showing the three lobbies of the massive hotel. There was also a glass case holding a portrait and a small statue of Lenin.

"We have never done anything like this before," the manager was saying, folding his hands on the desk and making it clear to Rostnikov that he viewed his request as a very serious one. He was a tall, sharp-featured man with steel gray hair. Rostnikov felt that the man would project the same significance to any request that disrupted the normal routine of the hotel.

"It is very important," Rostnikov said. He had declined a chair, hoping that he could intimidate the manager by standing over him, but when that proved useless, he had backed away and become as matter-of-fact and business-like as he could.

"You will have to sign a form accepting full responsibility," the manager said after taking a call during which he did not remove his eyes from Rostnikov.

Rostnikov nodded.

"I will also have to call your superior to confirm that this has been approved," the man said, reaching out to take yet another call.

Rostnikov had not considered this possibility, and while the manager was on the phone, he looked at Lenin for help.

"Yes," the manager was saying into the phone, running a hand through his carefully combed hair. "If you expect that many employees. As long as we do not go over the one hour allotted for each. Yes, I know it is the hotel Party's responsibility to keep up the moral level of all employees, and I am not in any way suggesting that we limit the lectures. In fact, I think the subject for this week is excellent. Let me see . . ." He took his eyes off Rostnikov long enough to find a blue sheet of paper on his desk. "'The Ideological Struggle between Socialism and Capitalism in Today's World—How It Can Be Stepped Up.' I will, of course, attend if at all possible. By all means. Let us meet on Tuesday. Eleven in the morning."

With that the manager hung up, shaking his head.

"We have over three thousand employees in the hotel, Chief Inspector," he said. "Can you imagine the logistics necessary to ensure that they all have time off to attend lectures for the collective?"

"Considerable," said Rostnikov.

"Considerable," agreed the manager. "Now, I will have to call your superior."

"Procurator Timofeyeva," said Rostnikov. "She is well aware of the circumstances surrounding this investigation. Unfortunately, she is in the hospital with a heart condition, and she doesn't have a phone in her room. If you wish," he said looking at his watch, "we have just enough time to get to the hospital, talk to her, and get back to the hotel, but we'd have to hurry."

The manager's gaze looked on Rostnikov as the bank of telephone lights blinked their demand. Rostnikov was counting heavily on the man's unwillingness to take time out from his busy job to make such a check. He might send an assistant, in which case Rostnikov would have to work something out to fool whoever was sent. He was not at all sure he would be able to fool the manager.

"Ah," sighed the manager, tapping his fingers on the desk. "We'll forget about it for now, though I would like an official memo from him."

"Her," corrected Rostnikov. "Comrade Timofeyeva is a woman."

"Her," said the manager, bowing his head slightly to acknowledge his error. "I'll have a statement of responsibility prepared for you to sign when you are finished. You are confident that Herr Bintz will make no complaint?"

"He will make no complaint," Rostnikov assured him.

The manager reached for the phone and, before answering, looked at Rostnikov and opened his hands in a so-be-it gesture. Rostinokov nodded and turned to leave the office.

"Yes, we have an interpreter for Gujarati," the manager was saying into the phone, "but I'll have to check on who it is and whether he is on duty. I'll call you . . ."

And Rostnikov was gone. He had already checked with his office and had been given a message from Ivanolva, the man who had been trailing Bintz. It was quite evident that the German was out for the afternoon. In fact, according to Ivanolva, he was at the Moskva Swimming Pool with his Intourist guide. So Rostnikov had plenty of time.

He took the elevator up to the German's room and entered, using the passkey the manager had given him. Although Rostnikov had taken a few trips in his life, always on police business, he was not particularly adept at packing clothes, and he was surprised at the large amount that Bintz had brought with him. The oversized shirts and four suits constituted a wardrobe far larger than Rostnikov's, but then, Bintz was a reasonably well-known capitalist filmmaker. It took Rostnikov almost half an hour to pack everything. He had estimated that it would take much less time.

There was no need to call the airport again. He had already called from a street phone that could not be tapped or traced. The next trick was to get the suitcases to a taxi.

He did not want the KGB men to see him and get curious. But Rostnikov had thought of all of this. He had also taken the packet from his pocket and put it in one of the suitcases, hiding it among a pile of scripts and notes.

He had investigated enough cases to know that the Soviet authorities would almost certainly not disturb the luggage of a German tourist, especially one who had been invited to the Moscow Film Festival. Actually, those leaving on Moscow flights were seldom given any trouble, which surprised many tourists. Rostnikov was also sure that Bintz would not be subjected to search in Berlin. He had checked and found that West Berlin's customs officials were even more lax than Moscow's. It was the British, French, and Americans whom tourists and businessmen complained most of.

Rostnikov struggled down to the elevator with the luggage and descended to the second floor. Then he found a freight elevator just off a second-floor ballroom. The elevator was large and almost empty. The man who ran it questioned him and he showed him his police indentification and told him in serious tones that he was engaged on official business that the man had best ignore.

The man was a Muscovite and knew well how to ignore what he was told to ignore.

"Is there a freight office?" Rostnikov asked when the elevator stopped on the ground floor in a service area behind the main ballroom.

"There," said the man, pointing, and Rostnikov lugged the suitcase forward, kicking a light brown leather case along the floor. He pushed the freight office door open, dropped the suitcases, and ignored the gray-capped young man at the small desk, who scowled up at him. Rostnikov fetched the leather case, then whipped out his identification before the man at the desk could speak.

"I will have a taxi come by here within the hour for these cases," Rostnikov said. "Watch them and tell no one they are here. If you wish to check up on me, call the hotel manager. He has been informed of this."

Before the man could answer, Rostnikov left the office.

The man might call the manager. In all likelihood, however, he would prefer to remain unknown to those in power. Even if he did call, the manager would confirm Rostnikov's mission and probably pretend he knew more about these secret doings than he actually did.

Rostnikov found a stairway as quickly as he could, made his way up two flights, and caught the passenger elevator down to the lobby where the KGB men could pick him up again.

Choosing a taxi required some care. Fortunately, the first one he hailed was driven by a bearded young man with a massively bored look on his face.

"Kropotkinskaya Embankment," Rostnikov said, settling in the back seat. "The swimming pool."

The driver twisted around to examine Rostnikov briefly, trying to imagine what this creature would look like in a bathing suit. And then he drove.

"I have taken down your license number and your name," Rostnikov said to the driver a few blocks later. He had not bothered to look back for the KGB men.

"My number?" asked the driver.

"I am with the police, Chief Inspector Rostnikov." He held his identification up for the man to see in the rearview mirror.

"What have I done?" the driver whimpered. "If this is about that girl, I didn't know she was a—"

"It's not about the prostitute you front for and not about the illegal vodka under your seat," said Rostnikov. "When you drop me, I shall pay you enough to return to the Hotel Rossyia. There you will go to the service loading dock, and pick up six pieces of luggage. The man in the freight office will know about this. You will then take the luggage to Sheremetyevo International Airport and check it through for the seven P.M. Lufthansa flight to West Berlin in the name of Wolfgang Bintz."

"I can't remember all that," the man protested.

"I've written it down," said Rostnikov. "I'll give it to you when we get to the pool." He did not want the men in the trailing KGB car to see him hand the driver anything but the fare. They might stop the driver and question him.

"All right," the driver said, sullenly pulling on his beard.

"If you fail to do this, Rasumi," Rostnikov said, "you will be in deep trouble and it will involve more than a few bottles of vodka or a prostitute."

"I'll do it," the young driver said quietly.

"Fine." Rostnikov sighed, and leaned back, and they said no more during the trip. When they arrived at the pool, Rostnikov paid him only slightly more than the trip would cost. Too high an overpayment might make the man suspicious.

When he had pulled away, Rostnikov turned toward the pool. It had been a dozen years since he had been in the pool. As a young man, he had been forbidden to swim there by his father. The pool had been built on the site of the massive Church of the Savior, and his father remembered being part of the crew that had been ordered to destroy the church in 1931. His father was not a religious man, but he did not like the Stalinist move to destroy the old and put up the new.

"It's too much like Mussolini in Italy," he had said once as they walked down the street, and Rostnikov's mother had almost cried in fear as she begged him to be quiet.

When Rostnikov did finally go to the pool after his father died, he felt guilty that he enjoyed it. It is the largest open-air pool in all of Europe, and there are often as many as two thousand people in the water at a time.

The water is changed three times every day by a huge filtering station, and the temperature is controlled for year-round swimming. Even on the coldest winter day, swimmers can splash about comfortably and watch the steam rising into the frigid night air.

Rostnikov paid his fifty-kopecks admission fee and went into the changing rooms. It was crowded this warm July day, and it took him only a few minutes to find what he was looking for. A rotund man with a pleasant red face was leaving with a small freckle-faced boy who was probably his grandchild.

"Pardon me," said Rostnikov, stepping in front of them and smiling to keep them from panicking. The smile on the man's face faded quickly, and his grip tightened on the little boy.

"I'm here with my grandson," Rostnikov said apologetically, "and I forgot my bathing suit. It was stupid, I know." He hit his forehead with the flat of his hand. "I see that you are on your way out and I'm sure your suit would fit me. I'd be happy to pay seven rubles. I don't want to disappoint the boy."

Rostnikov looked across the crowded changing room at a thin child of about six. He lifted his hand and waved to the boy, who didn't see him.

"It is a strange request," the man said, looking down at his own grandson.

Rostnikov shrugged. "It would be a great favor," he said.

"All right," the man finally agreed. He let go of the boy's hand and fished a damp pair of blue trunks out of his sack. Rostnikov fished out seven rubles, and they made the exchange.

"Thank you," he said, knowing that the man had made a fine profit.

"I'm happy we could help," the man said, and led the boy away.

Four minutes later, Rostnikov, feeling extremely conspicuous even in the large crowd, went out of the changing room where he had deposited his clothes with the attendant, and made his way to the pool deck. He knew he was not a common sight with his washtub body and his heavy leg, but no one seemed to pay much attention. He slowly circled the pool along the metal railing, looking for Bintz and Ivanolva. He spotted the policeman first, leaning against the wire fence.

"Chief Inspector?" he said.

"Could I be mistaken for anyone else?"

"No." Ivanolva was about thirty, good-looking, and well built. He would look far better in a bathing suit than I, thought Rostnikov.

"Where is the German?" Rostnikov said, backing away

from a boisterous teenage couple who were pushing each other and giggling.

"I do not always understand youth," said Rostnikov as the girl turned and plunged into the water, splashing a startled woman.

"They are playing," explained Ivanolva.

"I recognize that it is recreation," said Rostnikov, watching the teenage boy shout and leap into the water. "It is the nature of the joy derived from the game that I fail to appreciate."

"I think—" Ivanolva began, but Rostnikov interrupted.

"The German," he said.

"There," said the younger policeman, nodding.

"Point to him," said Rostnikov. "I'm not hiding. Look at me. Could I hide?"

Instead of answering what he hoped was a rhetorical question, Ivanolva pointed. Beyond the white bathing caps of two nearby women, Rostnikov spotted the German's white hair and massive body. Bobbing dutifully and not at all happily at his side, a bathing cap on her head, was Ludmilla Konvisser, the Intourist guide who had been assigned to Bintz.

"You are finished for the day," Rostnikov said over his shoulder to Ivanolva.

"Yes, Comrade," Ivanolva replied and went off as quickly as he could.

Rostnikov moved to the edge of the pool, squatted, and put a hand in the water, prepared to make a face at the cold, but the temperature was fine, so he sat at the edge of the pool and eased himself in. He made his way through the maze of bodies and sloshed in front of Bintz, whose eyes were shut. Ludmilla spotted Rostnikov and said, "Chief Inspector, what—"

Bintz's eyes opened and Rostnikov noted that there was no fear or surprise. He seemed to expect to see a policeman in front of him.

"Tell me, Inspector Comrade," he said in English, "do you find it as easy to float as I do?"

"It is our bulk," said Rostnikov, also in English.

Bintz nodded and closed his eyes again before speaking. "A whale and a walrus afloat on a Sunday afternoon."

Though not particularly fond of being called a walrus, Rostnikov had to admit to himself that the image was apt.

"Can we talk?" Rostnikov asked, making it clear that it was an order.

"Could I refuse one who follows me to the depths?" Bintz said, opening one eye.

"Comrade Konvisser," Rostnikov said, looking at the young woman, "could we . . ."

She nodded, plunged under the water, and swam away.

"A good-looking young lady," Bintz said, closing his eyes again. "Very *krasse'vliyaya*, is that the word? But very cold. Why are so many young Russian ladies cold?"

"She has a job," Rostnikov explained, "and it does not pay to be too friendly with foreigners. Young Russian ladies are not cold."

"What," grinned Bintz, "is your basis for comparison?"

"I admit I have none," Rostnikov agreed, looking about for his KGB tail and Bintz's. "You know you have been followed?"

Bintz laughed, eyes still shut, only his head bobbing on the surface. The two men were surrounded by the clamor of voices, but they were close enough so that they could speak in low tones and make each other out. A woman elbowed Rostnikov and moved away without apology.

"Besides your young man," Bintz said, "there is a very serious gentleman with glasses wearing a suit and tie standing just behind the fence in the corner behind me."

Rostnikov saw the man without turning his head.

"KGB?" Bintz asked, opening both eyes.

"Yes," said Rostnikov.

Bintz grunted, his guess confirmed. "There is someone else who may be watching," he said. "Did you know that?"

"Yes," said Rostnikov.

"Are you here for the reason I think?" Bintz said.

"I believe I am," said Rostnikov.

"Would you mind telling me what that is so I won't make a complete *dummkopf* of myself?"

"World Liberation," said Rostnikov. "I have reason to think you are involved in a terrorist act."

Bintz shrugged, sending out a circle of waves.

"Ha," laughed Bintz, but there was no mirth in his laughter. "Bintz doesn't kill real people. Bintz is known for the many he has slaughtered on film. For me, destruction and violence are ritual acts. When my people fall, they rise to act again another day, and my audience knows this. I know difference between movie blood and real blood. Movie blood washes away. This is exhausting my English."

"What were you supposed to do?" Rostnikov went on.

Bintz looked around the pool for the first time and then back at Rostnikov.

"I was supposed to blow up this pool," he said. "Can you imagine such a thing? There are children in this pool."

"How were you to do this?"

"A button," Bintz said. "A little black box, just like in an English movie."

"When?"

"At seven." Bintz shrugged. "The woman calls and says I am to do it at seven. I never saw her."

"If you do not plan to set off the bomb," Rostnikov said, sidestepping a man with glasses who floated by on his back, "what are you doing here?"

"I came to find the bomb and dispose of it. If I have a black box with a button, others might have a black box with a button. You don't believe me?"

"I believe you," said Rostnikov. "I found your black box in your hotel room. If you meant to use it, it would be here, not there. You could have told the police," he added, crouching down in the water and then floating on his back.

"It will be difficult enough to remain alive when that woman finds that I do not blow up this pool. I don't also confess to Russian police that I am involved with terrorists. But what difference? You have me. I swim, and we go."

"The bomb?" asked Rostnikov.

"I am a maker of movies," said Bintz with pride. "I work with pictures and spaces. I found the bomb by moving along the edge of the pool and reaching into all the drains. It is now inside my bathing trunks."

Rostnikov stopped floating and looked at Bintz.

"I'm very cool, *nein*?" said Bintz. "Like Charles Bronson."

"Very cool," agreed Rostnikov.

"Don't worry," he said. "I take great care. Even if one of them watches me, I have an hour. I must swim long enough so all of those trailing behind me single file can see that Bintz really wants to swim and is not here just for some mischief. But so . . . you are going to arrest me?"

"No," said Rostnikov. "I'm going to save you. Let's leave, and I will explain. I trust Comrade Konvisser will not follow us into the men's changing room?"

"Unfortunately, you are right," Bintz sighed. "Let's give them a sight, you and I, and get out of the pool together, huh? The level will go down an inch, and small children will stand at the shallow end with their noses above water."

It was with some difficulty that Bintz managed to get Comrade Konvisser to leave him with Inspector Rosnikov for the day, but she finally agreed, and as they changed clothes in the men's room, Rostnikov outlined the details of his plan. Bintz gave him the enormous swimming trunks containing the bomb.

"Then you are agreed?" Rostnikov said, slipping on his trousers.

"The risk is mostly yours," said Bintz. "A young man helped me take my pants off when I came in, but I am for obvious reasons unable to get them back on. Chief Inspector, if you would . . ."

"Of course," said Rostnikov and, with the bomb jiggling under his arm, he helped the massive man get dressed.

Outside the pool, Rostnikov found a sewer outlet and bent to tie his already tied shoes. He dropped the trunks he had obtained from Bintz and let them tumble through the hole. It was most likely that neither of the KGB agents noticed. It was clumsy, but Rostnikov did not relish the idea of carrying the burden any farther.

They found a taxi and headed for a restaurant that Rostnikov had chosen carefully. In the cab, they didn't speak nor did they turn to see if their entourage was behind them.

Rostnikov had eaten in the restaurant once and had bad
reports on it from others. In a city where service was generally poor in restaurants, the Destrovya on Arbat was in a
class by itself. The meal would take several hours to serve.
Best of all, Rostnikov knew from experience, there was a
rear exit near the rest rooms.

"I think we will catch her," said Rostnikov once they
were seated by a surly waiter. "The woman who threatened
you."

Bintz shrugged and reached eagerly for the menu.

The service was almost as slow as Rostnikov remembered it. The KGB men had discovered each other and
were watching from a far table. The restaurant was not at
all crowded.

"We shall see," sighed Bintz.

In the next hour, Bintz managed to eat an amount that
awed Rostnikov, who could eat with the best. The German
downed a crab salad, *kholodets*—a beef, veal, and chicken
gelatin appetizer—an order of chicken Kiev, a bottle of
white wine, and a whole loaf of bread.

When Rostnikov returned from the bathroom, Bintz had
finished Rostnikov's remaining beef Stroganoff and had
ordered a special dessert.

"I'd like to stay for the dessert," he said, wiping his
mouth and rising as Rostnikov sat.

"I'm afraid not," said the chief inspector. "The exit door
is to the right of the men's bathroom. I'll eat your dessert."

"Thank you, and good luck," said Bintz, putting down
his napkin and walking toward the rear of the restaurant.
He carried himself with great dignity in spite of his weight.

Rostnikov ate some more bread and made sure that neither of the KGB men had followed Bintz. Why should
they? The man had simply gone to the men's room before
his dessert was served.

The ride to the airport was approximately 32 kilometers.
In five minutes, if he had no trouble finding a taxi,
Bintz would be on the Leningrad Highway. He would
pass the massive Dynamo Sports Stadium and go by the

Petrovsky Palace where Napoleon had once stayed after being driven out of the Kremlin. Then, Rostnikov imagined, he would pass the monument in honor of the Moscow defenders who drove off Hitler's army, speed by the few remaining *isby*, or log cabins, and pull in to the airport.

If Rostnikov had timed it correctly, even allowing a margin for error, Bintz should make the plane and be well on his way to West Germany at about the same time that the KGB men began to wonder why he was staying so long in the bathroom.

Again, assuming nothing went wrong, Bintz would land safely in West Berlin before the KGB even thought of checking his room, let alone flights out of the country.

When the KGB man with the balding head showed the first signs of concern, Rostnikov beat him to it by examining his own watch, rising with annoyance, and stalking toward the rear of the restaurant. This caused the KGB man to sit down. Rostnikov checked his watch once more and slowly returned to the table.

Still looking annoyed, he called the waiter and asked for the nearest phone. His KGB man followed, leaving Bintz's man to head for the toilets. Rostnikov's first call, well out of earshot of the bald man, was to the airport. The flight, he found, had just left. His second call was to Sarah, as planned.

"Yes," she said.

"I will be home soon," he said and hung up. If they asked whom he called, they would have no trouble confirming the call home.

It was done. He paid the check, which was more than he had ever paid for a meal in his life, and went home. It was seven o'clock, the very moment Bintz was supposed to have detonated the bomb.

There was only one place it could be, Karpo concluded, looking at the copies of the maps he had given Rostnikov. It was not likely that she would attack another movie theater. He was unaware that a bomb was being planned for

the swimming pool and that Rostnikov had effectively de-
fused it.

What he did know was that the woman had only a few
hours if she was to board the plane on which she had a
reservation as Louise Rich. He assumed she was probably
on her own at this point.

Karpo sat erect at his desk, demanding that the maps
yield more than they had to give.

The target had to be something that, when destroyed or
damaged, would deeply affect the Soviet Union and whose
destruction could not be hidden from the outside world.
Thus, it would have to be something very public.

"Something irreplaceable," he said softly to himself,
looking up. His eyes went across the room to Zelach, who
had just finished a report and was about to go home, but
Karpo's gaze had caught him in a moment of guilty thought
about a bribe someone had offered him, and one he was
seriously considering. How much could it hurt to forget
about a few illegal telephones? It wasn't political, probably
not even very criminal, and the amount of the bribe was
considerable. Yes, Zelach had made up his mind to accept
the payment, until he found himself gazing into the steely
eyes of the Vampire. The man, he thought, is a damned
fanatic. He can probably read my mind. Zelach wilted
under the intensity of Karpo's stare and resolved to turn in
the capitalist offender. He got up, walked past Karpo with
a grunt, and headed out.

Karpo scarcely noticed him. It would be the Lenin Mausoleum, he decided. If he had read her ego correctly—the
use of exotic poison, her impersonation of Aubrey's
widow, the murder of the Frenchwoman—everything indicated that she had a massive sense of her own power.

Of course, he could be wrong. He knew he could be
wrong but, by the same token, he had little choice, and so
he folded the maps neatly, put them into his top drawer,
and rose slowly. His left arm ached slightly, but it was a
dull ache, as if he had slept on it. There was no migraine,
though he had expected one. It was time.

* * *

Vladimir Ilich Lenin died on January 21, 1924. A wooden mausoleum pyramid was designed and built within two days of his death to hold the embalmed body. In January of that year, the mausoleum was rebuilt and stood until 1930 when it was replaced by the present mausoleum of red granite and black labradorite. The stone structure is exactly the same shape as the wooden one it replaced, but it is permanent. The entrance to the mausoleum, which faces Red Square and the massive GUM, or State Universal Stores, is marked only by the name of Lenin, encrusted in dark red porphyry.

The mausoleum is an essential stop for Russians visiting the capital. It is both a political and cultural mecca and very nearly a religious one. Thousands visit the tomb each month to enter solemnly and gaze at the perfectly preserved face of Lenin, and most of those who come make a point of being in the square to watch the changing of the guard at the mausoleum, which takes place every hour, day and night. The guards, dressed in gray uniforms with two rows of brass buttons down their chests, carry their rifles in their left hands pointing straight to the sky. If the square is not too crowded, a visitor can hear the guards' black boots strike the pavement as they march from the mausoleum, which lies in the shadow of the Kremlin Wall.

Since it was a Sunday evening and nearly seven-thirty, Karpo did not arrive in time to watch the changing of the guard. Lenin was the symbol of all that Karpo believed in. A photograph could suffice to remind him of the leader, but the mausoleum was the central symbol for the entire nation. And he had made it his responsibility to protect it.

He stood on 25th October Street at the corner of the square scanning the crowd of tourists for a familiar face. But it was still too crowded for him to be confident of catching all the faces in the crowd. This was both a disadvantage and an advantage, for if he did not see her, then she would also have difficulty seeing him.

The clock in Spasskaya, the main Kremlin tower, told him that it was now twenty minutes to eight. He maneuvered slowly, carefully, and watchfully through the crowd.

People were gathered in clusters before the bronze doors of the red pyramid of the mausoleum. He slowly approached the mausoleum, glancing at the two uniformed guards who stood stiffly at the door with rifles bayoneted and ready at their sides. Karpo joined a group of about twenty men and women being led by a guide, who jabbered at them in heavily accented German and pointed beyond the mausoleum to the towers of the Kremlin.

It was time either to move toward the greatest humiliation of his life or to engage in the most meaningful act he had ever performed. In his pocket was a small book containing the constitution of the Soviet Union. He took it out and pretended to look at it as if it were a guidebook.

Easing away from the tail end of the crowd of Germans, Karpo, eyes on the book, said in a clear voice to the guards, "I am a police officer. My name is Karpo, and I have reason to believe that an explosive device has been placed inside the tomb."

He lifted his eyes to the two young, clean-shaven faces and noted that the one on the left reacted slightly.

"Do not react," Karpo went on, raising his head as if to admire the inscription over the door. "The person who intends to detonate this device may well be watching. I will remain where I stand while you do whatever you are supposed to do in an emergency."

Karpo, without watching, turned his back on the two guards, glanced up at the Spassky tower and let his eyes drift around the square once more, but there was no sign of the woman. Of course it was possible that she would send someone else, but he doubted it. This was her moment.

Behind him he could hear a movement, slight but distinct. He assumed that one of the guards had a microphone or some other device with which he could summon help. Karpo hoped this was true, for he could not stand there for more than a few minutes without attracting attention, especially if the Germans moved away and no other group moved close.

He turned again, glancing along the wall and beyond the marble stands at the foot of the Kremlin tower to the

Nikolsky tower and the gate below. Two men in uniform were moving forward quickly, hands on their flapping holsters. Karpo sauntered in their direction through the group of Germans, still trying to look like a tourist, but knowing that he would fool no one.

He intercepted the two men about a hundred yards to the right of the mausoleum and kept his hands in front of him and clearly visible.

"Major," he said, stepping in front of them.

The major, a hard-faced man of about forty-five with jaw clenched, flipped open his holster as the officer behind him took two steps to one side and did the same.

"If you will be as inconspicuous as possible," Karpo said, noting that a few people were looking their way, "you can remove my identification from my right coat pocket. May I warn you that someone may be watching us? If we do not act with speed and caution, we may be too late."

The major nodded toward the other officer, a young lieutenant, who advanced on Karpo, one hand still on his open holster. Reaching into the policeman's pocket, he removed the wallet and handed it to the major, who opened it, examined it, and looked at Karpo.

"Lieutenant Aronsov will remain with you while I check on your credentials," the major said softly.

"There may not be time," Karpo said, looking at the tower clock which now showed fifteen minutes to eight.

"Damn you," hissed the major. "Why didn't you go through proper channels with this?"

"There was no time," Karpo replied evenly. "I wasn't sure until a short while ago." He did not add that he was not certain even now.

The major's hands drummed against the leather of his holster as he appraised Karpo. Evidently he was properly impressed.

"Come," he said. He walked past Karpo and the lieutenant and headed directly for the mausoleum. Karpo turned and followed with the lieutenant behind, watching him.

"No one can enter the mausoleum carrying anything,"

the major said, "not a briefcase, flight bag, camera, anything."

"The detonator would be quite small," said Karpo.

The major grunted, pushed aside a startled Asian tourist and strode to the bronze door.

"With a dozen men we could do this in one minute," the major said impatiently, "but I suppose . . ."

"It would be rather conspicuous," finished Karpo, "and the terrorist might simply decide to detonate if she is watching. She might do so anyway."

"She," grunted the major, waiting for the guard to open the bronze door.

"Yes," said Karpo.

They entered and picked up an echo in the near darkness.

"And what we have already done might be sufficient to set her off," the major observed, nodding at the lieutenant to move. The major did not take his eyes off Karpo. The lieutenant moved swiftly, clearly knowing every inch of the interior, every place a bomb could conceivably be placed. Karpo watched, wanting to help and knowing that he would not be allowed to. The slight hum of the air conditioning played above the rapid movements of the lieutenant as they moved down the stone staircase. The light around the sealed case was dim, but the young officer's hands were swift. Karpo watched with fascination as the young man moved behind the glass-covered face of the corpse of Lenin.

"Here," cried the lieutenant, emerging from the far side of the casket holding up the small black box. "Plastic on the outside held it in place. No way to judge how powerful it is."

"One of her bombs went off a few hours ago at the Zaryadye Cinema," said Karpo.

"That was a bomb?" asked the major. "We heard . . ."

Karpo nodded.

"Out with it," the major said, and the lieutenant moved swiftly to the stairs.

"I suggest you put that in your pocket," Karpo said,

hearing his voice echo back. "If she is out here and . . ."

The young man looked at the major who shrugged and said, "The important thing is to get out of here with it. Let's go."

"I'll take it," said Karpo, moving forward as the lieutenant passed him. He grabbed the small box and heard both men respond almost immediately with drawn guns.

"If I were the one, I wouldn't have waited till I was in here," he said.

"What do you—" began the major, holding his pistol aimed at Karpo's chest. "Forget it. We'll deal with this outside. Move." He motioned with his gun as Karpo plunged the box into his pocket and moved quickly up the stairs through the cool tomb.

Beyond the bronze doors, the sun nearly blinded them. Karpo had been ready for this, and he dashed forward into a crowd of sailors and began to run across the square. He was heading toward an open area not far from the Lobnoye Mesto, the Place of Execution, the Skull Platform of white stone more than four centuries old where the czar's edicts had been proclaimed and public executions carried out.

There was no place to dispose of the bomb. Whichever way he turned he would be heading toward a national monument. The major and the lieutenant would have followed whatever procedure had been established for bomb disposal. It would have been impossible to impress the urgency on them, because they did not have his understanding of the woman.

Knowing the sailors were behind him, he ran on, pushing through the crowds and dashing across the open spaces, trying to figure out the least damaging place to put the bomb in case she was nearby. And then luck intervened. Standing in front of him, perhaps fifty yards away in front of the Place of Execution was a blond tourist in a blue suit. She was carrying a camera and wearing dark glasses. Karpo headed toward her and glanced up at the Spassky clock, which showed that it was only a few minutes to eight.

At first the woman ignored him, but when it became

clear that he was coming directly at her, she turned to face him. Behind her a young couple examined the Place of Execution.

When he was no more than twenty yards from her, the woman removed her dark glasses and fixed him with a look of black hatred.

"Stop," she commanded, and Karpo stopped. Behind him the soldiers brushed people aside and moved toward him.

Karpo turned his head in the direction of the running boots and saw the lieutenant in advance of the major and another armed soldier.

"That is the woman," Karpo shouted back to the young man who, panting, looked beyond him and stopped.

The lieutenant glanced at the woman and then at Karpo and saw the same look on both faces that he would never be able to describe adequately, though at the inquiry that night he would make an attempt at it. But whatever it was he saw convinced him, and he turned, still panting, and intercepted the major and the soldier with the rifle.

Karpo turned back to the woman, who held her camera in front of her. He hoped that the soldiers would back away, keep their distance, and clear the area.

"I said stop," said the woman, in almost unaccented Russian, but Karpo did not stop. "Do you know what this is?" She held up the camera.

In response, Karpo took another step toward her. He was now no more than a dozen paces away, surely well within the destructive range of the small device he now removed from his pocket and held in front of him.

"You've failed," he said.

"I'll try again," she said, her eyes looking beyond Karpo at the soldiers. "If you don't want me to press this button, you will give me assurance that the soldiers will remain where they are until I am gone."

"I can give no such assurance for the soldiers," he said, taking another step toward her.

The young couple who had been examining the Place of Execution moved past the woman, talking to each other, ignoring the conversation between her and the tall, cadaverous man.

"There is no place for you to run, Louise Rich," he said.

His use of the name stung, and the woman shook her blond hair out of her eyes.

"That's not my name," she said.

"I didn't think it was," said Karpo.

"But you know about my flight reservation," she said, "and the identity I've been using."

"And so," Karpo said softly, since he was close enough, "your options are gone."

"Limited," she corrected, "but not gone."

"Perhaps," he said with a shrug.

A draft of wind came across Red Square behind Karpo, blowing the woman's hair back and creating an image of her against the background of the Cathedral of Saint Basil the Blessed that drilled itself into Karpo's mind. At this moment, bomb in hand, facing this enemy of the state, he felt an emotion he wanted to deny but couldn't. Determined in the face of certain defeat, she looked quite beautiful.

"How did you find me?" she said quietly in a voice that matched his own as she looked over at the soldiers.

"Reason, a process of elimination, and a little luck," he admitted.

Her eyes were on him, her lips pale. He considered turning away, recalling a faint childhood image of Medusa, but he kept his gaze steady.

"We are alike," she said through clenched white teeth.

And Karpo realized that in some way she was correct and that he stood here now looking at an important aspect of himself which, until this moment, he had denied. The realization shocked him.

"In some ways," he said.

"You won't back away, will you?" she said with admiration.

"I can't," he said.

"In a moment or two that soldier will raise his rifle and

shoot me," she said, nodding beyond Karpo. "You know that."

"Yes," he said.

"And what would you do in my place?" she asked.

Karpo was silent.

"What is your name?"

"Karpo, Emil Karpo. And yours?"

"That," she said with a grin, "you will never know."

Karpo felt a surge within and about him, an explosion of love, regret, and death as he leapt toward the stone platform.

Roman Tibiliski was standing across from the State History Museum at the far end of Red Square seven hundred yards from the Place of Execution. He was telling his co-manager from the Gdansk Steel Mill that the building they were looking at was the headquarters of the KGB, which was as wrong as one could be about a building, but Tibiliski, at the age of sixty, was a massive, confident man with a gruff, assured style that usually masked his ignorance.

He had just turned to Waclaw Wypich, his co-manager, to add a few erroneous details to his description when the explosion occurred. He found himself looking directly at the flash of red, followed almost instantly by a whooshing sound and a ball of smoke.

Tibiliski had no idea what the explosion was, but he felt that he ought to explain it. "Look," he shouted to Wypich, "the fireworks. The Sunday fireworks in Red Square. They've begun early."

Wypich, who believed almost nothing his older co-manager said, nodded knowingly, which was his means of getting through life minimally scathed.

"Shall we take a look?" Wypich asked.

Tibiliski could now see the rushing of soldiers and the scurrying of people in the crowd. It dawned on him that he had been quite mistaken about the cause of the explosion.

"No," he said knowingly, "it's not worth looking at.

Let's move on into October Square and have a look at the Sports Palace."

The major, who had been more than fifty yards away when the explosion came, had been knocked backwards and lifted into the air. He had struck the soldier behind him, whose bayonet pierced the major's right arm.

The lieutenant was ten yards farther back, gently but insistently urging bystanders to move away from something they could neither see nor understand. He felt only the warm blast and turned to see the smoke.

His first act was to go to the major, who lay wounded. Beyond the immediate scene tourists and visitors were running, screaming, or standing in confusion. As far as the lieutenant could tell, no one except the major was seriously injured unless, of course, one counted that mad-looking woman with the camera and the policeman named Karpo. The woman was quite dead. Karpo was a bloody blot huddled against the platform; however, he was still breathing.

FIFTEEN

"**K**ARPO HAS BEEN INJURED. HE MAY BE DYING," SAID Tkach, putting down the telephone and turning to his wife.

Maya looked at her husband's pale face and knew that he was about to collapse. She took his arm and eased him into a chair.

He had come home from the hospital and immediately assured her that he was all right, that he had escaped with a few stitches and a slight shock, but now a second shock, a more profound one, had hit him.

"It could have been me," he whispered. "It was a bomb, a bomb like the one . . ."

He let his voice trail off and looked at her for an answer but she didn't have one. Fortunately, his mother was sleeping in the other room when the call came just before midnight on Sunday.

"It could have been me," he repeated.

"Yes," said Maya, "but it wasn't."

He had turned on the light in the room to answer the phone, and now the dim yellow glow on her face and in the corners of the room frightened him and she knew it.

"Maya," he said looking at her.

"I know," she answered.

"Karpo," he said.

"Do you want to tell me what happened?" she asked, not wanting to hear about it but knowing it would help him to talk.

"Not now," he said, brushing his straight hair back like a little boy. "Maya, if we have a boy, we will call him Emil."

"Yes," she agreed, knowing they would do no such thing, "we will call him Emil."

It took them an hour to get back to sleep, but sleep they did.

Anna Timofeyeva lay in her bed at midnight unable to see in the darkness but quite able to hear the breathing of the woman in the bed next to her and the snoring of the woman across from her.

No one had told her about what had transpired, for the doctors had given specific instructions that she was not to be excited. In fact, she was supposed to be asleep at this very moment. They had given her a pill to make her sleep, but they had not accounted for the determination of Anna Timofeyeva.

She had always considered sleep a waste of time that she could use to perform productive work. She worked well at night, in the moments just before sleep. At home she kept paper at her bedside to write down ideas about cases that she worked out in the darkness with Baku snuggled against her leg.

Rostnikov had assured her that the cat was taken care of, and the doctor had assured her that, with caution, she could return home and resume a limited work schedule after proper treatment. She would undergo that new rehabilitation technique for heart attack victims, learned from a South African who had defected to the Soviet Union. The South African would work with her himself.

Anna Timofeyeva was eager to get back to work. She could not think in this bed, could not think in bed without the cat, could not think with these hospital noises and the pill she was fighting.

She had faith in Rostnikov, she told herself, but there had been something in his tone, his movement. He'd held something back when he visited her. But she must have been mistaken. It must be the illness, the medication. Rostnikov would not hide anything from her.

A twinge hit her just below the breast bone. Angina, the doctor had called it. She considered cursing it and changed her mind. If rest would return her to the desk in Petrovka, then she would try to rest.

Unlike Tkach and Anna Timofeyeva, Rostnikov did not sleep. Neither did Sarah. Part of the reason for his restlessness was the condition of Emil Karpo, but Rostnikov did not blame himself. He had considered doing so, had sat up drinking tea and talking about it to Sarah after he returned from the office, but he could find no logical reason to blame himself for Karpo's condition.

The guilt I feel, he finally decided, is not because of Emil Karpo.

Some time after two in the morning Sarah went to bed, knowing she would not sleep. Rostnikov chose to sit at the table touching his trophy and deciding on how long to wait until he called Drozhkin. He expected that the colonel would eventually call him, but he could not wait too long.

When dawn came, Rostnikov moved to the window and looked across the wide street at the apartments where others were rising to meet Monday. Lights were on, and people were boiling water, rubbing their sleepy eyes, brushing their teeth. Unlike Rostnikov, they did not sense the significance of this Monday.

If Karpo survived, Rostnikov might change his mind, his course of action. But he could not wait. Instead, he told himself that if Karpo died, it was but the final reason for him to act. It was the cutting of a tie.

Sarah rose at eight and silently made breakfast. She wore a long white linen nightgown, and her hair was down.

"Shave," she said.

He got up, made his way groggily toward the bathroom

and shaved. In the small mirror he examined his dark face.

"It is time," he told himself. "Time, you dull-looking oaf."

"I'm calling," he told Sarah as he returned to the room and picked up a piece of bread and butter. She nodded and sat down with her tea and toast to watch him. He reached out a hairy hand and touched her before picking up the phone.

Though it was before eight, Drozhkin was in and took the call almost immediately.

"A somewhat disappointing conclusion to the case," the colonel said icily.

"In many ways," Rostnikov agreed.

"Yet," said Drozhkin, "it could have been worse, much worse. Your man Karpo still lives."

"He is still alive," Rostnikov confirmed.

"You will, I am sure, accept responsibility for what has taken place."

"I will take responsibility for that which was within my scope of authority," Rostnikov said.

The silence went on for about five seconds during which Rostnikov looked at his wife and nodded.

"The German," Drozhkin said finally.

"The German," Rostnikov echoed.

"You will have to explain," Drozhkin's voice was somber.

"I plan to do so, Comrade Colonel. If I may, I would like to discuss it with you this morning."

"Come to my office," said the colonel. "As soon as you can get here."

"No. I will meet you in the little parkway in front of the Polytechnical Museum," Rostnikov said, "right near the entrance to the Dzerzhinski metro station."

"Comrade," Drozhkin said ominously.

"I'll explain, Colonel."

"We shall see," said Drozhkin. "Twenty minutes."

Rostnikov hung up.

"He will come," Rostnikov said softly.

When Rostnikov limped up the stairway of the metro

twenty minutes later, Colonel Drozhkin was standing at the corner squinting into the morning sun and looking at Lubyanka across the Dzerzhinski Square. The man, Rostnikov could see, looked older, smaller, more gnarled, and tougher outside his own environment. The colonel was wearing a slightly rumpled dark brown suit. He looked at his watch to indicate that Rostnikov was wasting his valuable time.

"I hope there is a point to this secrecy, Rostnikov," he said in greeting.

"There is a point, Comrade," Rostnikov answered, assuring himself that no one was close enough to overhear him. "Shall we walk?"

"No," said Drozhkin irritably, "we shall not walk. We shall stand here and talk briefly. What is it that you could not say in my office?"

"Your office is wired, is it not?" said Rostnikov.

"Does that require an answer?"

"No," Rostnikov replied, "but I thought you might prefer that what we will say be kept between us."

Drozhkin's eyes narrowed, and he pursed his lips.

"Weigh carefully whatever it is you are about to say, policeman," he said softly.

"I shall," Rostnikov responded with a smile. They stepped out of the flow of traffic and walked toward the grass.

"And be brief," warned Drozhkin.

"As you wish," agreed Rostnikov. "In the past six months, I have been involved in two investigations that have brought me in contact with the KGB and with you. In both cases, I have come across information that might be a source of some embarrassment to the parties involved."

Drozhkin stopped walking and glared at Rostnikov.

"Are you going—"

"I am in a dangerous position," continued Rostnikov looking past the colonel. "I know more than I should about the supposed murder of a dissident by a madman who was manipulated by the KGB."

"You are a fool, Rostnikov," Drozhkin whispered.

Rostnikov shrugged. "Perhaps, but it was something we both knew," he said, "just as we both know that the two explosions and a number of very public deaths in the past three days have been as much the responsibility of your apparatus as they have been of me and my men. In short, you have been hiding behind me, Colonel, because you wanted a scapegoat in case that woman and World Liberation were not stopped."

Drozhkin's face was quite red, but Rostnikov did not look at him.

"What have you done?" said the colonel, grabbing Rostnikov's jacket. It occurred to Rostnikov that he could lift this man up and throw him into Kirov Street with very little effort.

"Just what you fear," he said. "I made copies of all the papers and interviews and investigation reports on both cases and copies of the tapes of all conversations I have had with you in the last week. Those documents have gone out of the country and now rest safely in West Germany."

"You are a traitor," hissed Drozhkin.

"No," said Rostnikov rubbing his neck. "That material would be an embarrassment to our country. It would not constitute proof of anything. What it would do, Colonel, is raise a series of very small questions, a few news stories that would result in waves that would wash you out of power. You have survived a great deal, Colonel, but I don't think you would survive this."

Rostnikov looked down at the colonel and imagined the thoughts that were racing through his mind.

"No," said Rostnikov. "Bintz has already put the material where even he cannot get it. In the event of his death, it will be released. If I do not contact him periodically, he will order its release. Even if he is tortured, he cannot retrieve the material. We worked it out. I'm afraid, Colonel, if anything happens to me or to Bintz, you will be in quite a bit of trouble."

"All this to ensure your safety, Rostnikov," Drozhkin said.

"No, Colonel, I want more than my safety. I realized

when this investigation began that I was a dangerous man in your eyes, that you would have me watched, and that my future was precarious at best. I also know that, given enough time, you will find a way to get around my plan."

"So . . .?" prodded Drozhkin.

"I wish to emigrate," said Rostnikov, looking around the square. "My wife, my son, and I want to go to America."

"That is impossible," said Drozhkin. "I can't—"

"You can. I'm sure you can," Rostnikov insisted. "This is not a decision I wished to make, but I can see no other way for me or for you."

"And if I choose to sacrifice myself instead?" Drozhkin said. They had walked down Serov Passage circling the Polytechnical Museum and, to a passerby, they would have looked like two old friends on a morning stroll.

"It would be a waste," said Rostnikov, "and would accomplish nothing but the end of your career and probably my life."

"It might be worth it," said the smaller man.

"I have gambled that you will not find it so," said Rostnikov.

"What will prevent you from releasing this material after you leave the Soviet Union?" asked Drozhkin.

Rostnikov carefully hid his relief. The colonel's question told him that he might well have won the battle. "What would my reason be?" Rostnikov said. "To punish you? To embarrass my country?"

"No," said Drozhkin. "Your word is not enough. I risk a great deal if I agree to this scheme, perhaps even . . . No, your word is not enough."

"There's nothing else I can give you," Rostnikov said, stopping to touch the colonel's arm. Drozhkin moved away from the familiarity.

"Your son," Drozhkin said, and Rostnikov could see that a smile was forming in the corners of his wrinkled mouth.

"My—"

"Your son will remain in the Soviet Union where I can watch him," the colonel explained.

"A stalemate," sighed Rostnikov, biting his lower lip.

"A stale—" Drozhkin began and looked at the chief inspector. "You knew I would propose this, didn't you? You expected this?"

Rostnikov did not reply.

"We should have recruited you into the KGB long ago," he said.

"I appreciate the compliment," said Rostnikov. "Do I take it that you agree to my proposal?"

"You are not concerned for your son?"

"I'm concerned," said Rostnikov, "but he has committed no crime, and he is unaware of all this. He is an innocent Soviet citizen in your care, and I'm sure you will take care of him. Once my wife and I leave, his safety will be your responsibility."

Rostnikov had not anticipated Drozhkin's reaction. The small man stopped and began laughing. He laughed, a hacking little laugh, until he choked and Rostnikov feared that he might actually die on the street and ruin the well-laid plan.

"You are threatening me?" Drozhkin finally spat out. "You're going to come back from some capitalistic country in the dead of night as a tourist and beat me to death or release your tapes and papers?"

A young woman passing by wearing a white T-shirt with "Dallas Cowboys" stenciled on it gave the colonel a curious look and walked on.

"It can be done," said Rostnikov.

"There is nothing more to say," Drozhkin said. "Go back to your job, your home, and worry."

"It is imperative that I have a decision on this within a month," said Rostnikov.

"Or what?" asked the colonel, stepping away from him. "Do you know what will happen to you and your wife if the material is released?"

"Yes," said Rostnikov, "the same thing that will happen if it is not released and I remain here. This conversation commits me, Colonel. You know it, and I know it. We are too old to play such games, and we have other work to do."

"I will not be denied the last word, Chief Inspector," said the colonel. "I'll do what I can to stop you."

With that, the colonel turned and walked quickly back toward Dzerzhinski Square.

In the Moscow office of *Pravda*, Viktor Shisko sat waiting for the call from Comrade Ivanov. He was in no hurry. He had endured similar waits during the past thirty years, and things could have been much worse.

Somewhere a committee of Party members was meeting to determine what to tell Ivanov to pass on to Shisko. Viktor drank a cup of coffee, knowing it was not good for his weak bowels, and checked his watch. His lunch would be late today.

People moved around him from desk to desk, talking, working, writing, but the level of sound was low, quite unlike the bustle of the newsroom in the American movies he had seen. Viktor had never visited an American newsroom, but he had seen *All the President's Men* and, long ago, *The Front Page*, and he wondered what it would be like to go out and actually investigate a story and then return to a madhouse of an office and write it.

When the call came at a little before one, Shisko took it, wrote down the information on lined paper, asked two questions, and promised to call Comrade Ivanov back in less than an hour with the story for his approval.

Viktor was surprised at the information Ivanov had given him. Rarely had such a story made the news, though he well knew such things happened. By two o'clock he had finished the story and called Comrade Ivanov, who checked it with someone else and called Viktor back at three-thirty. At that point it was decided that the story could run:

MOSCOW, July 23 (Pravda)—English filmmaker James Willery, 36, was killed in Moscow when a gas main exploded destroying a wall in the Zaryadye Cin-

ema today. The gas main defect also caused a small
eruption almost immediately after the explosion in Red
Square though little damage was done.

Screenings scheduled for the Zaryadye Cinema for
the Moscow Film Festival now under way will be held
in the Metropole Cinema until repairs can be made,
which should take no more than two or three days.

The gas mains that caused the damage were part of a
system that remains from before the Revolution. The
few hundred feet of piping that failed will be replaced
immediately to ensure that such an accident will not
occur again, according to the Moscow Energy Board.

Willery, whose film *To the Left* was shown at this
year's festival, was a prominent socialist filmmaker
who had been invited to the festival because of his in-
novative approaches to socialist film.

No one else was injured in the accidents.

Lieutenant Galinarov sat at his small desk absorbed in
the duty roster in front of him. His head was cradled in his
hands as if he were deep in thought. Iosef Rostnikov concluded that he was trying to give the impression that he
was deep in thought over who would be responsible for
barracks duty today or whose turn it was to pick up fresh
sheets on Tuesday.

Iosef stood patiently before the desk and waited while
Galinarov played out his scene. For three or four minutes
Galinarov examined the sheet, grunting occasionally,
feigning concentration, or reaching for a drink from the
glass nearby, which he kept filled from a bottle of Pepsi
Cola, but which, Iosef was sure, did not contain Pepsi.

"Yes," he said finally, taking a drink and looking up, "it
can be done."

Iosef said nothing.

Galinarov's next move was to examine Rostnikov from
head to boots.

"You have finished cleaning your weapons?"

"I have, Comrade," Iosef said.

"And do you have any outstanding obligations for the
next four or five days?" Galinarov asked.

"My only obligation is to remain alert at all times and be ready to be transported to wherever my unit might be needed in five minutes' notice," Iosef said. It was the required response, but he could not discern why Galinarov was putting him through this secular catechism.

"That is good, Corporal," Galinarov said. "And do you remember what you are to say when questioned by civilians or if the subject of your tour in Afghanistan is brought forth?"

"That all discussion of that subject is military and confidential and that I can say nothing of it," answered Iosef.

Galinarov nodded and then looked back down at the duty roster. "I suppose it can be arranged," he sighed. "Rostnikov, you are to receive four days' leave to visit your parents in Moscow."

"For that I thank you, Comrade Lieutenant," Iosef said, knowing that Galinarov surely had nothing to do with the granting of such leave and certainly, if given the opportunity, would have fought it. The business of examining the duty roster to see if he could let Iosef go was a childish attempt at reminding Iosef of his authority.

Galinarov reached under the duty roster, removed a folded sheet containing orders for leave, and tapped the sheet against his palm as if still considering whether to grant this favor.

"I'm not sure you deserve this, Rostnikov," Galinarov said. Iosef looked into the man's eyes and could now see that he had been drinking heavily. It was a bit early on a Monday evening to look as far into alcohol as the lieutenant did, and Iosef concluded that the order to give his hated underling leave had been most painful.

"I think you are right, Comrade," Iosef said somberly. "I don't deserve this. Since you do not want me to have it, I will, regretfully, go back to my duties." His face a blank, Iosef turned and took a step toward the door.

"Rostnikov," the lieutenant's voice shot past him.

"Yes, Lieutenant?" Iosef said, turning around with as innocent a look as he could present.

"I hate you. You know that, do you not?"

Their eyes met and locked.

"Yes, Comrade," said Iosef, holding out his hand for the folded sheet of paper. Galinarov threw it at him. Iosef caught it neatly and thrust it in his pocket. "Will there be anything else?"

"When you return from your leave, there will be a great deal else, Corporal, a great deal else." Galinarov drank from his glass without removing his eyes from Iosef. "You are dismissed."

Iosef turned his back, took three smart strides to the door, opened it, then looked back and said, "Thank you again, Comrade, and I hope you have a good week. May I bring you something from Moscow, a bottle of brandy?"

"You speak when you should be silent and are silent when you should speak," Galinarov hissed. "I will teach you when to do which."

"Yes, Comrade Lieutenant," said Iosef, and he went out into the corridor.

He marched slowly out of the building and across the open field, looking neither right nor left. Galinarov was probably standing at the window of his small office watching. Not until he had entered the barracks and closed the door behind him did he reach into his pocket and remove the leave orders. They were effective immediately. He hurried to his locker, waving the paper at Misha Svedragailov, who lounged in his bunk reading a newspaper.

"Why are you looking so pleased?" asked Misha. "Galinarov fall into the pisser?"

"No!" shouted Iosef. "I've got a leave, four days, starting now. If I hurry, I can catch the afternoon train to Moscow."

"Moscow's not such a safe place to visit," answered Misha with envy obvious in his voice. "I was just reading that they had some gas main explosions, one right in Red Square."

"I'll risk it," said Iosef, removing his small travel bag and filling it with underwear and shaving gear.

"You'll call my father?" asked Misha, going back to his paper.

"I'll call your father," agreed Iosef, slamming the locker and turning to leave. "Good-bye."

The bus to Kiev was ten minutes late, which meant that he had only fourteen minutes to get his ticket and catch the train, but make it he did by running and moving to the front of lines, a privilege of the military.

It wasn't until he was on the train pulling out of the station that Iosef allowed himself to think. He felt wonder and anxiety about seeing his parents for the first time in a year, a great eagerness to see the familiar buildings of Moscow, and a curiosity about who had tugged at the strings to get him this leave and for what reason.

ABOUT THE AUTHOR

STUART M. KAMINSKY is the author of five Inspector Rostnikov mysteries: DEATH OF A DISSIDENT, BLACK KNIGHT IN RED SQUARE (an Edgar nominee), RED CHAMELEON, A FINE RED RAIN and A COLD RED SUNRISE. He now teaches film history, criticism, and production at Northwestern University, where he is a professor and head of the Division of Film. He lives in Skokie, Illinois, with his wife and three children.